TALION JUSTICE

A FRANK LUCE THRILLER

RICK BOSWORTH

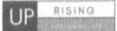

PROLOGUE

"The U.S. Army—my army—was in the field long before the ink dried on our Declaration of Independence," U.S. Army Chief of Staff Matthew York said, his voice rising. "And in all those 231 glorious years, do you know how many men have had the audacity to refuse the Medal of Honor—our country's highest award for valor?"

York did not pause long enough for me to answer.

"None!" he shouted, making a zero with his thumb and forefinger as he leaned across the table, neck veins straining, eyes afire. "Not one, Major Luce. There has never been a soldier in this republic's history who hasn't bowed his head for his commander-in-chief to place that medal around his neck."

York held his gaze, the same one that had chilled the blood of friends and foes alike on distant battlefields over the past three decades. It hit me like a gut punch. They were right. York was a fighting general. All six feet two of him. He had only recently been promoted to CSA and given his fourth star, which made him the highest-ranking active-duty officer in the U.S. Army. York reported only to civilians, specifically the Secretary of the Army, who answered to the Secretary of Defense, who answered only to the president.

York's sharp eyes wandered over my face, as most people's did now, and lingered on my left eye, scarred and still swollen from shrapnel I'd picked up from an ISIS IED in Afghanistan. The scar, still red and inflamed, started below my eye, split my eyebrow in half, then faded as it stretched for my hairline and angled away from my nose. The army doctors were amazed I'd regained my sight, and said the scar would be less noticeable in time. I didn't care. About the scar, at least.

This was the last place I wanted to be. Stateside. Away from my men. Answering to the number one man. I had tried to settle this properly, observing my chain of command, who now flanked me in York's vast office at the Pentagon. Sitting to my right at the grand conference table was my boss, Colonel Roland Velazquez, a squat, fleshy man who failed to impress even in the pressed uniform of a full bird colonel. He was the bad cop, the one who had yelled and dressed me down for embarrassing him in front of the brass. Velazquez had threatened and cussed like a petulant child. He'd ordered me to accept my MOH. I'd respectfully refused. Sir.

Next came Velazquez's boss, one-star Brigadier General Margaret Fitzgibbon, the good cop, now seated to my left. Fitzgibbon was an attractive woman, late forties, slender and tall, with sandy hair worn in a tight bun. She seemed genuinely baffled by my refusal to accept our country's highest military honor. She had questioned me as to my reasons, and I had given her the whole story. She'd listened with the practiced empathy of a human resources director. She had then spoken of honor, tradition, and duty. How things were not always black and white, especially in battle. I'd told her I saw no gray that day. I spoke of my men; she spoke of her army. She saw my resolve and accepted her failure to convince me otherwise. She'd still issued me an order, for the record, which I had also respectfully refused. Ma'am.

Less than one week later, I was summoned to Matt York's office. This was an order I could not refuse.

York settled back in his chair, his scowl replaced with a searching expression I took as paternal.

"What's the problem here, son?" York asked.

"It's all in my report, sir," I replied, hoping to expedite this. The air in York's commanding presence felt thin, like summiting Everest. My breathing became rapid and shallow. I was not acclimated to this altitude, as Fitzgibbon and Velazquez were, having base-camped at the Pentagon while I was over in Afghanistan fighting another kind of war.

"I know what's in your report, Major, and I know what General Fitzgibbon has briefed," York said. "I want to hear it from you."

I looked into York's dark eyes and saw the warrior, aged but unbowed, behind the reading glasses perched at the end of his nose. Still fit and able to lead in battle. I made the split-second decision to trust this man, trust that he would see my refusal for what it was—an honorable stance on principle.

So I drew a deep breath and began.

It all happened one July day in 2006, the summer of my 30th year. I was leading my company in a convoy through a contested pass in the Kunar Province in Afghanistan. As we came to a choke point in the road, I saw it was blocked by hostile local tribesmen. I knew an ambush when I saw one, and ordered fire just before the IEDs went off, the sequence a technical violation of a standing order not to fire upon locals except in self-defense. Armored transports were blown skyward; a chaotic firefight ensued. The fog of war, as they say. I lost ten good men that day, took many more of the enemy, and almost lost my eye. They say I fought heroically, running from Humvee to Humvee, firing on the enemy and pulling wounded men from burning wreckage. It happened so fast; one moment calm, the next chaos. All instinct and adrenaline. I did it to save my men. I did it because other men were trying to kill them. I guess that makes me a hero. If true, I saw a lot of heroes that day.

So I passed the army's MOH valor test. But it was messy. First, I had intentionally violated a standing order by proactively engaging the enemy. When questioned, I acknowledged my action and said I would do it again if faced with the same circumstances. I got bawled out by my colonel for this, but he was a West Pointer like me and I got off easy. And the army could overlook this act of insubordination when committed in the heat of battle by a bona fide war-hero-in-the-making.

But the army had a much bigger problem. During the after-action review, it came to light that one of the most beloved soldiers in my company was killed by friendly fire. It had only been two years since the Pat Tillman fiasco, and the army scrambled into damage control. At first all appeared proper. Army CID rushed in. Statements were taken.

Evidence gathered. Everyone in the company knew the truth of what had happened. We mourned all fallen soldiers the same and tried to quietly console the soldier who had accidentally killed his comrade. The poor kid was inconsolable. He left the army soon after. Went home, then got and stayed drunk. He shot himself in the face and was dead before his 22nd birthday. Another casualty in the pass that day.

They nominated me for the MOH before the CID investigation was even concluded. I was honored on behalf of my company. I saw it as a team rather than an individual trophy and had every intention to accept it as such. Then I read the MOH award narrative. A nice piece of fiction. It captured all my feats of derring-do and graciously omitted my insubordination. But most importantly, it also ignored any facts surrounding the friendly fire incident. I read this as a betrayal of two brave soldiers who had died that day: one in the pass and the other six months later by his own hand in Portageville, Missouri.

At first, I respectfully requested my MOH narrative be rewritten, which was denied. I then less respectfully demanded this, which got me a curter rebuke. I tried to withdraw my nomination, but the army explained that it was not my prerogative to do so. Finally, I resorted to my last option: I advised my command that I would respectfully refuse the MOH if awarded, which came out like Lyndon Johnson's refusal to seek a second presidential term in 1968: "I shall not seek, and I will not accept, the nomination of my party for another term as your president."

As one would imagine, my command in Afghanistan was not amused, and they shipped me stateside. I would be the Pentagon's problem now. First the headshrinkers took a whack at me, and finding nothing wrong, handed me over to

Velazquez. A little good cop/bad cop later, and I ended up in the big man's office, baring my soul.

York looked down at the conference table, rubbing his temples hard with the fingertips of both hands. He blew out a deep breath and looked at all three of us across the table. Velazquez squirmed in his seat. I could smell the fear leeching off him. Fitzgibbon cleared her throat and began to respond. York raised his hand for her to stop, and she broke off in mid-word, as if choked.

York looked only at me now.

"That's one hell of a story, Major," he said. "I have spent some time on the battlefield myself, and I want you to know I understand. Things can get complicated if we lose our focus on what matters most. Sometimes we have to sacrifice for the greater good. Sometimes the most courageous thing a soldier can do is to mind his tongue and salute. You understand that, don't you, son?"

That's when I knew I was done. I had trusted this man to champion the truth, to do the right thing. Eventually, I would come to learn that these concepts were subjective and pliable in the hands of the powerful.

But today was the day when I learned my truly big lesson—that evil thrives when the good do nothing. York could have ended all this with a stroke of his pen. He could have provided justice for all the heroes who'd sacrificed their lives in the pass that day. Could have kept me in the army, too, serving my country with distinction for another twenty years. But he didn't. He would do nothing.

I boiled inside, shook as I fought to hold my silence.

"Major Luce?" York bit off the last word.

Fitzgibbon exhaled a breath she had been holding since I'd begun talking. Velazquez straightened up in the seat to my right. He raised his hands from beneath the table and placed them in front of him, fingers laced. I gave him a side glance and saw the corners of his mouth rise in a grin.

"Sir?" I mustered.

"You will not be the first soldier to refuse the Medal of Honor. Not on my watch. Of this I can assure you."

I started to respond when, under the table, Fitzgibbon placed the heel of her shoe on top of my foot and pressed down hard. I swallowed my response.

"You will go to the White House when told, and you will bow your head and accept your MOH with the grace and humility of all who came before you." York squared his shoulders back and gripped the table in front of him. "This is a direct order, Major Luce. Do you understand?"

I cleared my throat and tried to respond. No words came.

"Am I understood, Major?" York shouted.

I nodded in resignation, my eyes downcast, shoulders slumped. I felt York's glare radiate upon me, like the heat of the sun.

"Your answer, Major!" York demanded.

I looked up from the tabletop and locked eyes with York. I heard the leather of Fitzgibbon's seat squeak as she squirmed in her chair. She could endure my silence no longer and began to issue an apology. Again, York raised his hand to silence her, and again she obeyed.

I straightened myself in my chair, feet braced flat on the floor. Fitzgibbon's foot flopped off mine and fell to the floor with an audible thump. She quickly tucked it back under her seat.

I had run my conscience as far as I thought it could go. Maybe this would be best for everyone. Maybe everyone was better off not knowing the truth. Certainly it was in the best interest of the U.S. Army. And wasn't that what this was all about anyway? It certainly was not about what was best for Frank Luce.

What I didn't know, couldn't know then, was that the answer I was about to give would change my life, dramatically and forever. I would do nothing. And evil would flourish.

"I'll take your answer now, Major," York said.

"Yes, sir," was what I said.

And so it was that I accepted the MOH.

I resigned my U.S. Army officer's commission less than one year later.

PART I

_____

We set ourselves to bite the hand that feeds us.
    — Edmund Burke

CHAPTER ONE

AUGUST 6, 2016
HOSPITAL EMERGENCY ROOM
WASHINGTON, DC

JILL EVERETT WAS MIDWAY THROUGH THE DAY SHIFT AT George Washington University Hospital. She had been a nurse for nine years but had only worked day shift for the past eight months, since she had taken sole custody of her nine-year-old daughter after she and her husband divorced. She had spent her entire career at GWU Hospital, all of it on the night shift, before her marriage fell apart. Everett found the day shift nurses aloof and unfriendly. She missed her night shift friends dearly.

Which was odd, because everyone liked Everett. Patients most of all. She bounced around the wing, all five foot three inches of her, spreading a flawless smile and her goofy sense of humor. Just shy of thirty, she still had her college gymnast body, although she'd lost some weight with the recent stress of her divorce. She'd shorn her flaxen hair to shoulder length and kept it pulled back tight into a stubby ponytail at work.

Everett was attending to an elderly patient on the end of the wing and had the woman giggling. Another nurse, prim and stern, popped her head in the door and announced that Everett had a phone call at the nurses' station. No chitchat, all business. The old woman made a sour face at the other nurse's back. Everett just rolled her eyes and said she would be right back.

She hustled down the hall in her red Crocs and grabbed the telephone. It was the vice principal of her daughter's school. Everett attempted small talk, but this was the third time they had spoken in the last two months and the vice principal was beyond cordial banter now. She explained that her daughter Kate had had a fight with another girl in her fourth-grade class, and that she had to come and pick her up. Now.

Everett asked for details. The vice principal informed her that Kate had slapped another girl, that she ran a zero-tolerance school, and that Kate had been suspended for three days. She said Kate was awaiting pickup in her office right now. Everett said she was currently on shift and asked if the vice principal had called her ex-husband. Yes, the VP said, but he wasn't answering his phone. Everett sighed and said she would be right down.

Everett handed the phone back to the desk nurse and rubbed her face with both hands. She turned to walk towards her boss's office when she spotted Naomi, her only friend on shift.

Naomi shrugged, mouthed "What's up?" from across the nurses' station. Everett shook her head, and Naomi followed her out into the hallway. "What's up, girl?" Naomi asked. "Was that your dick ex-husband?" Naomi was half a foot taller than Everett, a proud first-generation Jamaican who hid her soft heart behind piercing dark eyes and a no-nonsense demeanor.

"Nah," Everett responded. "It was school. Kate got in another fight. She got suspended this time. She's in the vice principal's office now. I gotta go get her."

"Shit," Naomi said. "Dr. Douche is on shift now."

Everett grimaced. "Yeah, I know. He hates me."

Naomi looked around. "Just go. The school's not far. I'll cover for you. Shoot down there, pick Kate up, and bring her back here. We'll find something for that little troublemaker to do till end of shift."

"Thank you! Thank you!" Everett exclaimed, and ran to get her coat and keys. She returned to Naomi, hugged her, and said she would be right back. She took two steps toward the door and stopped dead in her tracks.

Everett smelled it before she heard it. Heard it before she saw it. She'd worked long enough in the ER to know what this was. The pungent, acrid odor. The rush of gurney wheels and EMT chatter. The doors then flew open and in rolled another dying homeless man. Everett gagged as the gurney whooshed past her. ER policy dictated that they would extend treatment to the homeless only if their condition was life threatening.

One quick look at the guy and Everett knew he was in big trouble. Everyone knew that Everett was the best trauma nurse on shift, probably the entire hospital. And she loved saving lives. For her, it was what gave her job real purpose.

Everett's eyes followed the gurney down the hall until she saw Naomi, who waved her over.

"Go on, scrub in," Naomi said. "I'll pick up Kate."

Everett squeezed Naomi's hands and thanked her. Then she got to work.

———

The EMTs gave a quick rundown of the patient: forty-year-old Caucasian male; unconscious; extensive bleeding, loss of blood; stab wounds and blunt force trauma; pulse erratic and dropping; intubated, breathing labored.

"Looks like his buddies gave him one hell of a beating," one of the EMTs said. "Found him in an alley eight blocks from here. No defense wounds. Must have got him while he was passed out. Poor bastard." The EMTs wrapped up with the efficiency of a racecar pit crew. On to the next one.

Everett leaned in to get a good look at her patient. This one smelled the same as the others, but he was different somehow. He wore the same long hair and shaggy beard but was better groomed. His clothes tattered but clean. She parted his lips with gloved fingers. He had all his teeth, and took care of them too. She started administering to the man, hooked him up and got his vitals stabilized.

Dr. Aarav Chabra (aka Dr. Douche) walked up to Everett as she worked through her trauma progression. He looked over her shoulder, calm as a Sunday morning.

"What do we have here, Everett?" Dr. Chabra asked. "Another homeless warrior?"

"This one's life threatening, Doctor. He needs emergency medical treatment. Stat."

"I'll be the judge of that, nurse," Dr. Chabra said curtly. He asked Everett for the patient's vital signs and medical treatment rendered. He barked a few orders, then turned on his heel to leave.

"You're not done here, Doctor," Everett said.

"The patient is stable. Not life threatening," Dr. Chabra said, not turning around. "Call me if—"

A piercing alarm sounded as the patient went into full ventricular fibrillation, making Dr. Chabra jump.

"He's coding, Doctor," Everett shouted, as she turned to the crash cart and reached for the defibrillator. She handed the paddles to Dr. Chabra, who gave the patient a few jumps, to no avail. He waited a few moments, then gave a few more. He stepped back and placed the paddles down.

"I'm gonna call it. Time of death is—"

"No!" Everett screamed.

She pushed Dr. Chabra out of the way, grabbed the paddles, and gave the patient another jump. The rest of the trauma team rallied around Everett, crowding Dr. Chabra away from the bedside. He grumbled in the background as the team continued to work frantically. Everett ordered epinephrine and kept paddling. After several minutes, she recovered a thin but steady heartbeat. They restored the patient's vital signs and kept his airway open. This man would not die tonight.

Dr. Chabra stalked out of the room, sputtering something about insubordination.

———

End of shift. It had been a long day for both Everett and her daughter Kate, who had spent most of her day on the wing doing homework and playing on her iPad. Everett would have to make arrangements for someone to watch Kate during her three-day suspension. Her ex-husband would be of no use there. Everett wondered if her daughter needed to see a counselor, if maybe she was acting out because of the divorce. The thought saddened her. They would have a long talk tonight.

Naomi sat with Kate as Everett ran up to the ICU to check on her patient. It wasn't every day she saved a life, and besides, she wanted to get another look at this man. She bounded up the three flights of stairs, entered the ward and checked in with the nurses. They were friendly, as usual. ICU nurses were the best. It must have something to do with the clarity one gets from facing down death every day.

Everett sat down with the nurse in charge, a woman named Marie, and got the update on her patient. He was in critical but stable condition and had not yet regained consciousness. The ICU had run a battery of lab tests on him, with results due back in a day or two. The man had no ID, but they were working on that too. Everett thanked the nurse and walked down the long hall to her patient's room, last door on the left.

She stood at his bedside watching him. He was one among many other patients in the ICU, separated by curtain partitions. The machines that kept him alive hummed, adding their voices to the mechanical ensemble. The nurses had cleaned him up, and the color had mostly returned to his face. His nose had clearly been broken, and not for the first time, it appeared. His eyes were swollen from the beating he'd sustained. She checked his hands, and the EMTs were right. No evidence he'd fought back or tried to defend himself. Looking closer, she noticed how clean and clear his fingernails were. Odd for a homeless man. Straight white teeth as well. Again, odd.

Everett fiddled with the electrode patches on his hairy chest, checking for solid contact. Something red caught her eye. She brushed the chest hair aside and saw a tattoo. An emblem, about three inches square. It was a spread eagle on top of a shield bearing a helmet with a sword. Looking closer, she saw the words *Duty, Honor, Country*... then... *West Point*. Everett jumped back. Her patient was a veteran, a West Pointer. Her brother had graduated from the Point as well, class of '95. He was a full colonel now, stationed at Fort Bliss. Her dad had fought in Korea. Everett's pulse quickened. She had never encountered a homeless man from the Point.

She examined his face more closely. It was a ruggedly handsome face, under all the abrasions and the scraggly beard. He had sharp features and a strong chin. Everett reached out and traced a finger across his full lips. It was only then that she noticed the long-faded scar high on his left cheek. It split his eyebrow before moving up into his hairline. She ran her finger along the scar. The man had the face of a pride lion.

Everett knew a nurse at the VA. They had been college roommates and had stayed in touch. She would give her a call tonight.

She would help Everett put a name to the man in the bed.

CHAPTER TWO

AUGUST 12, 2016
HOSPITAL INTENSIVE CARE UNIT
WASHINGTON, DC

I AWOKE TO DARKNESS. MY EYES, DRY AS PARCHMENT, blinked open. I was in a room; looked like a hospital. I was flat on my back in a bed. The sound of rhythmic beeps and buzzes filled my ears. A man was groaning next to me. I tried to turn my body in the direction of this disembodied wail but was restrained by straps that secured me to my bedrails. I jerked, but the restraints held. I surveyed my enclosure, about the size of a prison cell, with curtain partition walls three feet from either side of my bed. The curtains were dark blue and plain. I was grateful I couldn't see the groaning guy next to me. I was glad he couldn't see me.

I was hooked up to a bunch of equipment, which added to the macabre symphony of this place. The wide-gauge needle stuck into a vein in the crook of my arm gave me the drugs and nutrients that kept me alive. I wanted to pull the tube out of my nose, but they had strapped my arms to the bed as well. I became aware of the awkward pressure of a catheter in my penis. At least I hadn't been conscious for that. My entire body ached. I tried the restraints again, choked back a flash of claustrophobia when they again held firm. All I wanted to do was get out of this bed.

My head was fuzzy. My memory of how I got here was a jumble of disjointed images, like a poorly edited movie. I hovered above myself, winced as the blows again found their mark. I saw the fists, then the feet. And some kind of bat or stick. I was in an alley. It was dark, but the streetlights showed my attackers' faces in shadow. I recognized a few of them. Other homeless guys from the block. I didn't care enough to fight back, which only emboldened them more. They pulled at my pockets, stole my bag and all my meager possessions. They bounded off, laughing and cavorting as if at Mardi Gras.

They left me to die. I didn't care. I closed my eyes and awaited death.

But now I know death did not come for me that night. That made me neither happy nor sad. Just *empty*. Why Death had passed over me in that alley that night was his business. I realized this largesse only meant I had more days to fill, more life to squander. I turned my head away from the groaning man, closed my eyes and silently cursed the skeletal demon and his scythe. If the man in the black hooded robe comes for me tonight, I will not fight back.

———

A nurse awoke me with a gentle shake. She had shiny blond hair pulled back tight. She smiled wide when my gaze met hers. Her eyes, unlike my own, were clear and danced with life. She wore different scrubs than the ICU nurses.

"Good morning," she said. "My name is Jill Everett. I work here at the hospital in the ER. Do you remember me?"

I just looked at her in silence as her eyes roamed my face.

"You were in pretty rough shape when you got here. We thought we were gonna lose you." Everett looked over my head to the monitor that displayed my vital signs. "You've been upgraded to fair condition. Your lab work's not back yet, but your vitals are stable. Glad to have you back. You were in a coma for six days; did they tell you that?"

I looked away. They had drawn my curtains back enough for me to see to the left and right of me. The groaning guy was gone, his bed empty.

"Are you in any pain?" Everett asked. "Can I get you anything?"

I shook my head no. Everett's face went slack, and her smile faded. Extinguishing her light made me feel bad. Shame, my long-lost friend. I tried to answer her but choked on the grit lodged in my throat. I cleared it out with a loud grumble. The voice that filled my ears was foreign to me.

"Take these straps off me," I said.

"You need them," Everett responded. "The nurses say you kept trying to pull out your nose tube and IV. You need your fluids and medications. It's what kept you alive these past six days."

I just looked down at my arms, strapped down to the bed at my sides. A medical straitjacket. Everett's eyes followed mine.

"If I get the nurse to remove your limb restraints, will you promise me you won't pull out anything?"

I nodded.

"Do you promise me, Frank?"

My stomach knotted. No one else at the hospital had called me by my name. Everyone referred to me as John1. I had assumed I was booked in as just another John Doe vagrant, living on the streets of our nation's capital. I didn't know what the 1 stood for. I didn't have much use for ID, having drifted around the country these past five years. And whatever I did have had been taken from me in the robbery that had put me in this bed.

I searched Everett's face for answers. Her smile slowly returned. She glanced around the room, then approached closer and leaned over me.

"I know who you are, Frank Luce," she whispered. "I saw your tattoo. Had your blood sent to the VA. A friend of mine ran it for DNA and checked the army database. Sent me what she could from army records. It was not a lot, but enough."

I shifted in the bed. Tried to get away but couldn't move. Damn straps.

"I knew you went to the Point from your tattoo. My brother did, too. Class of '95. But I had no idea you were awarded the Medal of Honor. My friend told me the army was fast-tracking you, and then—bang!—you resigned less than a year after the award." Everett grabbed the plastic bedrails with both hands, then lowered her face towards mine. She smelled good. I had forgotten how good a woman could smell.

"Your file said you went to work for the USIC," Everett said. "I had to look that up: United States Intelligence

Community." She lowered her voice again. "Is that like CIA or something?"

I paused as my senses, now alive, took her in. She smelled like lavender. On a Rocky Mountain summer breeze. What to say? I had to say something, as flowers are not to be ignored.

"Something like that," was all I could muster.

Everett looked me up and down. "What happened, then? You're—"

One of the ICU nurses came in and approached my bed. She placed her hand on Everett's shoulder, causing her to flinch.

"I see you've finally met John1," the woman said to Everett. She turned to me. "You know, this lady has been up here to see you almost every day this week. Glad you two are getting acquainted." Everett stepped aside and gave the ICU nurse bedside access. She gave me a once-over and looked satisfied.

"Yeah, John1 was just telling me how grateful he is for all the ICU nurses have done for him. Isn't that right, John?" Everett asked me with a smile and a nod of her head.

"Sure," I said. It'd been a long time since I played ball.

"Thank you John1," the ICU nurse said, with a pat to my leg. "I'll be sure to pass that along to the other nurses."

"And John1 says he's ready to have his limb restraints removed. Right, John?" Everett said.

I said I was. The ICU nurse made me promise to behave myself. I gave her my word, which she considered for a while. She then sighed heavily and said she would remove them, but that they were going right back on if there was any monkey business. She actually used that exact term. I chuckled despite myself. In my defense, monkeys *are* funny.

The removal of the straps was heaven. I flexed my arms and shook them out. Readjusted myself in my bed.

The ICU nurse told Everett to wrap up her visit, said I needed my rest. We both watched her walk across the ward to another patient.

Everett quickly replaced the ICU nurse next to my bed.

"Thank you," I said, still shaking the blood back into my limbs.

Everett smiled, then grew serious. "Look, Frank, we don't have much time. You're obviously—"

"I'm obviously what?"

"I didn't mean it like that," Everett stammered. "I meant, well, you're on the street now, Frank, and have been for quite some time, I suspect." She cleared her throat. "I can help. I mean, I want to help. There are services. I can put you in touch with some good people I know. They'll help you."

"Why don't you go help someone else? I don't need it."

"Everyone needs help now and then, Frank. Let me help you. You can trust me."

I looked away. Trust and I had been estranged for many years.

She was like a gawker at a fatal car accident, unable to turn away from the carnage. And I was the state trooper controlling the accident scene, running police tape around the accident perimeter, shooing away bystanders.

But I did not tell Everett any of this. All I mumbled was "Go help someone else."

Everett's eyes went cloudy. She stepped back from my bed, arms crossed over her chest. It was then I realized I had been wrong about her, that there was more to her than being the savior to my human wreckage. Her lower lip trembled into a frown; her face contorted in anguish.

We each held our silence. The beeps and buzzes in the ward now took on the cadence of a ticking clock.

"Just go," I said, and turned my face away from her. "Please."

Everett choked back a sob. I listened to her footfalls as she left my bedside and slowly walked away across the ICU.

I pulled the bedsheet up to my chin, squinted my eyes closed, and withdrew back into my darkness.

CHAPTER THREE

AUGUST 17, 2016
GEORGETOWN COFFEE SHOP
WASHINGTON, DC

PRISHA VEDA BAARI SAT AT A TABLE IN HER NEW LOCAL coffee shop. It was only a ten-minute walk from her tony townhouse in Georgetown, a historically upscale enclave of the movers and shakers in Washington, DC. There had been an incident at her old coffee shop, which involved Prisha screaming at the manager trainee and hurling a full cup of coffee against the wall just over the young woman's head. This outburst had earned Prisha a lifetime ban. She would have called corporate and had the trainee fired, but this establishment was a startup. So she'd calmly walked a few blocks over and found a new place to plant her flag.

From her very first visit, Prisha knew which table was hers. It was a four-top against the wall in the back. It was the only table that had an unobstructed view of both the door and the large window overlooking the street. The fact that this table was one of only two four-top tables in the busy shop mattered not to her.

Prisha was serious about her coffee. She typically had a cup in hand throughout her long workdays, which is to say most days. Like any addict, she had acclimated to the caffeine and sometimes took her last cup as late as ten p.m., to no effect. But she always took her first cup early. And in a coffee shop, never at home. It was one of the few things for which she was punctual, for punctuality led to routine, and routine made one predictable—a bad thing in her line of work.

Prisha had easily charmed Adam, the morning manager at her new shop. Adam was a young man, and Prisha had never had any problems gaining the affection of young men. Or men of any age, for that matter. Prisha was long and slender, with thick raven hair that fell below her shoulders and looked equally good worn up or down. Her dark eyes were large and expressive, in contrast to her sharp features. Almond skin gave her an exotic look that hit men like catnip.

After her successful exploitation of Adam, it was simply a matter of shuffling the pack order of her fellow morning coffee patrons. Prisha knew that they, like her, had their own morning coffee rituals. So she convinced Adam to let her into the shop fifteen minutes before opening, so that she was firmly ensconced at her new table when the early morning regulars shuffled in. The dirty looks and grumbling from the table's former occupants were of no consequence to Prisha; quite the opposite, in fact. She reveled in their discomfort and struggled to hide her smirk. It took only a week of this before the regulars had begrudgingly accepted their new queen.

And so it was on this warm Wednesday morning in August that Prisha was at her table sipping her second cup, which Adam had delivered to her upon her signal for a refill. As usual, she was facedown in her laptop, an oversized thumb drive protruding from the USB port, furiously tapping away at the keyboard, earbuds in both ears. The universal sign for 'Leave me the fuck alone.' Most people were happy to oblige.

But not all people. Prisha felt the women's eyes on her first. Didn't even have to look up, for she had the keen peripheral vision of an apex predator. Without any other discernible movement, she raised her eyes just enough to see three women standing nearby, large coffees in hand. They huddled together, speaking among themselves, with faces like curdled milk. They were not morning regulars and clearly did not know the drill.

What these three women didn't know was that Prisha's earbuds were all for show. They were always turned off in the shop, although she smiled and bobbed her head occasionally to indicate she was enjoying an imaginary song or video. Another thing these women didn't know was that Prisha's sense of hearing was as keen as her sight, even with the earbuds jammed into her ears. The ruse caused people to speak in normal conversational tones around her, and say things they might not say if they knew she was listening.

Prisha heard all the women's snark. How rude she was for taking up a whole table all by herself, and what a bitch she was for not giving the table up to them. One of them suggested they should complain to the manager. The other two eagerly agreed, and all three turned and headed for the counter to complain to Adam. Prisha's face creased in a mirthless smile.

The three women stood at the counter, backs to Prisha, gesticulating at Adam. Prisha caught his eye and winked. He smiled back. *A fait accompli*. Prisha went back to her laptop and in her peripheral vision saw the three women stomp out of the shop. She took a long pull of her coffee and signaled Adam for one more. She watched the little group bustle past the big window, and stared at them until one of the women looked her way. It was another power she had: her stare never went unanswered. Prisha nodded at the woman, held up her coffee cup in salute. The woman's face flushed, and she turned and tugged at the arm of the friend closest to her. The other two turned around and got the same coffee cup salute. Prisha smiled widely now, her full red lips pulled back to bare her prominent white teeth. She knew this was going to be a good day.

Prisha closed out the file she was reviewing and ejected the thumb drive. She placed it into a small plastic pouch, zipped it, then zipped the pouch into a second bag before putting it in the front pants pocket of her charcoal-gray Chanel pantsuit. Her last cup of coffee was half full. She raised it to her lips and almost choked as the shrill scream of a small child at the next table pierced her ears.

The child was under two years of age, red in the face and screaming at the top of his little lungs. Prisha was childless by choice. She hated kids of all ages. Screaming, obnoxious toddlers most of all. Hated them all fawning over children, and the aggrandizement of the mothers. Like they were all heroes for being born with eggs capable of fertilization.

This mother appeared to be satisfied to let her little demon cry it out. She made no attempt to stop the screaming, or even acknowledge it, as she calmly pecked at her iPhone. Prisha shuddered as she thought of what her father, a devout Wahhabi Muslim, would make of this. The West was still such a foreign land to her in many ways.

Prisha looked around the coffee shop at the other customers. The shop was rectangular, with the counter and bar area on one side and the tables on the other. The décor was a modern, industrial style; the stained concrete floors and tin ceiling magnified the child's screams. Most customers were clearly annoyed but braced their heads into tucked shoulders and avoided eye contact. A few women gave the mother sympathetic looks and tried to make light of the situation. The kid maintained his decibel level, undeterred.

For the second time this morning, Prisha activated the stare that could not go unanswered. This time a toddler would be the lucky recipient of her laser sights. Thankfully the boy's mother was hopelessly self-absorbed and didn't notice a thing. The child knew something was amiss but was slow and clumsy in his response. *C'mon, kid. Over here.* Prisha would cull this one from the herd. Sure enough, the child returned her gaze. The boy gagged as if a hand had been clamped over his mouth; his screams went from moan to murmur. His face then fell slack, confused. His eyes widened in recognition. He stared at Prisha, motionless. Prisha returned his stare with a tight smile that did not reach her eyes. The boy bobbed backwards as if struck by a blow, then turned and buried his head into his mother's side. *There it is! You little shit.*

Only the innocent—dogs and small children—can truly recognize evil.

The mother stroked her son's hair. He peeked out from

under her arm, looking uneasily back at Prisha. His mother followed his eyes. Prisha smiled and nodded, which the mother misinterpreted as more accolades.

Prisha packed up her laptop and surrendered her table. She intentionally walked past the mother, on the side of the table where the toddler was now seated, quiet as a mouse.

"What a beautiful boy you have," Prisha said as she approached, trying on her widest smile, meant to disarm the mother.

The mother beamed and accepted the flattery.

Prisha leaned in towards the boy and asked him what his name was. The child again buried his face tight into his mother, who chastised him in a singsong voice. Asked him to tell Prisha his name. The boy shook his head violently, refusing to turn around to greet the nice woman.

"That's odd," the mother said. "He's usually really outgoing."

"That *is* odd," Prisha responded. "Because I love kids, and they love me." She then told the woman about the two cute little nieces that she did not have, and how they adored their Aunt Prisha.

Her work done, Prisha walked out of the coffee shop and stood on the sidewalk. The sun was rising in a clear blue sky. It promised to be a hot and humid day. But Prisha had been born and raised in Saudi Arabia. The heat didn't bother her. She didn't even break a sweat as she walked around the block to her car.

———

Prisha accelerated her new Lexus past the main employee

gate and smirked at the thought of the incident here in 1993 that had cost two American lives. Amateur hour.

She circumnavigated the compound and arrived at the executive entrance. She flipped down the visor to check her makeup and tussle her hair, worn down today for this very moment. Prisha pulled up to the guard shack, opened her window and handed her ID to the new uniformed guard, a young stud recently discharged from the Marines. He smiled and blushed, called her ma'am. She continued her banter, winked at him once. His blush deepened. She welcomed him to the company and said she would see him around.

"You're good to go, Deputy Director," the guard said. He handed back her ID and gave the military arm chop that signified entry granted.

"Thank you," responded CIA Deputy Director Prisha Veda Baari.

CHAPTER FOUR

AUGUST 17, 2016
CIAHQ
LANGLEY, VA

PRISHA WAS RUNNING LATE, AS PER USUAL. SHE STOOD at the door of her boss, Robert Johnson, head of the CIA. She had swept past his secretary with nary an acknowledgment; the woman was one of the few at CIAHQ who was immune to Prisha's charms. Johnson's days as CIA director were numbered—Prisha would see to that. She would also take great pleasure in crushing the secretary when she could no longer hide behind her powerful boss.

Prisha stood outside the door and unbuttoned the top two buttons of her white poplin blouse. She closed her eyes, got into character, then blew out a protracted, silent breath. Eyes wide, smile firmly in place, she opened the heavy door and entered Johnson's office, then shut the door behind her. Because she knew better.

Johnson rose and emerged from behind his desk to greet her. He was a dumpy, thick- bodied man, a full two inches shorter than Prisha. He never removed his suit jacket in public. This gave him a perpetually wrinkled and slovenly look. He wore an ill-trimmed goatee, now full gray like his thinning hair. He stroked it with his right hand when he was nervous or anxious, a tell that Prisha had put to good use over the years.

Johnson's eyes went right for Prisha's abundant cleavage as she approached. Years before, a top-notch Beverly Hills plastic surgeon had given Prisha what Allah, in his infinite wisdom, had not, and Prisha still marveled at the power her breasts had over men. Prisha wielded them as a samurai did his sword. Men were such simple creatures, so easily manipulated.

"Morning, Prish," Johnson said in greeting. She hated when he called her that, but granted the fat bastard this indulgence. It was a small price to pay.

The hug that followed was tight and extended, lascivious to the outside observer. Prisha wriggled free. Johnson's hands came to rest high on her waistline, just below her bra. Prisha shuddered, then gently pulled his hands away. Her pasted-on smile hid her revulsion.

"Good morning, Bob," Prisha said. Without invitation, she took a chair in the informal seating area nearest the door, opposite Johnson's desk at the far end of his cavernous office. Experience told her to stay off the sofa. Johnson sat in the matching black leather chair across from her. She was grateful for the low table between them.

The office was opulent, its appointments more suited to a Fortune 500 CEO than the head of a government agency. But the CIA was unlike most government agencies, with its secret budgets and culture of deception. It was expected that taxpayer money would be diverted to provide for the comfort of not only the CIA director, but all Agency employees. Big, dark budgets were a piggy bank, with spending accountable only to Congress, who were themselves unaccountable. So it came down to trust— trust that the democratically elected representatives were monitoring these secret warriors, and that these freedom fighters lied only for the greater good. But Prisha knew better. She knew that trust was no absolute entity, or true emotion; rather, it was a commodity to be traded and exchanged, valued and devalued, bought and sold. Prisha was at home, at peace, in this world. This funhouse mirror world where reality was manufactured and nothing was exactly as it seemed.

Johnson had served his purpose. At his hand, Prisha had become the first woman appointed to deputy director, the number two at CIA. At thirty-four, she was also the youngest ever to have held this position, a fact that earned her the animosity and disrespect of most of the rank-and-file at the Agency. Though they hated Prisha, they also feared her, for she was well connected, both politically and within the leadership of the seventeen USIC agencies. Prisha was an expert Beltway infighter and had the scalps to prove it. She had been deputy director for seven years now and had matured into the position. She had built her fiefdom, her castle walls impervious to both breach and siege. No one dared to challenge her. Not anymore.

Prisha and Johnson met once a week. These meetings followed a similar pattern: they greeted, he groped, she parried, they sat, he flirted, she misdirected. Prisha would then walk him back to their meeting, like a dog on a leash. And so it was today.

"Bob, I need your support with POTUS tomorrow," Prisha said with a jerk of the leash. Prisha was briefing the president in the Oval Office tomorrow on the ODYSSEUS Project, a project she had taken over within a year of her ascension to DD/CIA. Prisha would brief the president in the Oval immediately prior to the PDB—the President's Daily Brief.

The PDB, a daily summary of high-level national security issues, had been presented to the president, in some form, since Harry Truman received the inaugural one in 1946. Over the years, the PDB had evolved to meet the needs and preferences of each president, and had expanded to become an all-source digital product that addressed both domestic and foreign threats. The PDB was now produced by the ODNI (Office of the Director of National Intelligence) with contributions from the CIA and the other USIC agencies.

Each president had received the PDB document in his own way. Some preferred hard copy, some preferred it digitally on a tablet, and some preferred the document be orally briefed. The current president, Morris "Mo" Udell, preferred an oral briefing. Accordingly, the DNI (Director of National Intelligence, and head of ODNI) briefed the PDB to POTUS at a daily meeting attended by key Cabinet members and advisors. D/CIA Johnson was one such key advisor, and he sat at the big adult table with POTUS. Prisha, by virtue of her pre-briefing, would be kissed into this PDB briefing as a "back-bencher" and relegated to the row of chairs that lined the wall of the conference room behind the adult table. Prisha did not mind sitting at the kids' table for this meeting, as it got her valuable face time with POTUS and the rest of the USIC sharks.

"ODYSSEUS is bleeding money, Prish," Johnson said. "POTUS knows it, I know it, you know it. But that's not the real problem. What he's really concerned about is the delay. He wants it operational. *Now*."

Prisha had known this complaint was coming, and was prepared to address it with POTUS tomorrow. She had appeased Udell before, but knew his patience, and her time, was running out. The dazzling complexity of ODYSSEUS's bleeding-edge technology gave her safe harbor for any number of jargon-laden excuses, but POTUS was mercurial and sometimes unpredictable. And the other USIC agency heads, envious of ODYSSEUS's multi-billion-dollar budget, were knives out, ready to strike at the first sign of weakness. The more Prisha delayed, and the longer ODYSSEUS stayed off-line, the more vulnerable she and it became. Covert funding in the intelligence community was a zero-sum game. And not for the faint of heart.

"We've had some difficulty with a few providers granting us complete access to their servers," Prisha responded, searching Johnson's eyes. "And some of the latest tech had issues in beta, but—"

"Shit, Prisha," Johnson said in a raised voice. "POTUS doesn't want to hear that." He threw up his hands. "And neither do I. You keep telling me we're close. But this damn thing is still on the drawing board, and I'm tired of getting my ass chewed over it. This is your project. Fix it!"

ODYSSEUS was Prisha's project. She was all in on it. All her ambition, her hopes and dreams, were wrapped up in it. It was her life, and would be her legacy. She knew it. She hadn't always known it, not at first. But she had seen it soon enough, had seen, clearly, what no one else had. And it was then that she had known that ODYSSEUS had to be hers.

Prisha had come to the CIA in 2005, a political appointment at the hand of an influential congresswoman for whom she had served as chief of staff. Her placement as a senior executive in the Directorate of Analysis had given her access to ODYSSEUS, which at the time had been more theory than anything. Nascent technology in search of a benefactor. One of many outside-of-the-box ideas the Agency big brains routinely hatched, most of which die in their infancy.

Her epiphany still gave her chills. She remembered it all as if it were yesterday: a sunny Tuesday afternoon; CIA cafeteria; she wore a cute little scarlet Oscar de la Renta outfit with matching lipstick; had veggie pizza and a soda. She had attended a routine ODYSSEUS briefing the day before, but was thinking of nothing in particular except her upcoming trip to Manhattan that weekend and how much she loved pizza.

It had hit her like a lightning strike, so much so that she'd choked on her mouthful of pizza so forcefully that it watered her eyes and drew concerned co-workers to her side. She'd washed down her clot of pizza with a large gulp of soda and waved away her benefactors. Electricity flowed through her. She had never before felt this intoxicating power. Prisha wiped her eyes dry and couldn't stop smiling. She saw it, and none of them did. She knew what she had to do.

After that, Prisha had screamed and moaned to get assigned full-time to the ODYSSEUS Project, and when her pleas were ignored, she made her boss, DD/DA Williams, scream and moan until she would no longer be ignored. D/CIA Johnson was not her first rodeo.

Prisha had gone over to ODYSSEUS full-time in 2007.

At that time, the project had consisted of a bundle of technologies that, in aggregate, formed the concept that would years later be termed cloud data storage. It later fascinated Prisha how readily hundreds of millions of Americans willingly surrendered control of their personal data. But who didn't like fluffy white clouds? Seemed innocent enough, and besides, it meant people could access their data wherever they wanted! Convenience trumped common sense. A wolf in sheep's clothing. Prisha chuckled at the irony of it all, a sheep's wool being so similar in appearance to those fluffy white clouds in the sky.

The NSA and FBI saw ODYSSEUS as collection—a surveillance or "pull" technology to spy on anyone they deemed worthy. The NSA would cast a wide net, collect everything and spend their time and budget sorting through the twenty-nine petabytes of data each day for their gold nuggets. The FBI, on the other hand, chose targeted surveillance, individuals or groups who posed a threat to national security.

The CIA took a more aggressive approach. They viewed the potential for ODYSSEUS differently. For them, ODYSSEUS was not a means of collection but a disinformation platform; a push technology to impact a target's beliefs and actions. In those early years, CIA leadership had had no real vision for ODYSSEUS. But Prisha did. By 2010 she was DD/CIA and had wrested complete control of ODYSSEUS for herself.

Everything had changed in October 2011, when Apple put the digital personal assistant app, Siri, on the iPhone 4S. Americans had fallen in love with it. The marketplace now had a convenient bridge to their fluffy cloud—voice command. But this bridge allowed traffic to travel in both directions. Siri was now in people's ears, sitting vigilant on every new iPhone. Amazon's Alexa had followed in June of 2015, but this time she lived in Americans' homes, inside the smart speaker called Echo.

This shocking abridgment of privacy and the fourth amendment had been welcomed wholeheartedly into the American home. Now anyone with the right access and technical ability could theoretically "push" information from the cloud into people's living rooms—and into their heads.

Prisha was no technophile, but she had spotted a command-and-control issue with ODYSSEUS and knew an opportunity when she saw one. Anyone else would have labeled it a vulnerability, but Prisha was not anyone else. The ODYSSEUS technology was highly complex and truly understood by few, least of all CIA executive management, Luddites all. Rather, they were reliant on the project experts to provide them with the truth of things they could not themselves see, touch, or even understand.

This ignorance and ill-advised trust created just enough of a gap for someone to slip through. Someone who desired to control a direct pipeline into the minds of hundreds of millions of Americans. Some sociopathic megalomaniac.

Someone like Prisha Veda Baari.

CHAPTER FIVE

AUGUST 18, 2016
HOSPITAL PATIENT ROOM
WASHINGTON, DC

I SURVEYED THE CACOPHONY AROUND ME. DAYTIME talk shows blared from nearby televisions, family visitors scurried around their loved ones, nurses came in and out to move or administer to patients.

I'd been out of ICU for five days, and now I had too many roommates. I paid them little mind in the hope they would leave me alone. All did, except my closest neighbor, Maurice, a talkative black man in his mid-sixties who wouldn't shut up. He appeared to be nice enough, though. A glass-half-full guy. Kept telling me his life story, over and over, and asking me a bunch of questions I didn't want to answer. Maurice slept a lot, which was good. I usually just waited him out until he tired of my silence and fell asleep.

Maurice was yammering on—to me or the television, I couldn't be sure—when a nurse approached my bed. She was new; I hadn't seen her before on the ward. An older woman with thin lips and a harsh look. She asked me if I could walk. I said yes. I had been out of bed yesterday for the first time and had shuffled down the hall, pushing a walker in front of me. She asked me if I could get up now and come with her. I nodded. Anything to get out of this bed and away from my new best friend Maurice.

The nurse helped me swing my legs to the side of the bed and stand up. A few people turned to watch the show. In here I sometimes forgot what I looked like. They had scrubbed me up good, but I still bore the wild hair and long beard of a vagrant. Most looked at me like I was contagious. I took no offense.

I shuffled down the hall with the new nurse at my side. We passed the nurses' station and I nodded a greeting to the shift nurses, all of whom I had seen before. None held eye contact with me, instead pretending to be distracted with other business. I gave my new nurse a side glance. She was all eyes forward, one hand lightly braced against my lower back.

New nurse rushed ahead of me. She held a hall door open and ushered me inside with a hand gesture. It took me a moment to shuffle through the doorway. I didn't like what I saw.

It was a small conference room. Jill Everett sat at a circular four-top table. Her eyes were puffy and red, and she teared up at the sight of me. Her hands were gripping a paper napkin, twisting and tearing at it. Jill had visited me in my room most days, sneaking me peanut M&Ms, my favorite contraband. We'd talked. She'd opened up and told me about her daughter and her divorce. I'd told her a little about my broken marriage, and my five years of wandering. We'd even laughed a few times. It felt good. She didn't push help on me, or ask me any questions she didn't want answered. Her visits had continued as my condition improved in my new room. I admit I looked forward to her visits. I liked Jill Everett.

Seated next to Jill was a female Asian doctor. She was petite, almost gaunt, with dark eyes and close-cropped hair. She looked too young to be a doctor. The name badge on her bright white lab coat said Ng. I wondered if that was a first or a last name.

"Please sit down, John," Dr. Ng said. I glanced at Jill and smiled. She had kept our secret. My smile caused her to sob. With difficulty, I sat at the table. New nurse took the chair next to me.

"My name is Dr. Ng," the doctor began. "And this is Nurse Holman." She pointed to new nurse.

The bottom fell out of my stomach. *Shit.* I knew what this was all about.

"Nurse Everett did nothing wrong," I said in a firm voice. "I was the one who did it. You have no reason to fire her."

"What?" Ng and Holman exchanged looks. Holman smirked.

"You have no right to punish her," I said.

Jill sobbed louder.

Dr. Ng paused. "I'm afraid that's not what this is about, John." She shifted in her chair. It screeched against the tile floor, and then the room went silent. The clock ticked. It was like the one I remembered from Eastern Middle School. Big round face with a clunky second hand that shook when it ticked. I counted the ticks going by: *one, two, three...*

"John," Dr. Ng said, and cleared her throat. "Your blood

work came back from the lab. And I'm afraid you have cancer."

So this means Jill's not getting fired? My first thought was one of relief, that this nice woman, now a single mother with a young daughter to raise, would not lose her job because of me. The thought caused me to smile.

"John, do you understand what I just said?" Dr. Ng asked, more frustration than compassion in her voice. "I just told you you have cancer."

"Yeah, I know," I responded, a smile still curling the corners of my mouth. "I heard you. I've got cancer."

"You've got acute myelogenous leukemia, or AML," Dr. Ng informed me. "It's the most common acute leukemia in adults."

She asked me if I knew about leukemia. I said no. She explained that they still didn't understand its exact causes, but that it was thought to occur when blood cells acquire mutations in their DNA. These mutations caused some cells to grow and divide more rapidly and to continue living when normal cells would die. Over time, these abnormal cells could crowd out healthy blood cells. In acute leukemia, the abnormal blood cells can't carry out their normal functions and they multiply rapidly, so the disease worsens quickly.

"You sure?" I asked.

Dr. Ng and Holman both nodded.

"How'd I get it?"

Dr. Ng responded that she couldn't say, that leukemia seemed to develop from a combination of genetic and environmental factors. A good lawyer answer to a medical question.

"How long do I have?"

Dr. Ng equivocated, said it depended on a variety of

factors. She started to run those factors down but was interrupted by Holman.

"AML has a survival rate of twenty-seven percent,"
Holman announced.

I received this news without any response.

"That means you have a twenty-seven percent chance of
still being alive in five years," Holman said. "With treatment.
And AML requires aggressive, timely treatment. Chemo and
radiation."

Everett sniffed and rubbed her swollen eyes. "We can get
you treatment, Fr—John. It's gonna be okay. We'll do everything we can."

Dr. Ng's eyes widened at Everett's outburst. Holman
shot daggers at her. They all knew the policy for treating
indigent patients—that all such patients, even the ones with
cancer, would not receive treatment unless on the verge of
death. I had just been told I had a twenty-seven percent
chance of living, and that hardly put me on my deathbed. I
was on my own to pay for my cancer treatment. They all
knew that. Even Everett.

Dr. Ng and Holman ran down my treatment options as if
reading from a manual, and had me sign something I did not
read. They feigned compassion, wished me luck, and left the
room.

Everett watched them go, then frowned and got to her
feet. She walked around the table and sat next to me. We
turned to face each other. She grabbed both my hands and
squeezed tight.

"That was a close one," I said. "Thought they knew
about the M&Ms."

"Frank!" Everett shouted, releasing my hands. "That's
not funny." Her eyes again began to tear. "This is serious."

"I'm just glad it was me instead of you."

"You can beat this, Frank," she said. "*We* can."

"Oh, this is 'we' now?"

"Do you have anyone else?" Her eyes narrowed.

I shook my head. She pressed for a name. I thought for a moment, but there was really only one person. Always had been. But I didn't want to get her involved in this.

"No," I said. "No one."

Everett sat back in her chair, shoulders slumped.

"You heard them, Jill. I've got no insurance. And no money." I squeezed her hand. "It's okay. Don't be upset. I'm not."

Everett rose to her feet again. "You can't just give up, Frank. There's gotta be a way. Don't give up hope." She placed her hand on my shoulder. "Trust me."

I wished I had hope. Wished I trusted her. But I didn't. In truth, I didn't care enough to care.

"Thank you for all you've done for me," I said, looking into her bloodshot blue eyes.

"What about the VA?" she asked. "I'll contact them. They'd help."

"They won't. Not the way I went out."

"Damn it. Then there's gotta be someone, Frank. Anyone."

I held my silence, tried to wait her out. But Jill Everett was tough. She jammed her hands into the pockets of her scrubs and dug in. She wasn't going anywhere.

Damn. Why couldn't I just die alone? That's how I'd pictured it. At least after I walked out of my life and hit the streets. I never imagined this obstinate, beautiful creature standing between me and my maker. Part of me wanted to tell her to piss off, to mind her own business. Tell her I was beyond saving, that she shouldn't bother. I would just leave this hospital and go back to the streets, and let the cancer have its way with me. Part of me wanted to say all that to her. But the best part of me, that tiny part hiding in the shadows, spoke up for the first time in five years and said no. This was not about hope or trust, for I possessed neither at that point. I simply could not bear to bruise the beautiful heart of Jill Everett. Sometimes the biggest decisions turn on the simplest of things.

"Sarah Reyes," I said. A rush of air escaped my lungs.

I'd thought her name a million times in the past five years, but not once uttered it aloud. In my mind, she was still Sarah Phillips, the girl I lost my heart to in high school, not Sarah Reyes, wife of DC cop Victor Reyes.

"Call Sarah Reyes."

Everett pulled a small pad of paper and pen from her scrubs, ready to take dictation. I didn't even have to search my memory for the telephone number. I carried it around with me always, just in case. I gave her the number.

"Call her. Tell her I'm ready to talk."

CHAPTER SIX

AUGUST 18, 2016
PARKVIEW MARKET
PETWORTH, NW WDC

PRISHA BAARI BROUGHT HER LEXUS AROUND FOR A
second time. It was close to midnight and the street was quiet
this Thursday night. Minimal foot traffic, just a few people
wandering back to their cars from the bars on nearby Upshur
Street. Parkview Market was dark, except for a light in the
window above the bodega. It was the boy's room—Yazid.
Prisha shook her head. That kid was always up. She
wondered if he ever slept. She was a nighthawk herself; only
needed five hours of sleep a night. The sleep deprivation had
no effect on her.

Prisha parked on the street and walked the two blocks to
the market. This section of Petworth was mixed commercial
and residential and not well lit. Prisha walked with purpose,

a pistol in her purse. She did not fear what might lurk in the shadows of these streets. She was a regular visitor and now knew this neighborhood as well as her own.

Parkview Market was far from any park, one of its many deceptions. It occupied the bottom floor of a beige two-story brick building that sat at the intersection of two busy streets. It was plastered with mismatched signage, like Post-it notes: Lotto tickets! Cigarettes! ATM/Internet! EBT! The Parkview signage itself had been hand painted, most likely in the 1970s, judging by its outdated font and faded condition. The proprietors, Yazid's parents, were villagers placed here by Prisha's Saudi Arabian benefactors. To the neighborhood, they were a quiet Muslim family running a family business. To Prisha they were watchdogs. Their instructions were to never leave the building unwatched, and to ignore whatever occurred in the locked basement at night. They knew better than to ask any questions. Curiosity killed the cat.

Prisha crossed the street and approached the front door. Above it and to the left was Yazid's lit window. An external air conditioning unit hung from it, dripping water to the sidewalk below. Antiquated satellite dishes crawled like spiders up the side of the building. Prisha passed an overflowing curbside trash can and stepped to the door. She glanced about, then inserted her key and silently opened the door. The bodega was dark and cramped, with narrow aisles of incongruous goods shelved with no apparent thought: produce next to cough medicine; beer across from bubble gum. Prisha was a regular visitor. She navigated the maze and found the basement door in the back without difficulty.

The door was hidden in the storage area of the bodega, among boxes of food and merchandise. This area was off limits to customers. A wayward customer would have to walk around the front counter to get to it, which was highly unlikely because Yazid's father was always standing there. The basement door itself was made of heavy blast-proof steel, camouflaged to look like a freezer. It was monitored by surveillance cameras 24/7. Prisha punched in the numeric door combination, waited for the metallic click, then turned the heavy knob, heaved the door open and walked down the creaky wooden steps. The basement had retained its damp, musty feel, despite all the remodeling they had done.

Prisha turned at the bottom of the stairs and saw her lead tech, Khabir Ahmad, standing at his bench in the low light. Ahmad was tall and rail thin, a twitchy man. A two-pack-a-day smoker with no fashion sense beyond khakis and white buttoned shirts, always tucked in and secured with the same worn black leather belt.

"Prisha," Ahmad said in greeting, without looking up from the private computer server he was working on. Ahmad was still uncomfortable working for a woman. Prisha knew she intimidated him, and used this to her advantage. Their relationship was awkward, but professional. All business. Prisha respected Ahmad's skills—he was brilliant with computers and signals and electronic intelligence—but did not fully trust him. He was from Pakistan, not Saudi. He had been recruited for ODYSSEUS by her benefactors, not her. And he was a hardcore fanatical Muslim. Prisha didn't trust anyone whose motivations she could not understand.

"Khabir," Prisha responded. "How are we doing?"

Ahmad turned to face her. "Good. Our work continues."

Prisha handed Ahmad the thumb drive. He dropped his eyes as their hands met. He nodded and placed the drive near one of numerous servers stacked side by side on his bench. Cords and power strips cluttered the space. Ahmad had hidden their electrical signature with the power company, but the sight of all this blinking and whirring equipment reminded Prisha how reliant she was on Ahmad's expertise. She did not like this vulnerability but was confident in her ability to keep Ahmad in line. He had come to ODYSSEUS early and was as committed to it as she was.

Regardless, ODYSSEUS was Prisha's project. And everyone knew it. She had worked on it full-time for nine years. As deputy director, she was the face to it. It was the only thing that kept her at the Agency—and in the United States, come to that. She would have preferred Switzerland or France, but since that day in the CIA cafeteria, she knew ODYSSEUS was her destiny.

It hadn't come to Prisha all at once, at least not the details. The details took years of painstaking research and development, billions of dollars, and adept bureaucratic maneuvering. What Prisha saw was the potential of ODYSSEUS. What it could be, how it could be used. Big picture stuff. Prisha thought and worked at altitude; she had staff and minions to handle the details.

At altitude, ODYSSEUS worked by hacking both the power and vulnerability of the human brain.

The human brain is remarkably modest in appearance, a spongy three-pound mass about the size of two fists put together. But it's the most complex thing in the known universe. It holds as much information in its memory as exists on the entire Internet, about two hundred exabytes. And it is a marvel of efficiency, using just enough energy to run a dim lightbulb. A computer with the same memory and processing power would require a dedicated nuclear power station.

The human brain is also utterly practical, without sentimentality of any kind. The five senses take in data, which is ultimately converted to electrical impulses that are carried to the brain via our nervous system. The brain interprets these electrical impulses, then tells you what to make of them. Everything we know about the world is provided to us by our brain. The brain views the world as just a stream of electrical impulses, and creates your reality from these impulses. In a very true sense, we all live out our lives in our heads.

But the brain can also be fooled. Through the power of suggestion, it is possible to implant false memories in about one-third of the population, which accounts for hypnosis and similar mind tricks. The trick lies in co-opting one of the five senses into collecting false data, converting it to electronic impulses (for your senses are agnostic conduits) and shooting these signals right into the brain. At a biological level, the brain does not question the validity of the signals it receives; it merely processes them.

Which one of the five senses to hack? How about hearing?

Hearing occurs in a series of complex steps that change sound waves into electrical signals. Our auditory nerve then carries these signals to the brain. But considering that the sound waves impacting our eardrums are actually silent, the biggest part of hearing isn't the sound wave itself, but the brain making sense of it. So what is heard is not what is—but what the brain says it is.

Prisha was no scientist but had several assigned to ODYSSEUS. They were the ones working out the details of all this. She only had to understand enough of the science to ask the right questions, the ones that would keep her scientists honest. What Prisha did understand, however, was steganography, and how it could be used to get inside people's heads.

Steganography is simply hiding information by embedding messages within other, seemingly harmless messages. It dates back to ancient Greece, where men of intrigue would tattoo a shaved messenger's head, let his hair grow back, then shave it again when the messenger arrived at his contact point. Whereas cryptography and encryption protect the contents of a message alone, steganography conceals not only a message's content, but the fact that a secret message is even being sent. The advantage of steganography is that the secret message does not attract attention to itself as an object of scrutiny. Encrypted messages, in contrast, no matter how unbreakable they are, still arouse interest and suspicion when discovered.

And so, under Prisha's tutelage, ODYSSEUS had become a top-secret CIA project to input false memories into the heads of the American people by grafting suggestive steganographic messages onto innocuous sound waves. What the CIA had needed was a delivery system to carry the ODYSSEUS messages to hundreds of millions of Americans. The introduction of digital personal assistants in 2011 had solved this problem nicely. Siri, Alexa, Google Assistant, and Microsoft's Cortana were soon answering questions and playing music for happy Americans all across the country. ODYSSEUS would hack these PDA systems, attach their messages, and let the music play.

Alas, ODYSSEUS had taken longer than Prisha had ever thought it would to go operational. The science and technology were constantly evolving, and the operations were maddening. All the big companies had denied the CIA access to their data infrastructures. Patriotic pleas and, later, boatloads of cash had proven unpersuasive. So Prisha had found the best hackers available and set them loose. But Apple, Google, and Microsoft were no mom-and-pop operations, and progress had been slower than anticipated. Nevertheless, progress was being made.

Prisha maintained control of, and funding for, ODYSSEUS through equal measures of charm, skullduggery, and ruthlessness. The scientists controlled the science, and she controlled the scientists. The few decision-makers Prisha answered to—D/CIA, POTUS—had made the mistake of trusting her without independent verification. No one was auditing her, not in any real sense. Prisha fully exploited this oversight.

"How long, Khabir?" Prisha asked. "Johnson grows more inpatient with every POTUS briefing."

Ahmad was meticulous in his work. He didn't like to be pushed, especially by a woman.

"The recent tests have been positive," Ahmad responded. "But I need more data, particularly on the Apple codec. And also I need—"

"How long?" Prisha said harshly, her eyes sharp.

Ahmad looked to his shoes. "Three to six months. Inshallah."

"Not a day longer." Prisha exhaled a protracted breath. "Do you have my stuff?"

Ahmad nodded, then grabbed a box from his bench and handed it to her. She slowly unpacked eyeglasses and a hair clip. She inspected them closely.

"The lenses are clear glass," Ahmad said. "Wear them tight against the bridge of your nose. The hair clip goes in the center of your head, in back. It will be important that you avoid any fast movements with your head when you are in the Oval Office tomorrow. The clip will not provide accurate acoustic measurements if you do this."

"I know, Khabir. I've done this before."

"Last time the data was incomplete," Ahmad said. "We haven't mapped the entire room yet. I need you to get Udell to give you a tour of his office. And turn your head when he speaks to you so that the clip can modulate his voice signature."

Prisha saw that Ahmad was clearly happy to be the one now issuing orders. He needed to be put back in his place.

"Got it, Khabir. Anything else?"

Ahmad flinched. His eyes blinked rapidly. Dry saliva was crusted at the corners of his mouth. "One of my best people is acting odd. He may be getting cold feet."

"Who?"

"Sweeney."

"What's the issue?" Prisha asked. "Personal? Financial?"

"I don't know. He's just acting a little...suspicious."

"Okay, I'll pass it along to Henrik." Henrik Karlsson was Prisha's head of security. Prisha clasped her hands together. "You got the thumb drive. I'm gonna go. Don't stay too late. Be out before daybreak."

"One more thing," Ahmad said. He tapped on his laptop, swiped the trackpad, then turned the monitor so Prisha could see it. It was video camera footage of the outside of the basement door. It showed fourteen-year-old Yazid tentatively trying the doorknob. Prisha felt her face flush. She clenched her fists at her sides.

"He's back," Ahmad said. "That boy has to be dealt with, or we will have to shut down this operation."

"I will deal with this," Prisha said.

"You said that last time, and—"

Prisha's eyes narrowed. It stopped Ahmad cold.

"I said I will deal with this, and I will. Understood?" Prisha's voice was icy. "We are not moving operations. We've been here for years. We're safe in this basement. The boy will not be a problem."

Ahmad bowed his head. "As you wish."

Prisha took her leave of Ahmad. She went back up the creaking stairs, checked the monitor at the top of the staircase, and, seeing no one, slowly opened the door, stepped through it, then shut and locked it behind her. She crept back through the bodega and then paused at the entrance, checking the front windows and surveying the street. Satisfied, she left the store and swiftly crossed the street, shoulders hunched and head down.

On the opposite sidewalk, she stopped and turned around. She stood next to a street lantern, under the canopy of a large oak tree that shrouded the street in shadow. Prisha's eyes followed this shadow to the spot above and to the left of the bodega's door. Yazid's window was still lit.

CHAPTER SEVEN

AUGUST 19, 2016
HOSPITAL CAFETERIA
WASHINGTON, DC

SARAH REYES STRODE INTO THE HOSPITAL CAFETERIA IN the lobby of GWU Hospital, pale blue eyes scanning the room. She was tall and lean, and although just shy of forty, still had the swimmer's body that had earned her a four-year scholarship to the University of Maryland. She had sharp Nordic features, and today she wore a smartly cut business suit and expensive heels, with her straw-blonde hair pulled back tight in a ponytail. She spotted the woman she was looking for and made her way across the room.

"Jill?" Sarah asked, extending her hand.

Everett took it and thanked her for coming. Today she wore her powder-blue nurse's scrubs with her red Crocs. A Styrofoam cup of black coffee sat on the table in front of her.

"I just got your message this morning," Sarah said. She slid out a chair and sat across the table from Everett. "What's this about Frank? You said it was urgent."

"Yes. It's—"

"Frank Luce, right?" Sarah interrupted. "Are you sure? I haven't seen or spoken to Frank in five years. No one has."

"He asked me to call you. He needs your help."

"He said that?" Sarah said, eyes widening.

"Not his exact words, no," Everett said. "But he's in trouble."

"What is it?"

Everett leaned across the table. "I don't know how to tell you this, but Frank has... leukemia."

Sarah gasped. The word hung between them.

"ALM. Acute myelogenous leukemia," Everett said. "It's an aggressive cancer, but it responds well to chemo and radiation. If we start treatment now, we could catch it in time."

"Shit," Sarah whispered.

"Problem is, Frank won't take treatment. Won't even talk about it. It's like he just doesn't—*care.*"

The two women sat in silence. Everett fiddled with her cup, picking at small pieces of Styrofoam with her red manicured fingernails.

Sarah shook her head. "Oh, Frank..." She blew out a breath. "What a waste."

"If you could just talk to him, maybe you can get him to come around," Everett said. "He's a little... down on his luck... but I think I can find a treatment center that'll take him on. Frank being a war hero and all." She looked down at the tabletop. "I don't want him to die in the hospital. Or on the street."

"How do you know Frank?" Sarah asked.

"He was my patient. Came into the ER almost two weeks ago. Got beat up real bad. His heart stopped a couple times. Almost died."

"Two weeks, huh?" Sarah asked. "I've known Frank since my sophomore year in high school." Frank had been the strongest man she had ever known. Her thoughts wandered to the beaten man, dying, alone in a hospital bed. His strong heart surrendering. She swallowed hard and tried to suppress her rising emotion.

"That's why he'll listen to you, Sarah," Everett said. She sipped her vending machine coffee and made a face.

Sarah cocked her head. "What is Frank to you, if you don't mind me asking?" She studied Everett. "Are you two dating?"

"No!" Everett said a beat too quickly. "He's just my patient... Well, he's become my friend. I come from a military family and I want to help him. That's it." Everett's face was flushed. She bit her bottom lip.

It was clear to Sarah that Frank was more than a patient or friend to Everett. She knew that look. She had worn it herself a long time ago.

Sarah had met Frank at Montgomery Blair High School; he was a junior, she a year behind him. Frank had relocated from Boston to Silver Spring, Maryland, three years prior. He had initially struggled in the new city, but he'd found his feet in high school. He was a popular but introverted kid, played varsity football and ran track. Sarah had grown up a tomboy, a competitive swimmer and basketball player. She had grown into her beauty in high school, but unlike every boy she met, seemed unimpressed by it.

Sarah and Frank had dated all through high school and

continued their relationship long-distance when Frank left for his plebe year at West Point. But one night, youth and impetuousness had won out, and Sarah had fallen for the charms of another boy. Afterwards, however, she'd been unable live with the guilt and had broken up with Frank when he returned that summer after his first year at the Point. It had broken Frank's heart, and she knew it. Sarah had never told him why she'd ended their relationship. That first summer had been rough, but they'd eventually reestablished their friendship. Sarah had always known Frank was the one, and thought one day they would reunite. But life happened, and they never had.

"I haven't heard from Frank in years," Sarah said. "Just two scribbled notes and some hang-up calls in the middle of the night. I don't know anything about him after he left my sister."

"Your sister?" Everett asked, voice rising.

"Yeah. Frank and my younger sister Nicole were married."

Everett raised her eyebrows. It was clear this was news to her. So Sarah filled her in.

Frank had returned to the Beltway after he resigned from the army. Sarah was in a committed relationship at the time and had convinced him to ask Nicole out on a date. Nicole had temporarily "withdrawn" from Florida State a year prior and was drifting in her life as well. They had begun dating, and to Sarah's shock and dismay, married a year later. Sarah hid her heartbreak and did her best to be a supportive sister and friend. It was hard. And despite knowing better, she had rebounded into the arms of Victor Reyes, metropolitan police officer and strutting Cuban peacock. This was the loveless marriage that Sarah was now trapped in.

"So, yes," Sarah said in a steady voice. "Frank and my sister were married for three years. Before he vanished. He didn't mention that?"

Everett shook her head. "No. He didn't tell me much about himself. Most of what I know is from his army records."

Frank's and Sarah's lives had diverged widely since Frank's army days. Frank had been a changed man after the army. Quiet and sullen, as if all joy had leached out of him. He went to work for the CIA as an analyst, a job he didn't particularly care for but was happy to have. Frank never told Sarah the circumstances behind the abrupt end of his once promising army career, but she had heard enough from her sister to know it had ended badly.

Sarah, on the other hand, was ascendant. She'd earned a master's degree in Cyber/Information Security at George Washington University, then was hired on as a consultant at the high-powered firm of White Rogers Young. While Frank was wandering the country penniless, Sarah had worked eighty-hour weeks and steadily advanced to a mid-six-figure position as executive vice president. Sarah's work hours and Victor's repeated infidelities effectively ended their relationship. Sarah had only recently accepted the failure and was currently planning to leave the marriage.

"This leukemia, ALM—how bad is it?" Sarah asked.

"It's bad. Frank needs to start treatment right away."

Sarah rubbed her eyes, exhaled loudly.

"What are his... chances? I mean, what are we looking at here?"

"ALM has a five-year survival rate of twenty-seven

percent," Everett said. "Much worse if he doesn't get treatment."

Sarah's stomach knotted. She bit down hard, her lips puckering into a thin line. She fixed her eyes on the ceiling until she caught her breath. She looked back to Everett, whose eyes were tearing up. Sarah now fought back her own tears.

"So..." Sarah's voice cracked. "What you're telling me is that Frank's dying."

Everett reached across the table and grasped Sarah's hands. "What I'm telling you is that he doesn't have to die. Not if you talk him into treatment. I think you're the only one who can, Sarah. You're the only one he'll listen to."

Sarah searched Everett's face. Everett held her gaze and smiled.

"Yes?" Everett asked.

Sarah gave Everett a tight smile and nodded.

Everett beamed. She again grasped Sarah's hands. "Thank you—*thank you!*"

"So, what do I do? How do we do... this?"

"Frank's up in the ward right now. Can you see him now?"

Sarah grimaced.

"It'll be okay," Everett said.

Sarah pushed a few strands of blonde hair behind her ears and rose from her seat. Everett stood as well.

"All right," Sarah said. "Where is he?"

"I'll take you to him," Everett said.

Everett followed Sarah out of the cafeteria, dumping her Styrofoam cup of cold coffee in the trash as she went. They walked to the nearest elevator bank. Everett pushed the button a few times. They waited in silence. Everett turned to face Sarah.

"Just one thing," Everett said. "Frank is—um... Well..." She paused, searching for the correct words. "He... he may not look quite like the man you once knew."

CHAPTER EIGHT

AUGUST 19, 2016
HOSPITAL PATIENT ROOM
WASHINGTON, DC

I'LL NEVER FORGET IT. YOU COULD SAY IT WAS THE FIRST day of the rest of my life.

Maurice was talking at me about something. I was looking at his face but not listening. He finally stopped talking, but only because he got up to go to the bathroom. I watch him shuffle across the floor, his ass hanging out of his hospital johnny. It was hard to hide the truth in a hospital. Death, illness, and close confinement had a way of bringing out the core truth in people. The fact that this place was having no effect on my core was beginning to trouble me just a bit. An itch I couldn't quite scratch.

I felt something, a presence, that made me turn towards the door. And just like that, there she was. A tremor ran through my body, actually shook me in my bed. I remember the squeak the plastic bedrails made when the bed jumped. I just stared in silence at her, mouth agape. Five years now felt like fifty.

Sarah froze in the doorway at the sight of me. Her hand went to her mouth. Her eyes said what her mouth could not. Her beautiful blue eyes, the same eyes I had fallen into long ago, now filled with tears at the sight of me. I choked and swallowed. It was the first whiff of shame I'd felt in a long time.

I sat up in my bed like a schoolboy, adjusting my johnny and pushing my long hair out of my face. It was no use. I was a mess. I didn't want her to see me like this. More shame. I cursed myself for giving Everett her phone number.

Sarah approached cautiously, as a bomb tech approaches an unknown ordnance. I tried to speak but couldn't find the words. She stood next to me now, tears rolling down her ashen face. I grabbed a fistful of sheet and swallowed hard.

Sarah wiped her tears away with a swipe of both hands. A smile appeared like a sunrise. Not a joyous, just-won-the-lottery smile, but something deeper. Compassion? Acceptance? Pity? Hard to tell. She reached out and held my hand. Her skin was smooth and warm. I squeezed back.

"Oh, Frank," Sarah finally said, in a voice barely above a whisper.

I said nothing, as there was nothing I really could say to her. I explored her face. God, she was beautiful. So beautiful it made me ache.

Sarah pulled up one of Maurice's visitor chairs and sat down, putting us more or less at eye level. I watched her face cloud up again.

"You left me... us," she said through tears. "I didn't know where you were. Whether you were alive or dead."

"I know," was all I could mumble in reply. "I'm sorry, Sarah. I really am."

She squeezed my hand again. "I don't know if sorry's gonna cover this, Frank." Sarah blew out a breath. Her words washed over me like a mountain stream, fresh and icy cold.

"I know."

"Interesting look you got going here, Frank," Sarah said, motioning to my unkept hair and long beard. "In a couple months, throw some powder in there, you can be a mall Santa." She chuckled.

"Yeah, sure," I responded. "Kids and dogs love me. You know that."

We both shared a long sigh.

Maurice returned to his bed. Sarah stood and offered back the chair. "Sorry."

His eyes ran her up and down. Maurice smiled wide. The man wasn't dead yet. He introduced himself, and Sarah did the same. Maurice then started talking as only he could. *Not now, Maurice.* I needed to put a stop to this.

"How about we take a walk?" I said to Sarah.

"Can you?"

"Yeah, sure," I said. "They gave me a cane yesterday. Good a time as any to try it out. Think they're gonna kick me outta here soon."

Sarah helped me out of bed. Her touch felt good. We bid adieu to Maurice and I clomped out of my room, Sarah close at my side, one hand gripping my arm for support. Slow progress, but good to be up on my feet and moving. People flowed by us on either side of the hallway, like I was a freeway accident not yet cleared. They wore tight-lipped smiles and faces that said they would rather be somewhere else. Not me. I was next to Sarah. No place I'd rather be.

We went past the nurses' station. Everett looked up and gave us a big smile and a wave. I nodded and Sarah said hello.

"She likes you, you know," Sarah said.

"Jill?" I paused to consider it. "No. She doesn't even know me. Just wants to save me, I think."

Sarah shook my answer off. We walked to the end of the hall and stopped by the stairwell door.

"Look," Sarah said, now facing me. I stood with my back to the wall. "Jill told me about your diagnosis." She cleared her throat. "Your leukemia. She said you are refusing treatment. Is that true, Frank?"

I looked past Sarah, over her shoulder. She was a tall woman, only an inch shorter than me. I tried to ignore the question.

"Frank, you have to go into treatment. You know that, right?" Sarah asked, with more urgency in her voice.

"I don't know, Sarah," I said, running my left hand over my head while maintaining my tight grip on the cane with my right. "I just don't see the point. I mean, the way things are."

"You don't deserve to die, Frank."

"Deserve's got nothing to do with this."

"*You* did this to yourself!" Sarah shouted. "Not the cancer—I didn't mean that. I meant your life. *You.*" She took a moment to collect herself, lowered her voice. "Why'd you do it, Frank? Why did you walk away?"

In the five years I was homeless on the streets, I often wondered what I would say to Sarah if this moment ever came. I had never found a good answer. I had none now.

"I don't know, Sarah," I began, and then the words just started to tumble out. "First the army thing, then the CIA fired me. I just felt so betrayed. And so angry. Then I found out Nicole was cheating on me. Looking back, I don't blame her, really. I was no joy to be around then. I lost everything I cared about. You were with Victor. For the first time in my life, I gave up. On myself. On the people around me. I never knew I had a limit, but I found it. Or maybe it found me."

I was breathless now. I gripped the cane and pressed my back tighter against the wall. Sarah's eyes bored into me.

"I guess... I guess I felt like I'd walked to the end of the earth," I said. My voice was barely a whisper now. "And instead of turning back I stepped off."

Sarah gripped my arm. "You could've talked to me, Frank. We could've—"

"I know, Sarah. I know. Pride and shame are a toxic mix. Like bleach and ammonia. It'll kill you." I managed a weak smile.

"The Frank Luce I know is a fighter." Sarah smiled back at me, her full smile. The one that melts my heart. "You can beat this thing, Frank. I know you can. You just have to want to."

She was right. I had lost my faith. In everything and everyone. Myself most of all.

"I can't afford this," I said, changing tack. "I'm broke."

"Don't worry about the money. We'll find you some resources and I'll get the rest. I've got some rainy-day money put aside."

My silence said all Sarah needed to hear. This was my rainy day, not hers. I would not take her money.

"Okay, Frank. I can see you won't do this for yourself, so I'm gonna ask you to do this for me. If you care about me, if you ever loved me, you will get into treatment." Sarah let go of my arm and took a half-step away from me. "If you don't— I'll never speak to you again. I'm not going to sit back and just watch you die on the street. I... can't."

There it was. We were five years apart, and already another separation loomed. This time at her hand. And this one would be final. I cared more for this woman than I did for myself. I had only been with her for minutes, but that was enough for me to decide.

"Okay," I said.

Sarah came in for a quick hug. I held her for a beat longer before she pulled away. We started back down the hallway to my room.

Sarah leaned into me. "You really need to talk to Nicole, tell her about this."

I nodded. "I know."

"Did she tell you she has a five-year-old son?"

CHAPTER NINE

AUGUST 19, 2016
WHITE HOUSE; OVAL OFFICE
WASHINGTON, DC

Prisha Baari stood to the left of President Morris Udell in the Oval Office. Not her first visit, of course, and she would ensure it would not be her last. Prisha smiled her best "big white teeth" smile and tittered convivially at everything Udell said that was remotely funny or clever. Powerful men often thought themselves clever, and Prisha would not disabuse Udell of this notion.

Prisha wore the clear glass frames and hair clip Ahmad had provided her last night. She momentarily turned her back to Udell, pretending to admire the wall art as the president and her boss, Robert Johnson, shared a laugh. *Got it.* She couldn't wait to toss her hair clip at Ahmad and tell him to never again question her talents. She spun back around and surveyed the Oval Office with Ahmad's spy glasses.

"Prisha?" Johnson said. "The president is ready for our briefing."

Udell smiled and gestured towards the sofa opposite his, by the fireplace. Prisha sat first, and Johnson seated himself next to her. The president then took his seat, and his chief of staff sat down to his left. Those formalities finished, Prisha discreetly examined Udell and his CoS. The two men were cut from different cloth. Mo Udell was a fleshy, gregarious man, with a balding pate and a bulbous nose. A career politician and populist president. His CoS, in contrast, was a retired three-star Marine Corps general, a stocky hammer of a man who ran the White House staff with ruthless efficiency. He was completely out of his depth as a civilian on Capitol Hill, however. The Beltway was a different kind of battlefield.

Johnson started speaking in the colloquial style that Prisha abhorred. She glanced over at the fireplace to her right. A portrait of George Washington hung over the mantel. She pictured herself in the portrait, wearing staid Burberry, or perhaps the hot red Chanel outfit she favored.

Johnson finished his introduction, then nodded to Prisha. She held the silence for a beat, felt the anticipation grow as the president and his CoS waited for her to begin. It was a little trick she had learned doing musical theater in college.

"Good morning, Mr. President," Prisha said, flashing her big, toothy smile. "Thank you for having me back to the White House, sir. It is always a pleasure to see you."

Udell nodded. Prisha noticed with satisfaction that his eyes flickered over her body, pausing on her chest long enough to give Prisha a hot flash. She had taken off her blazer as soon as she arrived in the Oval, and had intentionally worn a tight button-back blouse that clung to her Beverly Hills breasts. Unlike her boss, she now had the president's attention. She intended to keep it.

Prisha began her brief with a quick background of ODYSSEUS. She summarized the project technology, the lack of cooperation they were getting from the private sector, and how the CIA was stealing everything they could not beg, borrow, or buy. Prisha spoke of the history of the project, how it had been conceived as a last-chance, failsafe tactic to prevent large-scale domestic civil unrest should the president decide America was on the precipice of revolution or anarchy.

All this the president and Johnson already knew. What neither man knew, however, was Prisha's secret plan for ODYSSEUS. She would continue to push the project as she always had, spending huge piles of taxpayer money to get ODYSSEUS to an operational footing as quickly as possible. In this, her interest and that of the United States government aligned. The best lies, she knew, were the ones that most closely tracked the truth.

Prisha's plan differed from that of the CIA in only two areas: she would drill her own steganographic audio messages into the brains of the American population, and she would do this secretly, at a time of her choosing. She had already established a small team to accomplish her plan, a dark offsite team that had no connection to the CIA or the United States government. Sound experts like Ahmad and his team, her head of security Henrik Karlsson and his team, and a team of world-class virtual hackers to breach the big three (Apple, Google, Microsoft) and all other music and video streaming services.

When the time was right, Prisha would simply command Ahmad to create her audio messages, and the hackers would bury them in audio files on the servers of their targets. Music streaming services like Apple Music or Spotify pull from a database of the same fifty million songs. Billions of YouTube videos are watched every single day. And after Prisha gave the go signal, fully one-third of the people on Earth would cheerfully believe whatever message Prisha planted in their brain. She would own the world before anyone figured it out. And then, of course, it would be too late. Prisha knew a thing or two about power: how to seduce it, capture it—and wield it.

But ODYSSEUS was not operational just yet. Prisha needed more money and time. That's where Udell came in. She leaned forward slightly in her seat and went in for the kill.

"So, despite all the success we've had, ODYSSEUS will need an additional one hundred million in the upcoming fiscal year," Prisha said. She had learned to be bold with her demands, never equivocate or explain. These men were sharks and responded to the scent of blood in the water.

"In addition to the three billion? A budget enhancement?" Udell asked.

"Yes, sir," Prisha responded.

Udell squinted and sat back in the sofa. Prisha mirrored his movements like a tango partner, leaning forward just a touch more to better display her breasts. The dance had begun.

"How much longer?" Udell asked.

Johnson stirred on the sofa next to Prisha. She heard him take a breath to respond and beat him to it.

"ODYSSEUS will be fully operational in two to three

years, sir. At current funding levels and with the enhancement."

"I don't know," Udell said, rubbing his chin. He glanced at his CoS, who was shaking his head vigorously. "I know this project comes out of covert funds, which gives us more time, but I can't keep throwing money at this thing and getting no results."

Prisha jumped in and started to tick off some of the most recent ODYSSEUS successes, repackaging what she had already said, until Udell waved her off.

"I can't wait three years. I'll be too deep into my second term."

Aha. There it was. The lever she needed. Old Mo Udell was planning to use ODYSSEUS for his own political ends. She had him now.

"I agree, sir," Johnson chimed in. "Three years is unacceptable."

Prick, she thought, keeping her thousand-watt smile firmly in place. The buttons on Johnson's suit coat strained against his fat stomach as he repositioned himself on the sofa. Prisha's side of the sofa bucked like an earthquake tremor. *The bastard sold me out.* Prisha had long suspected Johnson would break at the first sign of presidential disfavor.

"How about eighteen months, sir?" Prisha countered. "Would that work for you?"

"Can you guarantee delivery?"

"With an additional two hundred million, I can have ODYSSEUS operational in eighteen months. Yes, sir."

It was an easy bet to wager. Prisha secretly knew ODYSSEUS would be operational in less than a year. Ahmad had committed to six months, max. Even if he was off by a bit, they would be ready next year.

"I like this one," Udell said with a grin, jerking a thumb at Prisha. "Okay, little lady. You got your two hundred million. You better give me my project."

Little lady? Prisha gritted her teeth. Mo Udell would live to eat those words. She would personally serve them to him. Prisha put on her big smile again and thanked him. His eyes wandered over her body once more. She gave Udell a knowing look, which he returned.

"Hey, Bob," Udell said, rising from the sofa. Prisha noted with satisfaction the inchoate erection beginning to tent the crotch of his dark suit pants. "Why don't you head into the conference room. Tell the others I'll be there in a minute for the PDB." He smiled at Prisha. "I'm going to give this little lady a tour of the Oval."

Johnson looked at Prisha and set his jaw. His eyes bored into her. She smirked, shrugged her shoulders. Johnson flushed red. He turned back to the president.

"Yes, sir," was all Johnson could say. He stomped out of the office. Udell's CoS followed.

Udell came around the sofa and stood close to Prisha, close enough for their shoulders to rub.

Udell gestured for Prisha to go first. "Shall we?" he asked.

Yes, we shall.

CHAPTER TEN

AUGUST 25, 2016
PIKE TOWERS APARTMENTS
COLUMBIA HEIGHTS WEST, ARLINGTON, VA

I JERKED THE WHEEL OF THE GRAY FORD FOCUS BACK around onto Columbia Pike and stomped on the accelerator. The four-cylinder engine groaned; the compact responded glacially. The light behind me had just changed, and a glance in my rearview mirror told me traffic was gaining on me fast. My hands gripped the wheel harder. I hadn't driven a car in five years and was not acclimated to the speed at which my fellow motorists traveled. Cars flowed around me. A large SUV blared its horn as it passed. I moved into the right-hand lane and tried to concentrate on the street signs. I almost missed it again. I jammed on my brakes and slapped my directional on. This didn't stop the elongated blaring of the horn of the guy behind me, or the stare-down he gave me as he passed on my left, close enough for our side mirrors to touch. I took the hard right turn with too much speed and drifted into the oncoming lane of traffic. More horns and anger. I pulled over to the side of the road and put the car in park. I wiped my forehead dry with the back of my hand, felt an ant trail of sweat march down my spine. Deep breaths failed to slow my racing heart.

I had been back in the world for only one week, discharged from the hospital the day after Sarah's visit. I had intended to go back to the streets, but Sarah would have none of that. I had protested to no avail, finally accepting her charity for the loving gesture it was. We compromised. The deal we'd struck put me in a hotplate studio in a rough neighborhood, instead of the more expensive option Sarah had proposed. It had also put me in this compact rental car en route to see her baby sister, and my ex-wife, Nicole. I had grown used to being invisible as a homeless man in America. This immersion back into society was a shock to my system; I was like a diver who had surfaced too fast and was now doubled over with the bends.

I checked the address on the scrap piece of paper in my lap. Looked at the number on the duplex across the street. Nicole's apartment was just a few doors down. The dashboard clock informed me I had five minutes before our meeting. I was sweating, my stomach doing gymnastics. I cranked the AC to high and rolled down the window for some fresh air. I still carried the look of a homeless man, my attempt to cut my own hair and beard notwithstanding. I didn't want to smell like one, too. I knew Nicole would not be as forgiving as Sarah had been.

Nicole was four years younger than Sarah, but age was not all that separated them. Nicole was built for speed.

Shorter and thicker than her older sister, with curves in all the right places. She had grown up a princess, fully aware of her beauty from an early age—unlike Sarah. Nicole had found makeup and boys before her older sister had. She had been the leader of the popular girls in junior high and had held this crown through high school graduation. I'd first met Nicole when I began dating Sarah. She was in seventh grade then and already stunning. Nicole was just discovering her powers then. She'd flirted with me, something both Sarah and I had found rather cute at the time. To Nicole, it was training, getting in her reps and honing her skills. By the time she entered high school, she was unstoppable. That was the year Sarah broke up with me.

I graduated West Point and fought the war on terrorism. Nicole graduated Montgomery Blair High School with a C-plus average and fought off frat boys at Florida State, the only college to which she'd applied. It took her five years to eke out a communications degree. She half-heartedly tried to put her degree to work, but mostly bartended at a campus hotspot.

Nicole partied her paychecks away, and by age twenty-three was back in Maryland on her parents' couch. She'd continued her Florida life in Silver Spring, bartending part time and partying full time. She paid her parents no room or board, and ate and drank mostly free thanks to the phalanx of suitors who pursued her with ardor. At this time, I was fighting in Afghanistan, brave enough for my country to put the Medal of Honor around my neck.

Nicole and I had our first date, courtesy of Sarah, less than six months after I had resigned from the army. At that time, we hadn't seen each other in over ten years. We had both grown but not changed much. We both wanted a little of what the other had, what we ourselves lacked. It was a bad match. We never really stood a chance.

The dashboard clock said it was time. I blew out a breath. My hand trembled as I shifted the car into gear.

I parked behind the apartment complex, in the back of the shaded parking lot near a full dumpster, its lid tied open with a rusted chain. The building was an eight-story structure, with walls of stained faux-brick and vinyl siding. Each floor was identical, which caused the windows to stack straight up the wall as if to impose some order on the place. The cramped balconies were filled with old bicycles, storage boxes, and plastic lawn furniture. Loud music and the smells of early dinner wafted from sliding patio doors.

Nicole was always late, a trait that had vexed me during our brief marriage. Right now, though, I took full advantage of the few extra minutes and gathered myself.

Five minutes later, Nicole walked out of the heavy metal back door. It slammed closed behind her as she released it. She took one final draw of her cigarette and stubbed it against the side of the building. She blew the plume of smoke down at her feet, then looked up. I flashed the Ford's lights and got her attention. She looked at me, squinted, then dropped her head and headed my way.

Nicole grabbed the door handle once, then twice, then bent down to the side window and gave me a look. I had forgotten to unlock the car door. I slapped at my door's side panel until I realized this rental did not have automatic doors or windows. Sighing, I reached over to open her door, only to be jerked back violently by my seat belt. This snapped me back into reality. I unbuckled myself and opened her door, cursing myself under my breath.

Nicole got in and locked her door. She gave the parking lot a quick scan, then turned to face me.

"Nice work, Romeo," she said with a tight smile that did not reach her dark hazel eyes.

"It's a rental," I said sheepishly. "I haven't driven much lately."

We looked each other over in the half-light. She still looked the same. Beautiful, but not as bright and shiny as before. Her long blonde hair was pulled back, with wisps escaping to frame a face now fuller and sallow. She took me in. Her face showed shock, then disappointment. To her credit, she kept these thoughts to herself.

Her silence hurt more than words. It hung in the air. My mind raced.

"You smoke now," I blurted out without thinking.

"Yes, Frank," Nicole deadpanned. "I do. I smoke now." She turned away and stared out the windshield towards the dumpster.

"I... I didn't mean... I mean..."

"Look, Frank," she said as she spun to face me again. "I can't stay long. My son's upstairs being watched by my neighbor. I'm only here because Sarah asked me to. She's helped keep a roof over Teddy's head since you left. Without her help we'd be—*homeless*."

Nicole bit off that last word. It hit its intended target. I dropped my eyes.

"Where the hell have you been, Frank?"

I tried to respond, but the words didn't come. Her eyes were afire now.

"Just fucking disappeared? No nothing for five years? Not knowing if you were alive or dead?"

Her eyes widened before she struck me with a balled-up fist. I think she was aiming for my head, but I leaned away from her and the blow landed on my shoulder. She yelled and slapped at me some more. I took it as my due. After a while, she stopped, breathing heavily. I gave her time. She gathered herself, then tucked strands of tousled hair behind her ears.

"This is my life, Frank!" Nicole said as she waved her hand across the windshield at the parking lot. "This is what it looks like."

I said I was sorry. And meant it. We sat in silence, both looking straight ahead.

"Sarah said you had something important to tell me?" she said after a time.

No other way than to just come out with it. So I told her. Told her about my hospital visit. How the doctors had found my leukemia. She was stunned, and we stumbled through all the questions one asks when you share this kind of news. She asked what type of leukemia it was, how I might have gotten it, what the symptoms were. All the while grappling with the news itself. I had the big C. Then came the serious talk.

"How... serious is this?" Nicole asked, tentative with her words now. "I mean... how much time?"

"They said it's an acute cancer. The survival rate's about twenty-five percent."

"So, how long?"

"About five years."

Nicole's eyes narrowed; her forehead wrinkled. "You're gonna die, Frank?" Her voice broke. "You're gonna die," she repeated, this time a statement whispered to herself.

She looked down, shook her head and began sobbing. It grew louder, and her whole body began to shake. I was surprised by this outpouring of emotion. Tragic news, sure, but I thought Nicole had already buried me and our marriage. I was touched, but unsure how to respond. I placed my hand on her leg and gently patted it a few times.

"It's okay, Nicole," I offered. "It's gonna be okay."

This seemed to make it worse. Nicole wept openly. This lasted three minutes by the dashboard clock. It felt much longer to me. She gathered herself, then wiped at her face with both hands. I remembered I had some fast food napkins in the glove box and reached across her to retrieve them. I offered her several. She took them with a flash of a smile, wiped her eyes and nose, pushed her hair back. I held my hand out, and she gave me the soggy brown napkins. I threw them back in the glove box and clicked it closed.

"What happened to us, Frank? Our lives? What a fucking mess." She began to sob once again.

"It's okay, Nicole. It's—"

"No, it's not okay, Frank," she said flatly. "You don't understand. It's not okay."

"What's not—"

"It's been really hard," she continued. "Getting good shifts at the bar. Finding a good man who's willing to commit to raising another man's child. Especially one like Teddy."

"What's wrong with Teddy?" I regretted the words as soon as they left my mouth.

Nicole's eyes narrowed. "There's nothing wrong with Teddy. He's a beautiful boy. Very smart. But he's a sensitive kid. Has a hard time making friends. His therapist says he has trust issues." Nicole snorted. "Can't say I blame him."

I asked her where the boy's father was, meaning Dave, the guy with whom Nicole had had a six-month affair. The affair that was the final straw that pushed me out of our marriage and onto the streets.

"He took off when he found out I was pregnant."

"Bastard," I said.

Nicole's eyes welled up with tears. One, then another leaked from her eyes and ran down her cheeks. She let them go. I watched them fall from her chin onto her blue cotton blouse. Her face contorted into an anguished mask. She raised her hand to her mouth and caught her breath.

"Dave had a vasectomy. He knew Teddy was not his son."

I was about to ask who the father was when it hit me. Hit me so hard I gasped. My mouth dropped open.

"You were the only other man I was having sex with, Frank," she said softly. "I knew Teddy was yours. And when he was born, I was sure. He moves like you. And his laugh..." Nicole placed her hand on my shoulder. "He's your son, Frank."

My field of vision narrowed. The world inside that car went into slow motion. The only thing I could compare it to was combat, when your eyes and ears send messages that your brain can't reconcile.

"No," I said, leaning away from her. "No, this can't be."

"You're Teddy's father, Frank."

I studied her face and realized it was true.

All the air rushed out of me. My emotions hit me like a rolling tide. I began to tremble. I sat mute for a long time.

"Does he know?" I finally whispered.

"No," Nicole said. "No one does. When I knew you weren't coming back, I changed my name back to Phillips. That's his legal name: Theodore Robert Phillips. There is no father listed on his birth certificate. I made it clear I wouldn't discuss the topic of Teddy's father. People suspected, I'm sure, but for Teddy's sake we all agreed to move on. Teddy thinks his father is dead."

"Why didn't you tell me, Nicole?" I said, my voice cracking. "I would've never left."

"You were already gone. You were the one who left, Frank. Remember?"

"You could've somehow got word to me through Sarah."

"Yeah. Nice of you to stay in touch with my sister and not your wife, Frank," she said with a snarl.

I looked at my lap for a moment, and then back up at her. "Why are you telling me this?"

"I had no intention to," Nicole said. "But with your... cancer, I think you have the right to know." Nicole began to gather herself. She sat up in her seat, flipped down the passenger-side visor to check her face in the mirror.

"Can I see him?"

Nicole sighed, and her eyes softened. "Better if you don't."

I dropped my chin to my chest. I just wanted to disappear.

Nicole scrounged in her bag, pulled out her smart phone and tapped at the screen. She found what she was looking for and handed the phone to me.

On the screen was a photo of a little boy who looked to be about five years old. His head was cocked to one side, his arms tucked against his side, feet together. The boy wore a melancholy expression. He had my green eyes and flat nose bridge. Nicole gave me a minute, then gently wrestled the phone from my hand.

I turned to her, struggling against a tide of emotion. "Can I come up and see him?"

"Better if you don't," she repeated.

I looked away, out the front windshield. My eyes stopped on the dumpster.

"I gotta go, Frank," Nicole said. She leaned over and kissed me on the cheek. I wished I had shaved off my bushy beard. "Take care."

She opened the door and stepped out; the little car shook as she closed the door after her. I shifted in my seat, my head bobbling on my neck. All my muscles had gone slack. I watched Nicole walk slowly back across the parking lot and out of my life. Her turn this time.

I sat there for hours, staring at the dumpster, as day turned into night.

CHAPTER ELEVEN

AUGUST 28, 2016
PRISHA'S TOWNHOUSE
GEORGETOWN, WDC

MEERA NAQUI BAARI WAS NOT HAPPY.

She wore the perpetual scowl she did every time she visited her daughter Prisha in the Western world. Prisha imagined the scowl appeared as soon as her mother hit U.S. airspace on her fourteen-hour direct flight from Riyadh. It certainly was firmly in place when Prisha picked her up at Dulles in her shiny Lexus. Driving an automobile was one of the many things Prisha would not be doing if she were still in the Kingdom and not among the infidels.

Prisha sat across from her mother at her cafe table in her Georgetown townhouse. The old woman had aged hard. Her coarse, wiry hair was almost fully gray. She wore it long and pulled back into a braid that ran down the length of her back. Dark moles formed a constellation on her face. Meera's body was short and thick, the opposite of her daughter's. She wore her standard *abaya*, a long black cloak that covered all but her hands and face. She smelled of ammonia and cumin.

Prisha tugged at the hijab she wore for her mother's benefit. She never wore it otherwise, and only indoors on these visits. She wore it loosely, such that her ears and raven hair were visible. This was the only sartorial concession Prisha made for these maternal visits. A cashmere sweater and designer jeans and heels completed her look. *Business on top, party on the bottom.*

Meera sipped her black tea, her eyes scanning her surroundings. High-end stainless appliance suite in the custom kitchen, digital music streaming through smart stereo speakers, a sixty-inch LCD television monitor mounted over the mantel of a gas fireplace. Meera flared her nostrils and curled her lip at these sights and sounds and smells of moral decay. She was a strict Wahhabi, and this was not her cup of tea. Not by a long shot.

Prisha had always bucked Wahhabism, the ultraconservative Islamic fundamentalist movement that emphasizes the importance of avoiding non-Islamic cultural practices and non-Muslim friendships. Prisha hated it for its prohibition of many social practices widely enjoyed by the rest of the developed world. Saudi Arabia, her birthplace, had a long history of exporting Wahhabism, which in turn has been blamed for fueling extremism around the world. Fifteen of the nineteen 9/11 al-Qaeda terrorist hijackers were Saudi citizens—a fact Meera Baari celebrated.

In addition to being her mother, Meera was also the broker between Prisha and her benefactors back in Saudi, the group of rich and powerful men who funded and supported her ODYSSEUS ambitions. At least Prisha thought of these men as her benefactors; Meera called them her patrons. The United States government labeled them designated terrorists.

As a broker, Meera visited her daughter three or four times a year for their information exchange. Meera passed instructions from the benefactors to Prisha, and Prisha provided her mother with ODYSSEUS updates and related intel for delivery back to the group. Prisha tolerated these meetings, but dreaded their arrival as one would a yeast infection, or perhaps food poisoning.

"Turn this music off, Prisha," Meera said.

Prisha did as she was told and bid adieu to Norah Jones. She snickered at the thought of giving her mother a little hit of Beyoncé or Adele, but did not want the poor woman to go into cardiac arrest.

"I worry, daughter," Meera said. "Worry you have been poisoned here in the West. How much longer must you be here?"

"As long as it takes to complete our mission, Mother."

"The patrons demand a time. When will your project be ready?"

Prisha calculated her response. She had tasked Ahmad to have ODYSSEUS operational in six months. She had just struck a deal with President Udell for eighteen months. She split the difference.

"Tell the benefactors ODYSSEUS will be ready in one year."

"*Alhamdulillah,*" Meera responded. Praise be to God.

Prisha nodded and hid her smile behind her coffee cup.

"You will return to the Kingdom in a year, then?"

"*Inshallah*," Prisha responded, knowing full well that Allah had no such plans for her.

"It is well. I have arranged a good match for you. He is a good Muslim from a prominent family."

Prisha knew where this conversation was headed and steered her mother back to business. Her mother asked her ODYSSEUS questions, Prisha provided answers. Answers with just enough truth to placate her benefactors, and to obfuscate her true plan for ODYSSEUS. A plan that only Ahmad and Henrik Karlsson knew.

Prisha had a little surprise in store for the benefactors as well. She would do her own bidding, not theirs. Until then she would enjoy the dance. The manipulation. The power. The danger. In the end, she knew her deceit would be a death sentence for her mother, even if she forsook Prisha as her father had done. No matter. In the afterlife, Allah would judge her mother pure. Prisha had no such concerns for herself. All she had to do was to continue to juggle her boss, POTUS, and her Saudi benefactors, and push Ahmad and her secret team to completion as planned. Once she had ODYSSEUS in her hands, it would be too late for anyone to stop her.

Meera closed her small notebook, laid her pencil down next to it. "The patrons will be pleased, Prisha. I will tell them of your successes upon my return."

"Thank you, Mother."

Prisha looked into the eyes of this woman and felt... nothing. She wondered if she herself would have been any different, if she had had the same upbringing as her mother: raised in British East Punjab, a mere seven-year-old girl at the Great Indian Partition of 1947, when East Punjab turned Hindu and Sikh overnight and over half a million Muslims were murdered trying to flee to West Punjab, the new Muslim enclave now known as Pakistan.

Prisha's father's family had also fled East Punjab during the partition, and the two had met in their early twenties in Pakistan. Her father's business interests had taken them to Saudi Arabia, where he had been active in the formation of OPEC and the nationalization of its oil reserves. Her mother had gone into academia and taught history at university, where she had become the faculty leader of various Muslim Student Associations.

Prisha, their only child, had been born in Saudi Arabia in 1975. She would never know when her parents had hatched their plot for her, but she chose to believe it wasn't until 1990 when American boots hit the ground in Saudi Arabia for Desert Storm. Or maybe it hadn't been her parents' idea at all. Maybe they had been approached by the shadowy men who she came to call her benefactors. It hardly mattered now. What did matter was that at the age of fifteen, Prisha had been selected to be a deep-cover sleeper agent in the United States. That her father had pimped out to an American GI to get her green card, and that her mother had been complicit in all of it.

Prisha regarded her mother across the table as she droned on about infidels and apostates. Prisha luxuriated in the exquisite irony of the moment, then excused herself to pour another cup of coffee. She strolled into her gleaming kitchen, running a finger along the obsidian granite countertops. Prisha poured herself another cup, and with her back shielding her mother, threw in a healthy shot of Irish whiskey.

What her mother did not know would not hurt her.

CHAPTER TWELVE

AUGUST 28, 2016
FRANK'S APARTMENT
FORT TOTTEN, UPPER NE WDC

I NOW LIVED UNDER AN OVERPASS IN UPPER NE DC. I'D
done this before; four months in Albuquerque, I believe it
was. But this was different. I had a roof over my head now,
courtesy of Sarah's rainy-day money. She'd wanted to put me
up in Dupont Circle and take me on a shopping spree—the
full makeover. But I'd refused her kindness and insisted on
my spartan lifestyle. I still had a hard time with charity, and
after five years of homelessness, anything nicer than this
would have given me vertigo.

The apartment building was six stories high and sat at
the end of a stubby dead-end road. My one bedroom on the
fifth floor faced the six-lane interstate that hovered over the

building to the northwest. The steady flow of traffic hummed past my window, like bees at the hive—all except for the big trucks that rattled the windowpanes. My building was an unpainted wood structure that had faded to a dull gray patina. The antique wrought iron fire escapes that climbed up the side of the building hinted at its age. The architecture and ornate trim, albeit neglected, suggested this building, like the neighborhood, had mattered once. Not anymore, it didn't. I wondered if any of the former residents had voiced their outrage as the city built an overpass that cast them in permanent shadow. If so, their voices had obviously gone unheard.

My new home had two rooms: a small bedroom and bath, and a larger room for everything else. I had thrown a bare mattress on the floor and called it good. Sarah had picked out my sheet and bedspread set on our trip to Walmart. We'd picked out my new wardrobe there as well, an assortment of knock-off jeans and shirts. Some of the shirts even had buttons. Boots, a black ball cap and an over-sized jacket finished the look. I'd insisted on shopping for my own underwear and socks. The rest of my furniture—two plastic lawn chairs and one round table—had come from Goodwill.

I ate off paper plates with plastic utensils, so no dishes to wash. My stove didn't work, so Sarah had bought me a hotplate. I kept it on top of the broken stove. I picked up a six-cup Mr. Coffee maker and a few bags of discount ground coffee. The novelty of cooking my own meals gave me joy. What a luxury it was to eat when and what I wanted. Mostly noodles, tuna, and jar sauce. It was great.

Sarah had given me a small allowance as well. That's

where all those noodles came from. This was the hardest thing to accept, but I'd only been out of the hospital one week and had nothing to my name. I'd protested that I'd pay her back every cent (and I would, somehow) and she'd just smiled. Sarah explained that her rainy-day fund was for her to leave her marriage and the philandering Victor. I asked her when, and she said soon. Sarah had worked hard at her career and was well off. She was looking at townhouses in Dupont Circle that were all seven-figure listings. We both knew what she was giving me was sofa-cushion change to her, but it meant the world to me. I loved her for it.

I had arranged my lawn furniture in the front of the big room, nearest the window and away from the kitchen area. The set was dark brown, lightweight and indestructible. It was comfortable enough, and I could move it about the room as I pleased. I grabbed my cup of coffee and took a seat facing the window. The windowpanes were permanently fogged up at the corners, which looked like spider webs. I leaned back in the chair and splayed my legs out. Blew out a few deep breaths, listened to the traffic. People going places. Myself? I wasn't so sure.

It had only been three days since Nicole had changed everything. I couldn't get the boy out of my mind. Kept seeing that photo of him, standing straight and awkward, head cocked at the camera. Eyes searching, no smile. I wanted to jump into that photo. Give him a big hug, tell him it would all be okay. Tell him he was not alone. That his father wasn't dead anymore. Or at least not yet.

Made me think of my own father, Arthur Edward Luce, a journeyman plumber who hadn't wanted to wallow in other people's shit all day and so became a small-time street hustler in one of the crews of Boston Irish mob kingpin

Quinn Doyle. Arthur was a good earner and even better with his fists, and gained a reputation as a man not to be trifled with. I'd worshipped my dad. But he'd loved the streets more than me, and my mom Emily and I hadn't seen him much. There were lots of rumors about him, his exploits and conquests. I think it was the rumors I'd loved more than the man himself. He died in the street when I was nine years old, two bullets behind his right ear.

So I never really knew my dad, and I'd vowed I would be different if I ever had a boy of my own. And now, as it turned out, I had a son who didn't know his father either. I tried to convince myself it was for the best, but Teddy's face would then appear to me as an apparition and I knew better. Or did I? *Hey, son. Good news, bad news. The good news is your dad's not dead; the bad news is that he's dying, though.* How could I ask this boy to put his faith and trust in me? Me, the man who had himself withdrawn from the world, surrendered his own faith and trust. I'd had my reasons, sure, but in truth they were explanations, not excuses. My government had betrayed my trust—twice—and I'd just stopped giving a shit. My son was too young for all this. A little boy without faith and trust was lost. Perhaps forever. I just couldn't let this happen. It was too late for me. It didn't have to be for him.

On my tippy plastic table sat a long-necked vase with two flowers sticking out. Daisies, I think. It was a housewarming gift from Sarah. The flowers were as incongruous here as Sarah was. And perhaps me as well; certainly the old me, not so much this gnarled version. I drained the last of my coffee, now cooled to room temperature, and placed the cup on the table by the flowers.

Next to these flowers sat the envelope Sarah had given

me yesterday. In it was a round-trip Amtrak ticket to Boston. I had officially been summoned by Quinn Doyle. And when Doyle called, one came.

Quinn Doyle and I had a complicated past. Doyle had been my father's boss and the only man he'd feared. Emily had always blamed Doyle for my father leaving the trades for a life of crime, and she resented him for it. My father had tolerated no disrespect of Doyle in our house, and so my mother had seethed in silence.

Emily had broken her silence when my father died, at least partly. She would rant against Doyle in private, but bit her tongue around others. My mother was a tough and outspoken woman, and had never had a problem speaking her mind before my father's death. This had led to arguments, and sometimes more, as my father got heavy-handed when he was drunk. But something had changed with Emily after my father's death. She feared Doyle now and showed him deference whenever he came around.

And Doyle had started to come around often after my father died. He made sure we had money and food on our table. He offered his protection, which in our neighborhood in South Boston was as if we had been kissed by God. I had taken my dad's death hard, and I guess I was looking for a father figure. Doyle became that to me, and I like a son to him. Emily had tried to intervene, but it was no use. I fell under Doyle's influence. Emily had screamed and forbidden me to see him, but no one told Doyle what he could and couldn't do. Doyle had started to groom me for the life. The life my father had chosen. I did not resist. In desperation, my mother had pulled me out of the eighth grade and moved us to Silver Spring, Maryland, to live with her younger sister. I'd hated her for it at the time.

My contact with Doyle had remained after the move. He was there for many of the milestones of my youth: school graduations; my championship football game in high school; my and Sarah's senior prom. He'd stayed in my life through West Point, and glowed with pride when I was awarded the Medal of Honor at the White House, an event he chose not to attend out of fear his criminal notoriety would detract from my ceremony.

Doyle had loved Sarah, and they had grown close. Our breakup broke his heart as well as my own. He'd supported me in my stance against the army and my marriage to Nicole. Doyle was one of the relationships I'd betrayed when I walked away from my life. Sarah had told him of my return, and he hadn't wasted much time in calling me to his side. Through Sarah, I had succeeded in delaying this trip by two weeks.

I grabbed the envelope and held the Acela ticket in my hand: Union Station to South Station. Four hundred fifty-seven miles, seven hours, and fourteen stops. And one giant leap into the past. I anticipated and dreaded this reunion with Doyle in equal measure. But knew I owed it to him, and knew I would go.

I rose from my chair and went to the kitchen to make my second cup. Then I walked back to the window and wrestled with the old double-hung frame, finally raising it a couple of inches to let in the smell of the summer rain. The traffic noise grew louder, like angry wasps buzzing through the window's aperture. I sipped my morning coffee and took in the view. The overpass stood over me, a giant billboard over it.

The billboard rose almost one hundred feet in the air, its concrete pillars at ground level as wide as a redwood. It tucked into the side of the overpass, enlightening the passing motorists about the miracles of Viagra, or how to get bailed out of jail, or the location of the nearest dollar store. But now this billboard was spreading the word about the A1 Pawn Shop, which claimed to offer the best deals in the District.

I had no interest in the A1 Pawn Shop, for I had nothing to pawn and objected to shylocking on principle. What had mesmerized me was the picture of the young woman pitching A1. She was presented in headshot, twenty feet high from head to shoulder. Her head extended another five feet above the rectangular billboard, calling even more attention to her. She was a young Latina, with dark eyes and silky black hair, which she wore long and parted over to one side. Her skin was flawless, the color of my milky coffee. But it was her eyes and lips that really got me. Her eyes danced with a youthful innocence that masked a glimmer of melancholy underneath. The full red lips were slightly parted; her open Mona Lisa smile said she was in on the joke.

This woman towered above me, like a beguiling angel. Her face filled my only window. I'd taken to calling her Angela, which I soon shortened to Angie. The longer I studied her face, those eyes, the surer I had become that she was looking right at me. Her face was burned into my brain. I found myself glancing up at her often. Her presence had become reassuring to me. I did not know why, nor did I care. I'd take it.

My eyes traveled from Angie down the long pillar that propped her up, to the street below. Off to the right, in the shadows, lay a homeless man, passed out. I felt a sting in my gut. I still remembered that life. I emptied my coffee cup with one last gulp.

I had a few extra bucks now. I slipped on my shoes and jacket. I would go down and shake the homeless guy awake, press a ten-dollar bill into his hand.

And say a proper good morning to Angie.

CHAPTER THIRTEEN

AUGUST 28, 2016
FRANK'S APARTMENT
FORT TOTTEN, UPPER NE WDC

I DROPPED THE DISPOSABLE RAZOR INTO THE SINK AND inspected the stranger in the mirror. I had not seen this man in years. I stood naked in my tiny bathroom; the door was open, with a view to my bedroom and mattress beyond. Between the shower and shaving, I had exhausted all the hot water, and finished with a cold shave that nicked my face and neck up good.

I had ventured out earlier today to get a haircut at a local shop. I had always worn my hair high and tight, an echo from my military life, I suppose, but now thought I'd do otherwise. I told the guy to cut my bangs straight across at eye level and shorten the rest to just above shoulder length. I hadn't had a haircut in years, and it was a mess. I felt bad for the guy and tipped him heavily when he was done.

Now, I pulled my hair up tight into a topknot. It felt tidier this way, kept the hair out of my face. Old habits, it appears, die hard.

The man in the mirror had a quizzical expression on his face. I ran my hand over his—my—smooth face, then to the triangular soul patch below my bottom lip. I tried on a smile but got only a grimace, and so let it fade. My face had gone gaunt, my features sharp as a hawk's. More than a few wiry gray hairs spotted my dark brown hair. The green eyes were flat, the whites a jaundiced yellow. I was shocked at how much I'd aged. That was enough for now. I turned from the mirror and got dressed.

I grabbed a can of beer and plopped into one of my lawn chairs, which I had positioned five feet in front of my window. Night was falling, and Angie was up-lit by the lights bolted along the bottom of the billboard. I turned my one light off, which put the room in near darkness. Better for me to see Angie, and her me.

"Yeah, it's just me—Frank," I said, tipping my can towards the billboard in toast. "Whaddaya think, Angie? You like?"

She held our stare.

"Here's to a new look... and a new life," I said, and took a hit off my beer. Then another.

Was a new life even possible? Or was it too late? What would the leukemia have to say about this? I was in day ten of my life with cancer, but I felt fine. No symptoms. I'd promised Sarah I would take treatment, and I would. But I was in no hurry for my body to be blasted with chemo and radiation.

I studied Angie's dark features. "You know, you remind me of someone." I chuckled, took a long pull from my beer. "Just a little."

I'd thought of my fall from grace often during my absence. My five-year odyssey, a journey I'd started as a soul-searching backpacker and ended as a hardcore homeless transient. It seemed to always come back to that one night, a Friday it was, that I had stayed at CIAHQ to work deep into the evening to meet a deadline. I'd got up from my desk to stretch my legs and ran into her at the elevator lobby. She had dark features, like Angie, but was of Middle Eastern descent. Her name was Prisha. She didn't give me her last name. We talked, she flirted. I was tired and lonely in my marriage. She invited me up to her office and we rode the elevator together. She had a small executive bar next to her desk. We drank bourbon and swapped stories. She poured us another, then sat down next to me on the sofa. Close. She kissed me softly. Then again, forcefully. We had sex on that sofa. Loud, animal sex. She was aggressive and liked it a bit rough. I obliged. We both finished quickly.

I regretted it as soon as it was over. By this time, I was certain Nicole was being unfaithful in our marriage, but I took no solace in that. This was not revenge sex. It had just happened, as the trite saying goes. I was ashamed, disgusted that I had broken my vow of fidelity. Nicole knew nothing of this. I knew it would never happen again.

The following week, I learned that Prisha was none other than Prisha Baari, the newly appointed Deputy Director of the CIA. I had stayed away from office gossip and news back then. I had heard we had a new DD, of course, knew it was a female, and had maybe even heard her name, but all of this was far from my mind that late Friday night in her office.

I avoided Prisha as best I could, hoping this thing would just go away. At first, she sought me out, even stopping by my desk a few times. She was charming, clearly wanting to continue our liaison. I was physically attracted to her, as I suspect all men were, but told her I was married and committed. This seemed to encourage her even more, and she got more reckless and brazen in her courtship. I finally had to shut her down, tell her to leave me alone. She'd turned on me instantly, cussing and threatening, and that's how we parted. After that final blowout, she gave me icy stares the few times we passed in the halls.

I was fired from the CIA, for cause, a month later. Some bullshit about me mishandling classified information. They pulled my security clearance and all my government benefits. No health insurance, no pension. And no security clearance meant I was basically unemployable in the Beltway. Cue the sad trombone.

I had no proof that my one-night dalliance with this black widow spider had anything to do with my firing and deconstruction, of course. But it did feel like this was the beginning of the end, the day the clouds gathered and never parted. The rain came soon thereafter.

I was lost in thought when I heard the pounding on my door. It clearly wasn't Sarah's knock, and no one else knew I was here. I approached and listened. I could hear someone shuffling and breathing heavily on the other side. I threw the latch and opened the door wide. A young guy, rail thin and jumpy, gave me a gap-toothed smile.

"Hey, man," he said, scratching at the scabs on his face. "You got any hero, man?"

"What?"

"C'mon. Big H. I know you holding. How much?"

"You got the wrong guy."

"No. They told me this was the place."

Great. The previous tenant must have been a heroin dealer. Just wonderful.

"Wrong apartment," I said.

I shut the door on the guy as he was about to start another round of gimme-my-stuff. There was a pause, and then the pounding began anew. The cussing followed. I shouted at him to piss off. He kicked the door and stomped away. I wondered how many more customers I might get this night.

I turned and walked to the kitchen, pleased to feel adrenaline in my veins for the first time in years. Fight or flight. Fight it would be.

I searched my kitchen for a proper knife but found none. I supposed Sarah thought me suicidal and didn't want anything sharp or pointy within my grasp. I realized I had never even noticed my kitchen was without steak knives. I searched the apartment for a suitable blunt object, but again nothing. I walked back to the kitchen, opened the drawer, grabbed a butter knife, and went back to my chair to await my next visitor.

For the next few hours, with the glowing billboard as my nightlight, I sat in my lawn chair, watching the night pass. I asked Angie about the previous occupant of my apartment and about our neighborhood. She had nothing good to say. It occurred to me that Nicole and Teddy lived in a similar neighborhood to mine. That they too must get unwanted knocks at their door. I now understood that they had lived in fear since I'd left, and that fear was all that Teddy knew. He had not been around for the good early years in Colonial Village, our suburban home three miles north and a galaxy away from the Pike Towers Apartments. How many nights had Teddy lain shaking in his bed, covers pulled tight over his head, while Nicole stood guard against the world?

I looked down at the butter knife clenched in my hand. I slowly released my grip, let it clatter to the floor. I flinched at the noise, my nerves now on edge. I heard footfalls in the hallway, but no visitors. I turned back to Angie and we had a long chat. It started to rain again.

I glanced down at the butter knife twinkling in the light of the billboard, still lying where it had come to rest on my filthy floor. Though dull, the blade had nicked the old gritty hardwood, revealing the lighter golden wood that lay beneath. I stared at it a while before it hit me. I shot upright in my plastic chair. The idea arrived fully formed and clear as truth can be.

I would find out why I had been wrongfully terminated from the CIA. I would fix it and get my government benefits and pension reinstated. Nicole and Teddy would get it all upon my death, enough to get them out of Pike Towers and back to where they belonged. I would put things back to the way they were. Nicole could use the money to buy a house in Colonial Village, our old neighborhood. A place with good schools and no fear. Teddy would make friends, live a good life. I would stop treatment when my benefits were restored. Nicole would collect soon enough.

A great weight lifted from my soul. I grabbed the arms of my chair lest I float to the ceiling. I smiled openly at the thought of Teddy in his new bedroom or playing with his new friends in the schoolyard. I heard his jubilant laughter. I looked to Angie through misty eyes. She agreed.

It was done, then.

I walked to my bedroom and stripped down to my underwear and T-shirt. I dropped onto the mattress and slid the butter knife under my pillow. I was asleep in minutes, the first solid sleep I'd had in a long time.

———

I awoke in the middle of the night to another loud banging at my door. I shook myself awake and fought to gain my orientation. *It's night. You're at your new apartment. Another fool's at your door.*

I grabbed my butter knife, took a solid grip of it in my right hand, then rolled off the mattress and took to my feet. I walked towards the door and thought of Teddy and my new plan. I gripped the knife tighter. Hope is a powerful thing. If this world wanted a fight, I was now happy to oblige.

CHAPTER FOURTEEN

TOMMY BOONE PARKED HIS F-150, CAMOUFLAGED IN primer, outside his trailer in Loblolly Estates, just southwest of El Dorado, Arkansas, near the Louisiana border. He stepped out of the truck and slammed the door with a grinding metallic clank. He patted himself down roughly and drywall dust enshrouded him. He coughed and swiped at the white cloud, a Marlboro screwed into the side of his mouth and a beer in his big left hand.

A barking dog rushed him. He was a pound mix, big and brown with patchy spots. His ribs showed. Boone calmly reached into his pocket, withdrew a hard dog treat and lobbed it overhand in the direction the dog had come. The dog spun to retrieve his treat. It clanked off the side of his shit-for-brains neighbor's trailer and into the weeds. The dog scooped it up and was chewing his nightly offering as Boone reached his own trailer.

He ducked as he entered, because Boone was a big man. Six foot four and wide, with a big bucket head and size sixteen boots. He was country strong and liked to throw things around, whether it be 4x8 sheets of drywall at work, or any takers at the local bars from Shreveport to Pine Bluff on the weekends. He had a patchy blond goatee and a prominent forehead big enough to project movies on. He saw the world simply, through squinted eyes.

He tossed his keys on the table by the door, watched them slide off and hit the floor. He left them there and headed to the fridge to get another beer. The fridge door creaked open to reveal two six-packs and leftover fast food bags. Boone grabbed a six of Bud and a bag of Taco Bell and headed across the room. He pushed some junk to the side of the table and sat down. The chair groaned. He dropped the evening's nutrition onto the table, then retrieved his laptop from under the sofa, where he placed it for safekeeping.

Boone lived alone, at least for now, until he could land wife number three. He had two ex-wives and four young children by three different women, and had declared bankruptcy twice in his thirties. Boone was in his mid-forties now and working as a drywall laborer for cash under the table to avoid his various spousal and child support orders. His good ole country boy act had worn thin. Any affability he once had was gone. Boone was now just bitter and angry. So angry.

The laptop was the most expensive thing Boone owned, if one counted possession as ownership. He had stolen it from a rich kid's closet during a big remodel job he had worked on six months ago. Boone figured the kid's parents could buy him a new one. He'd paid another drywaller, a young tweaker, fifty bucks to wipe the laptop clean, and another twenty bucks to hack into his neighbor's WiFi—the two young dumb-asses with the dog.

Boone fired up the laptop and logged on as he slugged down his can of Bud. He went to Fox News and clicked on the top story. It was a video of a Pentagon spokesman announcing the death of ISIS terrorist Wael Adel Salman, its minister of information and one of the few people who had direct access to Abu Bakr Al Baghdadi, the leader of ISIS. The U.S. had got Salman with a drone strike, hitting him on a motorcycle just outside a house in Raqqa, Syria.

Boone laughed. *Another raghead dead. Good. Kill 'em all.* He clicked out of the top story, then walked back to the kitchen for another beer and to look for more hot sauce to punch up his day-old tacos. Boone realized it when he was deep into the fridge, rooting around in taco bags. He jumped back and stood at attention. *No—it couldn't be.*

He rushed back to the laptop and rewatched the video. He paused it and leaned in for a closer look. Played it, then paused it again. His eyes were squinted almost shut now, his head inches from the screen. The woman in the background, off the right shoulder of the Pentagon spokesman. It was her! Boone whooped.

"God dammit!" Boone mumbled to himself. "Fucking bitch." Boone was sure it was her. Prisha Baari. His first ex-wife. Though he didn't consider her that. She was merely the first woman who'd screwed him over. The first of many in his life. Boone had to admit that Prisha looked good, though. And she was obviously a government big shot of some kind, getting face time at a major Pentagon news conference. He googled her and found her after he properly added the double "aa" to her last name.

Boone's mouth dropped open, his beer frozen mid-air in his hand. He read from the official CIA website:

Prisha V. Baari
Deputy Director, Central Intelligence Agency
Prisha Veda Baari was officially sworn in as Deputy Director of the Central Intelligence Agency (CIA) on April 18, 2009. She was thirty-four at the time of her appointment, making her the youngest deputy director in CIA history. As deputy director, she manages the Agency's intelligence collection, analysis, covert action, counterintelligence, and liaison relationships with foreign services.

Deputy Director Baari joined the CIA in 2005 as a direct SES placement in the Directorate of Analysis. In Washington, she has held numerous senior analyst and leadership positions, including Director and Deputy Director of the Directorate of Analysis, and Acting Director of the National Clandestine Service.
Deputy Director Baari is the recipient of the Intelligence Medal of Merit, and the George H. W. Bush Award for Excellence in Counterterrorism.

Deputy Director Baari earned a bachelor's degree in Political Science from Barnard College in 1997, and a master's degree in International Affairs from American University in 1999. Before joining the CIA, she worked on Capitol Hill from 2000 to 2004, rapidly rising to serve as Chief of Staff to Congresswoman Janet Mullins, Chair of the United States House Permanent Select Committee on Intelligence.

Deputy Director Baari was born in Saudi Arabia and
became a U.S. citizen in 1990. She has been an effective
advocate for Arab American causes and was active in
forming legislation in the wake of the 9/11 terrorist attacks.
In addition to English, she speaks fluent Hindi, Urdu, and
Arabic.

Boone's hands shook. He balled them into sledgehammer
fists. *Bullshit!* Boone knew better, because he had been there.
In Saudi. For all of it. A U.S. Marine in Operation Desert
Shield and Desert Storm, 1990 to 1991. Boone had been a
testosterone-filled nineteen-year-old kid who had never been
outside southwest Arkansas. He'd met Prisha on base; she
was one of the locals who helped keep the place running.
She was young and beautiful, and appeared interested in
Boone from the start. He couldn't believe his luck, and
because it was forbidden, they'd managed to hide their relationship from both their countries. The sex had been great.
Prisha certainly knew how to please a man.

At the time, Boone had considered this the best part of
his life: he was a Marine, young and strong, defending his
country against terrorists. He had a hot girlfriend on the sly.
Life was good. He was the cock of the walk.

That had all changed when Boone met Prisha's parents
and learned it wasn't luck that had brought them together.
Prisha had sat to the right of her father, avoiding eye contact,
as the old man ran it all down. He told Boone he knew of
their relationship, and that Boone had brought dishonor to
his family. The father said Boone had to marry his daughter,
that this was the only way. Boone had equivocated, and the
father had had to threaten to expose him to his superiors.
This made Boone angry, a fact he made known. The father

had then offered a significant cash dowry—$50,000—to set
Boone and his daughter up in the States. This was more
money than Boone had ever seen. It got his attention, and the
rest became mere details. In the end, Boone got his beautiful
Arab bride, his cash payout, a less-than-honorable discharge
from the Marine Corps, and a one-way ticket back to southwest Arkansas. And Prisha had gotten her green card. She
had divorced Boone within one year, after they had pissed
through the fifty thousand dollars.

Boone had learned some troubling things about Prisha
during their brief marriage. First, she had lied about her age
and was only fifteen when they met, sixteen on their
wedding day, which under U.S. law made Boone a statutory
rapist. And Prisha and her parents were not the moderates
they pretended to be, but strict Wahhabis who hated the
United States. Prisha was a convenience Muslim who had
developed a taste for alcohol behind closed doors.

Most of these revelations came after a night of drinking
and fighting; and man, did Prisha like to fight. She went from
fun to furious in a flash. And she was cruel, gloating about
her family's deception: how her father had pimped her out;
how Boone had not been the first American to taste, but was
the first gullible enough to bite; how easy it had been to fool
him; how she had never loved him or been faithful to him,
not even now in the States.

Boone looked around his shitty trailer and reflected on
the squalor that was his life. He threw his beer can across the
room, spraying foamy liquid everywhere before the can hit
the wall with a crash. He slammed the laptop shut.

Boone knew he had been stupid to agree to his green-
card marriage to Prisha; he was also painfully aware that he
had made a litany of mistakes over his life. He would never

be anything more than a good ole country boy. A bit of a hell-raiser, sure, but not a bad guy, all in all. But his life was shit and he knew it. Why should he be living like this? Boone had fought for his country and had nothing to show for it. Prisha was a lying bitch who didn't give a rat's ass for this country, and she was the hero? *The goddamn Deputy Director of the CIA?*

Boone was patriotic. He regretted what he had done—given Prisha green card status in his beloved country. He had no idea how Prisha had gotten full U.S. citizenship status, but knew it could not have been through proper channels. It troubled Boone that a woman such as Prisha was the number two at the CIA. She was dangerous. It troubled him more that she had won and he had lost. After a few more beers, he resolved to fix this.

Boone rooted around under the sofa again and came up with a tattered photo album. He flipped through it and then slid out what he was looking for. He held the faded wedding photo in his large, callused hands. It was the only thing he had left from the marriage. He looked so young and hopeful, his arm around his bride, a broad smile for the camera. Boone had had feelings for Prisha, despite everything, and had tried to make their sham marriage work. He studied young Prisha in the photo, the tight-lipped smile that never reached her dark shark eyes. She had never cared for Boone at all, had just wanted to leech off his citizenship. And now she was at the highest levels of government, and he was spending another night alone and drunk in his trailer. Trying to ignore the beat-bop of music that blared from his neighbor's trailer and crawled under his skin.

Boone slammed his fist to the flimsy plastic table, which sent his crushed empty beer cans crashing to the floor like fallen leaves. Enough was enough. Time to get even, balance the scales of Lady Justice. What she and her family had done —to his country, and to him—wasn't right. He might be just a good ole country boy, but he had a pretty good idea that the CIA and the American public would be awfully interested in this little piece of information. And that Prisha would be awfully interested in keeping it secret. He had a plan: he would blackmail the bitch.

Boone would make her pay this time. Really pay, not the pissant fifty grand he'd got the last time. This time Boone would add another zero. Prisha would find the money. She'd have to, or Boone would ruin her. Tell all he knew. She had everything to lose, and he had nothing. Going up against the CIA frightened him, but there was nothing more dangerous than a man who truly did not give a shit—like Boone. He didn't care if he got arrested, beat up, or worse. He wanted Prisha to pay for what she had done. And he wanted his money.

———

Boone found a pen and paper among the clutter of his kitchen counter. He scratched out a quick note, then taped it to the front of his refrigerator. The note was addressed to his children. It contained things he wanted them to know about their dad in case he didn't come back. He packed a quick bag, turned off the lights, and left his front door unlocked. *Steal all my shit. I don't care.*

He walked to his pickup. His neighbor's dog was lying by the door, in the glow of the porch light. The dog eyed Boone but did not charge. He let out a solitary bark, then put his head back down. Boone got into his truck, rooted around in the deep storage console between the front bucket seats, and tossed the dog his remaining treats. The dog sprang up, walked a few steps, and scooped a few up. He watched Boone as he chewed.

Boone put the truck in gear and headed north to seek his fortune.

CHAPTER FIFTEEN

SEPTEMBER 10, 2016
NATIONAL WORLD WAR II MEMORIAL
WASHINGTON, DC

I WAS WIDE AWAKE, LYING ON MY FLOOR MATTRESS AS I listened to the overpass traffic buzz by. Too nervous to sleep. I got up before sunrise, shaved and showered. I fidgeted in the mirror and changed my shirt twice. Like a nervous teenage girl before a big date. *I really wanted this boy to like me.*

I took the Metro to the National Mall and shared a serene early Saturday morning with Mr. Lincoln before the horde came calling. It was to be a beautiful September day in the District, full sun, light wind, with the temperature to reach into the high seventies by afternoon. It was cool now, with just a kiss of fall in the air. I bid adieu to Mr. Lincoln and walked east to the Washington Monument, where I spent another hour waiting. I stood at the foot of the great obelisk, leaned my back against the cool white marble. Closed my eyes and hoped some of the greatness of this man would seep into me. I could use all the help I could get today.

Having killed a couple of hours on the Mall, I slow-walked the half mile west to the World War II Memorial. The site of my big date. I crossed 17th Street and the three large lawn panels at the eastern memorial entrance. I veered left and found an unoccupied granite bench against the rampart wall at the curved southern approach. I was still early by thirty minutes. The elm trees behind me offered just enough shade to cast shadow on my bench, cooling the granite. The cold stone did not stop my nervous perspiration, now beginning to bead and run down my back.

I looked out at the memorial site, bathed in shards of morning sun. It was a park-like setting, a big granite oval centered by a grand water fountain and spread out over seven prime acres between Messrs. Washington and Lincoln. Bronze and granite statuary lined the oval, with twenty-four carved stone panels depicting the Atlantic and Pacific theaters of the great war. My bench was in the Pacific theater.

I licked my lips, checked my watch. A few minutes still. My heart sped up, despite the deep breaths.

It had taken me two weeks to convince Nicole to go along with my plan. I understood her skepticism. I'd earned that. But she knew me well enough to know I was serious about this, and that I did what I set my mind to. It all came down to Teddy. We were both doing this for him. She was allowing me back into their lives, would accept my government benefits package upon my demise in order to give our son a better life. Nicole had rejected most offers of money from Sarah and their parents, choosing instead for her and Teddy to go it alone. I respected her for this but couldn't shake the image of Teddy returning from his warehousing public school, shuffling down a long, littered hallway past the screaming neighbors to his squalid two-bedroom home.

Nicole had slowly come around to seeing my government benefits not as charity but as money I—we—had earned. Money that had been taken from us. She didn't like that any more than I did. So we agreed on my plan. I'd get my shot at redemption. I'd go to my grave knowing I had done *something*, that I hadn't just stood around watching while the world swallowed my son whole.

My one condition in all this was that I would get to meet my son. Nicole had been understandably cool to this idea, but I wore her down. We agreed I wouldn't tell him our big secret, that it was best for him to continue to believe that his father was dead. This stung, but Nicole was adamant that this was non-negotiable if I wanted to meet my son. I had ruminated on the fact that I posed a worse option for Teddy than him continuing to believe his father was dead, which made me worse than nothing at all. I also knew that I would have done better by him—by *them*—had I known. I resented Nicole for not telling me, not giving me the chance to be a father to my son. I knew all too well how hard it was for a boy to grow up without his father. But this was on me. I planned to make it right.

———

I scanned the growing crowd. They were fifteen minutes late. My mind went dark. Had Nicole lied to me? Was I a fool to have trusted her? Faith was fragile, like inching out on thin ice. I fell through into my icy water now, bobbing like a buoy, arms down at my sides. My core temperature dropped. My blood began to chill. I knew this feeling and fought against it, but knew I would submerge again.

Then I saw her. I leapt from the icy water and back into the Saturday morning sunshine. It was Nicole. Walking towards me, behind oversized sunglasses. She held the hand of a beautiful five-year-old boy. My son Teddy. He was the boy from the photo, come to life. I started to shake.

Nicole saw me and smiled, tight-lipped. She stopped and squatted down in front of Teddy. They had a brief conversation, and I saw Teddy steal a couple of tentative glances in my direction. Nicole kissed him, then stood up and strode towards me, Teddy in tow. Time slowed then jerked forward. My mind was taking photographs to preserve this memory. Then they were upon me.

I stood and immediately felt dizzy. I widened my stance in search of equilibrium. He was a small boy. Had our green eyes and my nose. He glanced up at me, then looked rapidly away. I was mesmerized. I think my gawking made him all the more uncomfortable. He tucked himself partially behind his mother's leg to shield himself from the strange man.

"Teddy, this is... a friend of mine, Frank," Nicole said, taking charge in the midst of this exquisite awkwardness. "Frank, this is my son Teddy."

He wouldn't look at me. I swallowed the lump in my throat. My eyes stung. My fingertips tingled. I bit down hard on my molars, which set my jaw and helped keep my emotions at bay. I looked at Nicole and she gave me a quick head nod intended to get me back on task.

I bent down to his eye level and offered him my hand.

"Nice to meet you, Teddy." My voice sounded faint in my ears.

Teddy turned away from me, tucked closer into Nicole.

"Teddy," Nicole paused to slide the boy out from behind her leg, "Frank is a friend of mine. Say hello to him."

Teddy looked at his shoes and shook his head no.

"Teddy, go on, say hello to the nice man."

Teddy mumbled a hello without looking up.

Nicole and I exchanged looks.

"It's okay. He's just a little shy around people. Especially people he doesn't know. But his therapist is working on that. Isn't that right, sweetheart?" She tousled his hair. He leaned against her leg. "He's even got a new friend at school. Brad."

"Brandon," Teddy said in a soft voice, addressing his mother.

They joined me on my granite bench. Nicole placed Teddy between us, a courtesy for which I was grateful. It was thrilling to have him so close. His silky dark hair, side parted and neatly combed. His feet hanging off the bench, swinging six inches above the ground. It took all I had not to wrap an arm around his small shoulders. Tell him everything.

We started with small talk, Nicole and I. Mostly pantomimed conversation for Teddy's benefit. He seemed to gradually relax in my presence. Nicole got him talking to me, one or two words here and there, but it felt good. He resisted my attempts at conversation. I fished for topics.

"Your momma says you like to play with army men," I said. "Is that right?"

Teddy nodded.

"Yeah, me too. Your momma told me you want to be an army man when you grow up."

Teddy shrugged.

I took a deep breath and tried to think of another topic, fast.

"My daddy was brave. That's what Mama says." Teddy looked up at me. "He won lots of medals."

My gut clenched. I flicked a look at Nicole. Saw her sad eyes and set jaw. She was gritting through this.

"The president gave my daddy a big medal. 'Cause he was really brave."

So my son did know me. The best part of me. I wanted so badly to tell him more.

I swallowed hard. "Teddy... I... he... your daddy... He..."

Nicole was shaking her head, eyes wide.

Teddy was looking up at me now. This time he didn't turn away. He wanted to know what I had to say about his daddy. He waited for me to finish what I had started. My ears buzzed; my eyes began to water. I bit down hard on the insides of my cheeks to stop this avalanche of emotion. Hard enough to draw blood, slick against my tongue. I flicked at the corner of my eye and leaned down towards my son.

"Yes, Teddy," I said. "I knew your daddy. He was a very brave man." I cleared my throat. "And I know he loved you very much."

Nicole began to sob, with a hand to her face to muffle the sound lest Teddy turn around. She shook herself, forcefully wiped her tears away. She gave me a weak smile and mouthed "Thank you." I nodded.

I turned back to my son. "Hey, Teddy, I've got an idea. Maybe you and me can be friends. Like you and Brandon. What do you say?"

Teddy shrugged.

"C'mon. It'll be fun."

"What kind of fun?"

"Whatever kind of fun you want. Sound good?"

This time he nodded. A bit of a smile curled the corners of his mouth.

"Friends then," I said, extending my hand.

Teddy shook it. His small hand felt soft in mine. I placed my other hand over the top of our handshake. It was as close to a hug as I would come.

This friendship pact ended our meeting. We closed with some more small talk, but Nicole and I were wrung out. We all stood.

"Time to go, sweetheart," Nicole said. "Say goodbye to your new friend."

My son took a step towards me and stuck out his hand. I almost stared bawling but held it together. I grabbed his hand and shook.

"Frank's a war hero, Teddy, just like your daddy," Nicole said.

I let go of his small hand. "I'll see you again, Teddy. And remember, we're friends now."

He nodded. I got another smile out of him.

Nicole approached me. Her eyes welled with tears. She threw her arms around me, held me tight.

"Thank you, Frank," she whispered, her lips to my ear.

"I'm sorry," was all I could think to say.

I slipped it into her pocket. The weight of it tugged her light jacket down. Nicole searched my eyes. She reached in and pulled out my Medal of Honor. She gasped at the sight of it.

"Give it to Teddy," I said. "When he's older. When he understands. Tell him his father was once brave, and that he loved him very much."

I turned and left, knowing not to look back.

I walked aimlessly, hands in pockets, eyes downcast, back towards Mr. Lincoln. Past happy tourist families I could not bear to see. I waited for tears that never came. Just a smothering emptiness. An infinite dark universe I was now ready to navigate in search of life.

My life.

CHAPTER SIXTEEN

September 10, 2016
Parkview Market
Petworth, NW WDC

THE NORDIC MAN PULLED OFF THE BLACK HOOD AND tossed it skyward. It fluttered down to the floor next to the man now blinking hard against the light from the bare bulb overhead. He was tied to a chair that was bolted into the floor. His face was swollen, his bottom lip split. He was a big man. He rocked violently in the chair, but the straps held. This chair had been designed to tame big violent men.

"Oh, Tommy," Prisha said, patting the man's arm as it strained against the straps. "Did you really think this was going to work?" She chuckled and shook her head.

Boone was wide-eyed. His thinning hair stood up tall on top of his head, from the static electricity of the hood removal. His bulging eyes went from Prisha to the Viking to his right, then back to Prisha.

"Where am I?" Boone asked.

Silence.

"Who is he?" Boone asked, flicking his big bucket head towards the Viking.

"That, my dearest Tommy, is Henrik Karlsson, my head of security. He's the man who put you in that chair."

Boone grumbled and shook against his restraints.

"U.S. Marine, yes?" Karlsson asked. "I myself was Swedish SOG—Special Operations Group." Karlsson took a step closer to Boone. "You fought well, my friend. There is no shame in being bested by the better man."

Karlsson had porcelain-white skin and pale, wide-set blue eyes. He had keen features, a jawline hard enough to crush walnuts. At thirty-six, his two hundred fifteen pounds were well distributed over his six-foot, four-inch frame. All broad shoulders and tapered waist. He had the physique of a rower: long ropey muscles, all sinew and no show. He moved with the grace and efficiency of a tiger. Karlsson was intense, laconic. Not given to bluster or grandstanding. A Swedish iceberg. His danger lay below the surface.

"You gotta admit, Tommy, this plan was asinine, even by your standards," Prisha said.

"What was I supposed to do?" Boone shouted. "You CIA motherfuckers don't put your phone numbers on your website."

Prisha got a genuine laugh out of this. Even Karlsson snickered. Boone joined in, and the three shared a moment of brief mutual revelry.

He had driven nonstop from Arkansas to Virginia. Boone had figured he'd find a number for Prisha, then pass along his demands and payment instructions. When he couldn't find any number for her online, he'd simply shown up at Langley and demanded to see her. The CIA security guards had detained him and contacted Prisha, who, in turn, had contacted Karlsson. It was Karlsson, not Prisha, who had come down to get Boone. He had subdued Boone without breaking a sweat.

The forced laughter abated as suddenly as it had begun, and with it any pretense that Boone was going to get what he wanted. It was time for Karlsson to get to business. He and Prisha began to question Boone to determine the extent of his knowledge. They took him for a dope but couldn't be sure. At first Boone resisted, foolish pride masquerading as bravery, but this soon gave way once Karlsson applied a few advanced interrogation techniques. Boone came clean. Told them all he knew—Prisha's Wahhabi extremist background, her green-card immigration fraud, his suspicions that she was up to something.

"What is it you think I'm up to, Tommy?" Prisha asked.

"I dunno. Something shady. Maybe you're a terrorist. A sleeper." Boone looked to Karlsson. His face was impassive. He turned back to Prisha. "I dunno. Don't care. Just give me my money and I won't tell anyone. Promise."

"Anything else, Tommy?" Karlsson asked.

Bone nodded his head vigorously. "No. That's it. That's all I know."

Karlsson and Prisha exchanged glances.

"Did you tell anyone about this, Tommy?" Prisha asked. "Does anyone know you were coming to see me?"

"No!" Boone shouted, with the innocence of a child.

Prisha believed him. Karlsson dipped his chin. He believed him too. Too bad for Boone. He had just given away the last leverage he had. It was clear to both Prisha and Karlsson that Boone knew nothing of ODYSSEUS. At least not yet.

Boone misinterpreted the silence. He smiled, thinking things had turned in his favor. Prisha almost felt sorry for him. She returned his smile, then signaled Karlsson. Karlsson pulled a small canister from his front pants pocket. He covered his nose and mouth with his free hand. Prisha stepped back and covered up as well. In one smooth motion, Karlsson brought the canister up and sprayed a fine mist in Boone's face, then jumped back next to Prisha. Boone coughed and whipped his head from side to side. He slumped in the chair and was fast asleep in thirty seconds.

Karlsson and Prisha retreated to the far end of the room, waited for the mist to dissipate. Karlsson looped the sheer mask over his nose and mouth and approached Boone. He put an ear to his chest and took a neck pulse. Got nose to nose with Boone. He watched and waited, then rejoined Prisha. The room was small and windowless, its walls and floor of poured concrete several feet thick. This "interview" room was behind a steel door adjacent to Ahmad's much larger laboratory in the basement of the Parkview Market.

"He's asleep," Karlsson said.

Prisha removed a cellular phone and two sets of earbuds from a latched case. She instructed Karlsson to put the buds in, with a tight seal in the ear canals. She did the same. They traded thumbs-up. They both approached Boone, who was still out. Prisha activated the ODYSSEUS app on the telephone and placed it next to Boone. She headed to the basement staircase, motioning for Karlsson to follow her. When they reached the top, they closed the basement door tightly, double-checked it, then went to a small storage room behind the front desk of the bodega. They grabbed a couple of Huggies diaper boxes and sat down opposite each other, close enough for their knees to touch.

The earbuds they wore were ODYSSEUS prototypes, made to block all sound waves coming from the app but permitting environmental noise. They were also paired so that wearers could talk to one another. Karlsson went first.

"Let's hope these earbuds work, and we do not succumb to the siren's song." He permitted himself a small smile.

"We've both been tested multiple times, and both of us are immune to suggestion," Prisha stated. "This only works on the weak-minded, the impressionable."

"How do we know it will work on him?"

They exchanged bemused looks and laughed. Yeah, it would work on Boone, all right.

The ODYSSEUS sleep app they were now beta testing on Boone allowed for the delivery of sound waves, encoded with suggestive messages, to the sleeping brain. This was the first test of this technology outside the lab on a live subject. If it worked, if Boone's brain received and acted on the encoded suggestion, it would be a major step forward for ODYSSEUS. Having full access to Americans while they slept would broaden their bandwidth by a third.

In truth, this app was not ready for testing, but Boone had presented himself at an opportune time and Prisha could not resist.

Prisha checked her watch. They had a few minutes.

She regarded Karlsson. He was a striking man, a man she would have pursued under different circumstances. But she needed him, and most men she bedded became disposable.

"Why do you do this, Henrik?"

He shrugged his shoulders.

"There must be a reason."

Karlsson thought. "When I was with SOG, I was a very good soldier," he said, breaking the silence. "I loved my team and loved Sweden. My country put me in military prison—two years—for putting an officer in the hospital. He gave me an order that would harm my men. I told him so. He didn't hear my words, so I had to get my point across another way. Some of my men testified against me at trial. When I left prison, I walked away from all of it. God. Country. Honor—as they see it. None of it mattered. So I took my skills to the open market."

"So you're a nihilist, then?" Prisha asked. "Life has no objective meaning or purpose? No intrinsic value... pointless?"

"If you say so, Prisha." Karlsson grinned.

"Okay, then, why *do* you do it?"

"Let's say it's for the money."

"I don't believe that for a second, Henrik."

Karlsson was quiet for a few moments before speaking again. "Why are *you* doing this, Prisha?"

Prisha thought about how to answer Karlsson. Wondered what answer he would like to hear. She knew exactly who she was. *What* she was. She couldn't let Karlsson see her. Not yet.

"For the money, like you," Prisha responded at last. Both of them were equally comfortable with her lie, and the conversation ended.

Prisha heard a loud thump on the ceiling. She looked up, as did Karlsson. It was the Muslim family, from Prisha's village in Saudi, who had been selected by her benefactors to be the caretakers of this bodega.

"How do you know the app sound waves won't go upstairs?" Karlsson asked.

"The basement's soundproof," Prisha responded.

"What if it's not?"

"Then we're going to have a bigger mess to clean up tonight than we thought." She checked her watch. "Okay. He's had enough time. The test was at maximum calibration; strong waves, short duration. High velocity. If we can get Tommy to do this, we can get them to do anything. Any time of day or night."

Prisha led Karlsson back down into the basement. Prisha went right to the phone and turned off the app, then double-checked it before telling Karlsson they were good. They both masked up and Karlsson sprayed another mist into Boone's face, this one the antidote to the first. They stepped back and waited for Boone to wake up. It took less than two minutes.

Boone awoke with a start, in a groggy stupor, eyes wild in his slack face. He struggled to focus. Prisha asked him simple questions at first. To get his mind back online, as it were. It didn't take long before he was back to full Boone.

It was then that Prisha started to warm him up. Reminded him how sad and pathetic his life was. How he had betrayed his country, and she him. Reminded him of what a failure he was, and how he had failed at this ridiculous blackmail attempt—his last shot. Suggested that no one would miss him were he gone.

This went on for fifteen minutes. Prisha pacing in front of Boone, talking. Boone listening in silence, head bowed, allowing this poison into his brain.

"How do you feel now, Tommy?" Prisha asked when she'd finished.

Boone just shook his head and began to sob. His big shoulders shuddered as he wept.

"What's the matter, Tommy?" Prisha knew what the matter was, of course. At her order, the suggestive message encoded for this particular beta test was suicide. *Do it now, Tommy! DO IT NOW!*

"Look at me, Tommy," she said in her sweetest voice. "It's okay, sweetheart. Look at me now."

Boone snorted and choked, then went silent. He looked up at Prisha and again burst into tears.

Prisha smiled and stepped to his side. She stroked his hair.

"It's okay, Tommy. No one will think less of you if you do it. It's the only way. You know that, right?"

Boone nodded.

"You're ready, aren't you?"

Boone nodded again.

"Henrik's going to loosen the strap now. Okay?"

Another nod. Karlsson approached and released Boone's right arm from the straps. Boone rotated it in two lackadaisical circles and let his hand fall to his lap.

Karlsson produced a Glock 9mm pistol with silencer. Prisha held out her hand. Karlsson spun it around and handed it to her grip first. Prisha regarded the weapon in her hands as she tightened her grip. Karlsson drew his own pistol and held it at waist level, muzzle lowered in Boone's direction. Prisha turned to face Boone.

"You want this, don't you, Tommy?" she said in a calm voice.

Silence.

"Say it, Tommy. Tell me you want it."

Boone whispered something.

"I can't hear you, Tommy. Speak—"

"Give me the damn gun!" Tommy roared.

Prisha smiled. Her big open smile. The full-octane one.

"That's my man," Prisha said, and handed the pistol to Boone.

Karlsson raised his weapon to Boone's chest, watching him intently.

Boone put the muzzle of the Glock under his chin and pulled the trigger. The hollow-point round tumbled and expanded as it traveled through his head, blew most of the top of his head off upon exit. Brains spattered on both Prisha and Karlsson. Blood gushed from the top of Boone's head like a fountain.

Prisha felt a mixture of adrenaline and arousal. She had never been so close to a killing before and had wondered how it would feel. Now she knew. She liked it.

"What if he'd shot you?" Karlsson said, shaking his head.

"That's what you're here for, Henrik," Prisha said with a smile, picking bits of Boone's brain from her hair. "Besides, I knew he wouldn't shoot me."

The ODYSSEUS bedtime app had worked. The beta test had been a complete success. And they had gotten rid of their Boone problem. Two birds, one stone.

"Let's not make a habit of you handing people loaded weapons," Karlsson said. He began to unstrap Boone, who had slumped to one side. He was a big man and would be hard to move. Plus, he had made a mess of the basement. It would be a long night.

Prisha came in next to Karlsson. She leaned over and looked into the gaping hole in Boone's skull. It was still bleeding profusely. She poked at the gray matter with her finger. It felt spongy.

"So," Prisha said as she flicked a piece of brain matter from her finger to the floor. "That didn't take long. Granted, Tommy's an imbecile, but it'll work on others, don't you think?"

Karlsson grunted.

"It'll work," Prisha declared.

Prisha poked at Boone's skull some more, then began to help Karlsson with the straps.

"I got this," Karlsson said. "Why don't you get out of here. Go home and get cleaned up."

"What, and let you have all the fun?"

PART II

All human laws are, properly speaking, only declaratory; they have no power over the substance of original justice.
— Edmund Burke

CHAPTER SEVENTEEN

SEPTEMBER 11, 2016
WEST CHEVY CHASE NEIGHBORHOOD
BETHESDA, MD

THE MOSQUITOES HAD FOUND ME AND WERE ENJOYING their feast. I dared not move, hidden in the tall bushes in some guy's side lawn. As long as I stayed still and close to the ground, I might not be seen. My hiding spot was not perfect, but it was the best I could improvise. It was the only place that provided any concealment to watch my old supervisor's house, located directly across the street in the swank Bethesda neighborhood of West Chevy Chase.

I had taken an early train to get here. Metro Red Line. I would stay here in the bushes as long as it took to catch him alone. It had been less than twenty-four hours since I had met my son for the first time. I was weaponized now. This guy would tell me what I needed to know.

About three hours and a hundred mosquito bites later, Doug Mitchell, my old supervisor at the CIA, emerged from his tidy two-story split ranch. Mitchell looked the same as he had when he'd fired me five years ago. A tall, light-skinned African American, still fit but graying a bit at the temples. Retirement on full government benefits had been good to him. He held a rambunctious chocolate Lab at the end of a six-foot leather lead. Time to walk the dog. Time to make my move.

Mitchell moved briskly down the sidewalk on the opposite side of the street. I gave him a four-house lead, then darted from the bushes and paralleled him from my side of the street. Luckily, the dog stopped him short to investigate something at the foot of a towering oak tree. I checked over my shoulder and, finding the street empty, crossed and closed distance. Both Mitchell and the Lab were preoccupied. I was not. I got to within grabbing distance.

"Hello, Doug," I said.

He didn't turn around. I said it louder. This time I got his attention. He casually turned around and looked me over. I expected shock, or even fear, but got neither. It almost seemed like he was expecting this day. The Lab jumped towards me, straining against her lead, panting and wagging her tail. Dogs loved me.

"Frank."

"Been a long time, Doug. You look well."

"What the hell are you doing here?" Mitchell scanned up and down the street.

"I came alone, Doug. Let's walk and talk. Your dog here —what's her name?"

"Violet."

"Violet wants a walk. So do I. As far as the neighbors

know, we're just two old friends walking a dog." I gestured forward at the sidewalk with my hand. Mitchell frowned but accepted my invitation.

Mitchell was an experienced CIA man, a mediocre case officer but an effective manager at Langley. Still, he had been trained like all the rest of them at the farm and was skilled in the subtle art of interview and interrogation. He played along now and hid any concerns he may have had. I was certain he didn't have a weapon, he left to wonder if I did. We both understood I had the upper hand if he tried to get physical.

I started slow. We swapped stories, took each other's temperature. Mitchell had been retired less than one year. He had two kids in college, out-of-state and non-scholarship, and their tuitions were more than his mortgage. He retired on Cialis and high blood pressure medication. Said his old football knee was bothering him again. I told him I had less than five years to live. It stunned him to silence and altered the posture of our conversation. As I had intended it would.

"You love your kids, right, Doug?"

"What do you mean?" Mitchell's eyes widened, his first tell of emotion.

"I just found out I have a son. Can you believe that? And I'm new at this, but I'd do anything for that little guy. Just like you would do anything for your kids. You've got two daughters, right? Where'd you say they went to school again?"

"What the hell do you want, Frank?" Mitchell flexed, jerking the leash back and causing Violet to turn and look.

I smiled.

"How'd you know I walked my dog every Sunday morning? Or even that I had a damn dog?"

"I didn't."

Mitchell's face twisted into a snarl. "You been watching my house, Frank? My family?"

"This is a real nice neighborhood, Doug," I said. "How'd you get in here on a GS-15 salary? Your neighbors must all be millionaires. High-speed consultants and corporate VP types. I'll bet you're the only government wonk on your block. Am I right?"

"I got lucky. Saved my money. Invested it," Mitchell responded. "Unlike you."

"You see," I said, turning to him and wagging a finger. "That's what I'm here to talk to you about." We both stopped walking and stood facing each other.

"They fired me, Doug. Stripped me of all my government benefits. My pension. You were their messenger, but I don't begrudge you that. I didn't do a goddammed thing wrong. We both know it. All I need to know is who did it, and why."

Mitchell swallowed hard; his prominent Adam's apple rose and fell. He started to speak, then stopped. I could see the gears grinding in his head.

"I don't know what you're talking about, Frank. And I don't appreciate you stalking me and my family."

"You *have* a family, Doug. I don't! I'm trying to get them back, before it's too late." I lowered my tone. "But I need your help."

"I can't help you."

"I just need a name."

The chocolate Lab smelled her owner's fear and came closer. She sat alert at Mitchell's feet.

"That was a long time ago, Frank. I just did what I was

told to do. I always liked you, Frank. It was nothing personal."

"And evil triumphs when good men do nothing."

"Fuck you, Frank," Mitchell said. "I can't help you. I'm not going to get involved in any of this." His eyes narrowed. "Look. You don't realize what you're asking." Mitchell glanced around, then leaned towards me. "There are powerful forces at play here. Best to leave this alone. Trust me. Walk away."

"Best for who, Doug?" I shouted. "I gotta make this right —right now—while I still can. And you're gonna help me. You owe me that, Doug."

"I don't owe you shit, Frank," Mitchell shouted back.

Violet started barking. The yelling and barking brought the neighbor out of his house. He was an old white guy, mid-seventies, with a bald head and big-frame eyeglasses. He stepped to us; we were standing on the sidewalk in front of his house. The old man greeted Mitchell by name and eyed me suspiciously. He asked Mitchell if everything was all right, while keeping his eyes on me. Mitchell paused, then told the old man everything was fine. Told his neighbor I was an old friend, that we were just happy to see each other. He apologized for the noise. The old man said okay, then studied me again, closely enough to describe me to a police sketch artist. He petted Violet, then walked back into his house.

"You got to get out of here, Frank. You don't belong. Somebody's gonna call the cops."

"I just need a name. Who and why, and I'm gone."

"I can't... You just don't understand, Frank."

"Then tell me, Doug! For my son."

"What about my family, Frank? My daughters? We both

saw what they did to you. Don't you think they'd do the same to me? I just retired, for Christ's sake."

Mitchell blew out a breath. Violet whimpered and jumped up, put her front paws on my chest. I grabbed them and eased her back down to the ground. She barked once, then again.

"I considered you a friend once, Doug. I need you to do the right thing here." I locked eyes with him. He squirmed. "I don't want to have to come back here and make things difficult for you. But I will. You know I will. Just a name, Doug. Give me a name."

Violet began barking again. I saw the old man finger open his curtain and knew the cops would be here soon. Neither Mitchell nor I wanted that.

"Tomorrow," I said. "Monday night. Seven p.m. Sharp. Where can we meet? Someplace good, near the Metro stop. I don't want to be walking all over downtown Bethesda."

Mitchell just stared at me.

"Doug," I said evenly. "Your neighbor just called the cops. Believe me when I tell you that it is in your best interest to leave now and meet with me tomorrow. Where, Doug? Quick. I need a location."

Mitchell turned and looked at the old neighbor's house. I followed his eyes. The front curtain fluttered.

"Now, Doug."

"Parking garage. On Waverly and Montgomery. Fifth floor, on the west end, near the Hyatt," Mitchell grunted.

"Okay. I'll be there. Seven o'clock tomorrow night. Come alone."

"Shit, Frank," Mitchell growled. "I'm retired. I don't need any of this bullshit." He spun around and strode away, pulling Violet with him. He hurried back down the sidewalk of his beautiful neighborhood, back to his beautiful house and his beautiful wife.

Mitchell did not look back at me as I stood on the sidewalk, watching them leave.

I turned and waved to the old man behind the curtain.

Then I got the hell out of there.

CHAPTER EIGHTEEN

SEPTEMBER 12, 2016
CIAHQ GUARD SHACK
LANGLEY, *VA*

PRISHA PULLED HER LEXUS INTO A SPOT UNDER THE shade of a magnificent American beech tree. She climbed out, hit the key fob and got the chirp. The morning was overcast, with an early fall nip in the air. A breeze kicked up and under her skirt, causing her to twitch. She had taken off her panties in her office and smiled at her little secret.

She had just endured an insufferable executive staff meeting that she'd thought would never end. Every Monday morning at nine a.m. She hated it. Prisha could not think of a worse way to start her week.

She had had quite the weekend. Boone's death had been less than forty-eight hours ago. She kept replaying it in her mind. His moronic face, all the pathetic whining. The suppressed *zip* sound of the bullet leaving the gun and entering Boone's head. The top of his head exploding all over the wall—and her. She was anxious, but not about the killing. She had no qualms about that. Prisha was thrilled that the ODYSSEUS bedtime app had worked, and relieved to be rid of Boone. He was a loose thread that needed to be pulled.

No, Prisha was on edge this morning for another reason entirely. She was aroused. The killing had turned her on, thrown a switch that needed to be addressed. For the past month, Prisha had been grooming the stud security guard for a moment such as this. Today would be his day.

Prisha walked towards the guard shack at the side of the rear executive entrance, just outside the swinging metal gate. The guard, Joel Zabel, was leaning into the window of a stopped car, checking the bona fides of the occupants. Prisha caught Zabel's eye and gave him a smoldering look. His look of confusion faded as his nostrils flared with the smell of her intentions. Zabel was young and strong, thick as a Clydesdale. Prisha's hot spot moaned. She walked right past Zabel and into the guard shack, nodding to the carful of executives as Zabel waved them through.

"Uh, ma'am—you're not supposed to be in here," Zabel stuttered. His eyes flicked down to Prisha's chest; her large breasts stretched the silk of her pink buttoned-down blouse. A blouse she'd had custom tailored for just such an occasion.

"Is that so?" Prisha responded. She raised her hand to her neck, maintaining eye contact, and undid one button. Then another. She stepped over to Zabel. He stood frozen in place. The remainder of the buttons yielded to her hand.

"What are you doing?" Zabel's voice trailed off to a whisper.

The silk shirt, untucked at the waist, fell open to reveal a black lace bra that barely contained her. Prisha grabbed his hand and pressed it against her right breast, then kissed Zabel deeply, her tongue probing his. He didn't push her away. She grabbed his crotch, rubbing up and down, slowly, then faster. Zabel rose to the occasion. Prisha kissed him again, with more force. Zabel grabbed her other breast. They came together like magnets. *Got him.*

It didn't take long. Prisha pushed Zabel against the desk in the corner of the shack, unbuckled his pants and slid them down to his ankles in one fluid motion. Her fellatio skills were legendary, and she finished Zabel quickly.

Prisha stood, wiping her mouth. "My turn." She slid Zabel out of the way, cleared the desk with an arm sweep, then hopped up.

Zabel buried his head under Prisha's skirt and got to work. She was ready for him.

They both heard the car pull up to the gate. Zabel's shoulders flinched. He started to withdraw. Prisha grabbed a fistful of hair at the back of his head and pushed him in deeper. Prisha moaned as she finished, then shrieked. She shrieked again, louder this time.

Zabel jumped to his feet and clasped a large hand over her mouth. His rough skin scratched her lips. Prisha bit down hard. His blood was coppery and slick in her mouth. She rubbed it over her teeth with her tongue.

Zabel snapped his hand back. He examined the bleeding wound. "Crazy bitch!"

The toot of a car horn spun Zabel's head around.

"Shit!" He grabbed his pants up from around his ankles, struggling to get them buckled back up.

Prisha watched Zabel's full panic with a sense of bemusement. She casually wiped his blood from her lips with the tip of her finger, inserted the bloody finger into her mouth, then sucked it dry with a slurp as she withdrew it.

Zabel watched the show as he stuffed his shirt into his pants. He shook his head and grunted as he fled out of the guard shack to attend to the waiting visitor.

Prisha straightened herself up and followed Zabel out of the shack. He was addressing a carload of visitors at the driver's side of the government sedan. Prisha recognized the group as West Wing White House staffers. She glided to the front passenger's window.

"Is this guy giving you a hard time?" Prisha said, in her playful, charming voice. The vehicle's occupants laughed. Zabel's face turned sheet white. Prisha worked the vehicle, told the occupants how good it was to see them again. She wished them a good day. Anger flushed Zabel's face as he watched Prisha's performance. He looked about to speak, but Prisha beat him to it.

"Good to see you again, Officer Zabel. Take care," she said with her big, open smile.

Zabel looked as if he might come around the vehicle at her. Prisha slapped the roof of the car and walked away. Two more vehicles had arrived at the gate and were now stacked behind the West Wingers.

Prisha ambled back to her car. The wind tugged at her skirt. It felt warm and wet. Rain was coming. She patted her skirt down with both hands. The itch was gone, her homeostasis restored. Today would be a good day.

She sank into the driver's seat of the Lexus and rooted around in her bag for her government phone, as she saw yet another car queue up at the gate. Good. She searched through her contacts and hit the button.

"Human Resources. This is Yvonne speaking. How can I help you?"

"Good morning, Yvonne. This is Deputy Director Baari. We've got a problem here at the back gate. There's a long line of visitors queued up waiting to get in, and the guard out here now is completely incompetent. We can't have visiting executives treated with such discourtesy. I want him gone by the end of the day."

"Do you mean switched to the front gate, ma'am?" Yvonne asked.

"No," Prisha replied as she watched Zabel hustle from one car to the next. "I want him fired and off campus by close of business today."

Another one bites the dust.

CHAPTER NINETEEN

I PULLED OUT MY PHONE FROM MY CARGO PANTS SIDE
pocket and pecked out a text message:

Me: *who's the guy?*

Doug: *what?*

Me: *4 cars down, gray chevy tahoe?*

(pause)

Doug: *what guy? What're you talkin' about?*

Me: *you see that raggedy dude come through...2 minutes* ago?

Doug: *yeah, smelled him too*

Me: *i paid the dude 20 bucks to roll through the fifth floor...said tahoe guy looked shady*

Doug: *i don't see no guy. homeless guy lying*

Me: *maybe you're lying*

Doug: *i came alone...fuck frank...we doin' this or not?*
(pause)
Me: *leave now. meet me outside lot exit.*

For two hours I'd been hiding behind a giant concrete pillar in the parking garage where we'd agreed to meet. I was relieved that my old supervisor had shown up, but still not convinced that Doug Mitchell could be trusted. In my world no one could really be trusted.

People were rushing to their cars now and peeling out of the garage, the five o'clock working drones reanimated at the end of another long workday. Most of the fifth floor had emptied out by six, and by seven o'clock only a few vehicles remained, including Tahoe man, just a few spaces beyond where Doug had parked.

I had to be sure Tahoe man was not with Mitchell, and the best way to do this was a quick change of location. Turn this thing from static to mobile and watch for the chaos.

I saw Mitchell's black Audi sedan pull out and leave without hesitation. A good sign. No one followed him. Another good omen. I dashed out from behind the pillar and darted over to the stairway entrance close to my right. I whipped open the door with a bang and ran down the concrete stairs, hand sliding along the railing for support. I almost sideswiped a woman as I flung myself to the second-floor landing, shouting my apology to her over my shoulder without slowing down. I was well past her when she screamed her profanity-laden response.

I reached ground level and pushed through the heavy door to the outside. It was plenty bright out and the garage security lights were not yet on. I spun my head around and found the vehicle exit to my left. The metal arm rose, and Mitchell's Audi appeared. He pulled through to let the arm drop, and stopped as he saw me sprinting towards him. I tried the door handle, flipped it up hard. Nothing. I banged my fist on the window. I heard the lock pop and jumped in.

"Jesus, Frank," Mitchell yelled. "Easy on the window."

"Drive! Drive!"

I flipped around to give the back seat a good look. It was empty. The Audi started to ping, telling me to fasten my seat belt. I did. I gave Mitchell turn-by-turn instructions, all the while checking my side-view mirror for any suspicious cars that might be following. Mitchell could easily have had someone following at a distance with GPS. I hoped not.

I instructed Mitchell to continue north on Rockville Pike. We went through a mile of city blocks and a few traffic signals. Mitchell bitched the whole way. I remained silent for the most part. We reached Walter Reed Medical Center in five minutes. I directed Mitchell to park in the center of a huge, mostly empty outdoor parking lot. He did.

"Turn off the engine and give me the keys," I said.

Mitchell rolled his eyes. "C'mon, Frank. I—"

That's when I slid that little 9mm out of my pocket and put it in my lap. Muzzle facing Mitchell, trigger finger on the frame. I'd purchased the gun on the streets from a guy I had heard conducted such transactions. I'd used the money Sarah gave me but didn't mention it to her.

Mitchell lurched away from me and the gun. His shoulder slammed against the side window. I motioned to him and he threw me the car keys. I caught them with my free hand and pocketed them.

"Fuck, Frank! What's the gun for?" Mitchell stared down at my lap. "Put that thing away. I didn't betray you." He exhaled with enough force to flap his lower lip. He ran a hand over his face. "Jesus, Frank. We're friends. I didn't betray you. You know that."

"So we're still friends, Doug?"

Mitchell nodded. But he still leaned as far away from me as he could. And he was breathing real heavy. I hoped it was just the gun.

"I'm glad we're still friends, Doug," I said, fingering the gun in my lap. "Because if you were the one to set me up, old friend, I'm going to kill you tonight. Right here in your new car."

Mitchell's eyes grew wider as he watched the gun rise from my lap and point at his chest.

"Do you understand me, Doug?"

Again he nodded.

"Good. Because I have nothing. Which means that I, unlike you, have nothing to lose. And at this moment, that's liberating. My nothing means everything right now. I really don't care if I live or die tonight. Imagine how little I care about you."

"I'm your friend, Frank." The pleading had begun. "I always tried to help you when I could. You know that." He shook his head. "But you were a hard man to help, Frank."

"Well, I'm glad to hear that, Doug. Because you're gonna help me now. And I'm going to make it easy for you." I placed the gun back down in my lap. "Who set me up, and why?"

Mitchell's shoulders slumped. He stammered.

"Who, Doug?"

Mitchell held his silence. He turned from me and looked out the front windshield. I repeated my question. The Audi went silent. I checked the mirrors for trouble, saw nothing troubling, and held our silence. It lingered. I could see Mitchell was weighing his options.

"It's not that easy," he finally said. "This thing—these people. It's big. Please, Frank. As a friend, I'm begging you to leave this alone." Mitchell looked at me now, on the edge of emotion. "What is it, Frank? Money? I can put together a little bit for you... if I—"

"So it was you?"

"No! It wasn't me! I just did what I was told to do."

"Told by who?" I raised the gun again.

"You don't know shit, Frank," Mitchell said, a trace of defiance in his voice. "Did you even know that you and I... our whole unit... were working on a secret project? That all our intel work went directly to people you don't want to know, who were doing things you don't want to know about?"

"I worked on overseas stuff," I reminded him. "War on Terrorism shit. Analytical papers. Emerging technologies."

Mitchell snorted.

"Tell me."

"I protected you all, don't you see?" Mitchell flailed his arms. "And I barely knew shit. Didn't want to know. I was so close to retirement. Just wanted to get the hell out of there in one piece."

"Tell me what you know."

A car passed by. The driver turned his head and looked right past us. He kept going.

Mitchell sighed deeply. His hands milked the steering wheel.

"ODYSSEUS," Mitchell said into the front windshield. "The project was called ODYSSEUS. It was very close hold.

Very dark. I never knew what they were doing with it. I swear."

"What is it?"

"I don't know. But I'd been a CIA case officer for too many years not to know when to look the other way. I never asked questions. Just did as I was told."

"You were a part of it, then?"

"No!" Mitchell shouted, turning to face me. He lowered his voice again. "But our work got funneled to ODYSSEUS. Half the Agency worked for the project in one way or another, I suspect. No one really knew."

"What does ODYSSEUS have to do with me getting fired?"

"I told you, Frank, I don't know anything." Mitchell shifted in his seat, broke eye contact with me. He was lying about not knowing anything. He knew something, all right.

I slipped my finger from the frame to the trigger of the gun. A subtle gesture that Mitchell understood. He sighed and continued speaking.

"All's I know is that some dumpy broad came to my office one day, shut the door, and ordered me to fire you by close of business. I of course protested, asked why. Said I would have to speak to my supervisor. The dumpy broad just laughed. Said this came straight from the deputy director. That it was a matter of national security, and that anything I did on your behalf from there on out would be considered direct insubordination, and that I would be following you right out the door. I was one year out, Frank. I had a family, a fucking mortgage, two daughters to put through college. I'd been with the Agency over thirty years. They threatened to take it all away, Frank. All of it! So I fired you. I don't know why you were fired, and I swear I didn't know they were going to fuck you over like that, strip your benefits and security clearance. I didn't learn that until after you were already gone."

I studied my old friend. He was shaking now. Adrenaline. He held my eyes. He was telling the truth about this part.

"Tell me more about this dumpy broad."

"I don't know her name. She worked for the deputy director. Prisha Baari."

Oh, shit.

CHAPTER TWENTY

THE WOMAN SAT IN ONE OF THE BEST SEATS IN THE house—sixth row, center stage. It was Saturday night at the Brooks Atkinson Theater, and the place was packed. *Waitress* was one of the hottest Broadway musicals of 2016, with music and lyrics by Sara Bareilles. It tells the story of Jenna Hunterson, a waitress in an abusive relationship with her husband. When Jenna unexpectedly becomes pregnant, she begins an affair with her doctor and, looking for a way out, latches onto a local pie contest and its grand prize as her last chance. The musical was nominated for four Tony Awards that year, including Best Performance by a Leading Actress in a Musical.

The lead actress was now belting out the show's signature song, "She Used to Be Mine," about a woman who ended up different than she thought she would be, and her struggle to reconcile that difference. The lead actress, a strawberry blonde from the Midwest with big blue eyes and full lips, held the audience in her sway. Even the woman seated sixth row center was mesmerized; she, too, had at one time wanted to be a Broadway star, having fallen in love with musical theater in college. But dedicating one's life to such frivolity was strictly forbidden by her parents and her religion. And besides, her parents already had their plan for her.

As the lead reached her apogee, the woman saw herself as a little girl, then flashed to her own lead performances in her college musicals, singing in jubilation to the cheers of the crowd. The woman at sixth row center sighed. As with Jenna Hunterson, things had ended up different from how she'd thought they would.

The woman stood with the others who applauded wildly during the curtain call. The crowd erupted as the lead actress was called back to the stage. The woman studied this All-American girl—her easy smile, the grace with which she accepted and returned the love of the audience. This actress had never had to fight for acceptance, as she had. Never been the different one, the outsider. Membership had been her birthright. The crowd knew it and loved her all the more for it. The woman now standing sixth row center did not.

The woman shifted her weight and looked around her. The audience was still roaring its approval, lost in rapturous applause. The woman grimaced and turned her attention back to the stage. She stiffened and slowed to a polite clap, wondered when this exhibition would end. This actress wasn't *that* good, after all. And not all that pretty either. Vanilla beauty. The woman knew that if she, too, had dedicated her life to the stage, it would be her up there now, basking in the love and acceptance of this audience. But a life of such folly was a waste, singing and dancing while the world burned. The woman grinned, remembering. She was the one who had the courage to do something that would really matter, and soon enough the entire country would be clapping for her, chanting her name.

Prisha Baari wiped her eyes dry and held her applause while the others continued to cheer.

———

"Wasn't the lead just wonderful tonight," gushed Tilly, wine-glass raised. "To Broadway—and girls' night out!"

Prisha joined the toast with her big, open smile. The other two women—Patricia, "Poppy" to all, and Leighton, who insisted upon being addressed as such—clinked glasses as well. All consummated their toast with a healthy sip from their glasses of hundred-dollar French Bordeaux.

They sat at a back table at a popular after-show spot a mere five-minute walk from the theater. It was a cozy place, one flight down from street level under a big awning. It had low ceilings, no windows, and aged wood plank floors that creaked underfoot. Their four-top round table was tucked up against an exposed red brick wall, opposite a long mahogany bar. The lights were dim and the place was humming with activity. The waitress came by, and they ordered their appetizer plates in place of dinner.

Prisha and the three women were college friends; Barnard College, Class of '97. Barnard College was a private women's liberal arts college located in the Upper Manhattan neighborhood of Morningside Heights, along Broadway between 116th and 120th Streets, directly across from the main campus of Columbia University. Indeed, Barnard was founded in 1889 in response to Columbia's refusal to admit women into their institution, just as with Radcliffe and Harvard. Unlike Radcliffe, which merged with Harvard in 1977, Barnard retained its all-female undergrad autonomy when Columbia went co-ed in 1983.

Prisha's parents sought pedigree and had thus enrolled her at Barnard, one of the Seven Sisters, that is, the seven blue-blooded liberal arts women's colleges in the Northeastern United States. But Prisha discovered that pedigree was not transferable, at least not among the seven sisters. She'd arrived at Barnard a gawky freshman, thin and long faced, with an oversized mouth and big teeth that made her reluctant to smile. Her English was good but tinged with the British accent she had acquired during her years at boarding school in London. All this, combined with the fact that she was a Saudi Arab in a time of escalating terrorism, was more than enough for the other pedigreed girls to cull her from the herd. Three such girls sat across the table from Prisha tonight, still clinging to the pack order that had been established in Brooks Hall dormitory freshman year.

All three girls had light complexions. Tilly, the most outgoing, was a ginger, petite and loud. Poppy, her opposite, had dark hair and eyes, and was the most thoughtful of the three. Leighton was the alpha female in the threesome. Her family went back generations in New York, her mother an active member in the local DAR chapter—Daughters of the American Revolution. They were very well off, her father having made his fortune with the rise of Big Pharma. Leighton had arrived at Barnard a vested trust fund girl. She smelled of that which the other girls coveted. As if by magnetism, a clique of girls were drawn to her. Prisha's dorm room had been down the hall from Leighton's, and she had watched with envy the swirl of activity that gravitated around that room. The peals of laughter, the pranks, the cute boys that were snuck in and out and sometimes spent the night.

It took Prisha almost a year to crack into Leighton's group—and she knew perfectly well why they had allowed her in. She was their token minority member. The brown-skinned girl. The exotic Arab from across the globe that the others magnanimously tolerated because she wasn't like "those other Arabs." Prisha had thought that this would change over time, once the girls got to know her, but it never did. The condescension was subtle, the ostracism complete. The other girls never let her in on the joke, refused her the punchline. Prisha resolved to get the last laugh.

"Oh my God, Leighton," Tilly said, bringing her hand to her mouth. "The lead tonight looked a lot like you."

Tilly and Poppy gazed at Leighton, both smiling.

"Don't you think?" Tilly asked. Poppy nodded.

Leighton waved it off but was clearly pleased at the comparison. The actress was beautiful and easily fifteen years younger. Prisha was pleased to note that privilege and age were beginning to catch up to Leighton. The cigarettes had robbed the shine from her complexion, and time had creased her forehead and the corners of her eyes and mouth. She'd kept her weight under control, but her face now looked angular, her features sharpened. Prisha had worked relent-lessly on her appearance since college, and it showed. Prisha had played to win, while Leighton had simply played not to lose.

Prisha rewarded herself with another glass of wine, and then poured Leighton another glass as well. It was Leighton's third glass; she was already well ahead of the rest of the table. Prisha gave her a heavy pour, which she readily accepted. It appeared Leighton liked her wine a little too much. *I can work with this.* Prisha ordered another two bottles of Bordeaux for the table.

The wine flowed freely as the four Barnard alums settled in and caught up. This had become their annual outing, dinner and a show, and had been started by Prisha in 2009 when she was appointed Deputy Director of the CIA. To the other three, this event was simply one of many "girls' night out" they enjoyed, but in truth, Prisha had initiated the outings to rub her friends' faces in her success. The three women, however, had proven remarkably intransigent. Prisha knew she would not get her satisfaction until she broke Leighton.

Tilly and Poppy gave their updates, which were essentially the same story: rich, unavailable husbands ten years their senior; high-performing children; Central American nannies and European vacations; some perfunctory charity work on the side. Poppy offered that she had caught her husband in an affair with his twenty-something assistant. All the women nodded knowingly.

Prisha then spoke of her own accomplishments. Briefing the president in the White House, testifying on Capitol Hill, public terrorism victories she had had a hand in at the CIA. All heady stuff compared to the lives of these three kept women. But the three stubbornly held rank. It was still freshman year at Brooks Hall.

"I give you credit, Prisha," Leighton said, draining her glass. "I don't know how you work for the CIA. They're so... *immoral.*" She paused long enough for this to land. "I mean, not you, of course. I meant, you know, the Agency and all."

Prisha poured Leighton another glass. Thought she had heard her slur a bit.

"It's important work, Leigh, work that needs to be done," she said, smiling and setting the bottle back on the table. Prisha had just lobbed her first bomb of the evening. Leighton loathed to be called Leigh. Tilly and Poppy winced when they heard the slight. Leighton appeared not to have heard it, however, and continued to work on her wine and glance about the restaurant.

"You were in the city on 9/11," Prisha continued. "You know better than most the importance of what I am doing—for our country."

Leighton waved Prisha off with a subtle flick of her wrist. "I knooow, Prisha. War on Terror. Blah, blah, blah." She slugged the last of her wine and knocked her fork to the floor when she returned her glass to the table.

Tilly dutifully retrieved Leighton's fork, wiped it with her cloth napkin, then gently placed it back on the table.

"I mean..." Leighton interrupted her thought to give herself a shaky pour from the second bottle. "I guess I mean... I just can't imagine being a government employee, is all." Leighton took a long sip and scanned the faces of Tilly and Poppy. They nodded in agreement. "Like—didn't you want to be an actress or something? Remember all the time you spent at MSM? You minored in theater. I always thought you should do that. But that's pretty hard, isn't it?"

A flash of white rage blinded Prisha. She leaned across the table and locked eyes with Leighton, who still wore her smirk. *Not for long.*

"So, Leigh, what's the latest with Thatch?" Prisha asked in a playful tone. "Have you seen him lately?"

Prisha already knew the answer to this question. Thatch

was Thatcher Kenworthy, Wall Street wonder boy and Leighton's old college sweetheart. He had recently graduated from multi-millionaire to billionaire, thanks to the sale of his brokerage house. Prisha had seen the *New York Times* piece on him. He still looked great: tan, fit, just the right amount of gray at the temples.

Leighton withdrew back into her seat at the mention of Thatch. He was her kryptonite. Prisha pressed on.

"I saw the article in the *Times*. Sold his company for 1.2 billion. Good for him." Prisha sipped her wine modestly. "He looked great, too. He was always such a good-looking guy, wasn't he, Leigh? It was a shame you two broke up. A real shame."

Leighton and Thatch hadn't just broken up. This had been Prisha's master stroke. It had taken her over two years to seduce Thatch, who had attended Columbia right across the street from Barnard. She'd studied him, his needs and vulnerabilities. Guys like Thatch had just about everything. So Prisha had focused on giving him things even the perfect Leighton could not. Prisha was a dark, exotic fruit and, unlike Leighton, eager to please him. She did things to Thatch that Leighton would never do. Thatch was young and full of himself, and Prisha had had him hooked by senior year. She'd insisted he break it off with Leighton, and he had willingly complied. Prisha had then immediately distanced herself from him, and they'd graduated estranged from one another.

But Prisha had accomplished her mission. She'd had her revenge on Leighton. Treachery trumped pedigree.

Prisha watched Leighton closely now, smiling and sipping her wine. She had found her mark, and she kept at it, adeptly picking at the Thatch scab until Leighton began to sob and broke for the ladies' room. Tilly and Poppy exchanged awkward looks. Poppy checked her phone. Tilly kept her eyes on the ladies' room.

"Anyone for another round of sirloin tips?" Prisha asked, flashing her brightest smile. "I'm starving."

CHAPTER TWENTY-ONE

SEPTEMBER 17, 2016
SCITUATE, MA

IT WAS A BEAUTIFUL DAY TO FLY A KITE.

The midday sun danced around the cotton-puff clouds, bathing the field in early fall warmth. A steady breeze off the Atlantic kept the heat at bay and the kites in the sky. At least, Quinn Doyle's kite, that is. He was an experienced kiter and flew a dual-line delta kite that resembled a stealth bomber. I stumbled with my single-line "Charlie Brown" kite, ignoring Doyle's instructions and dive-bombing it to earth on several occasions.

To anyone not paying close attention, Quinn Aidan Doyle looked like an ordinary man. A man of average size and weight, in his prime more than one hundred sixty-five pounds. He had a wide face, dark blue eyes and jet-black hair, which was now streaked with gray in his sixty-eighth year. His eyebrows had gone bushy, and he had taken to wearing knotted wool scarves and matching flat caps. But the eyes had not changed. There was something behind those eyes, something that could chill the blood of men twice his size. Dangerous men who knew the real thing when they saw it. The same eyes that twinkled at a good joke or a snort of smooth Irish whiskey. Doyle's men followed him out of love and fear, but mostly they respected him as a just boss who dealt straight. Those who didn't see him that way never stuck around. They had a habit of disappearing.

For decades Doyle had led the largest crew in South Boston, and on the streets was considered *the* Irish Mob boss in Southie. He had proven shrewd enough to keep one step ahead of the feds, and ruthless enough to keep his crown from all usurpers.

Doyle had given it all up within a year of my disappearance, proving you can leave the mob standing upright. He'd closed out all his accounts and left the city for Scituate, a pleasant seaside town thirty miles south of Boston near Plymouth Rock, where the Mayflower arrived. Scituate was part of the "Irish Riviera," a collection of seaside towns south of the city that the Irish have dominated since the end of World War II. In fact, the latest U.S. Census Bureau statistics showed Scituate to be almost fifty percent Irish, making it the most Irish town in the United States. All of this was just fine with Quinn Doyle.

Sarah's first call when she left my hospital bed had been to Doyle. The two were very close. Doyle took the news of my re-emergence with restrained composure, as he was a man accustomed to dealing with surprises, both good and bad. My summons to Scituate was not issued until a week after Sarah and Doyle's phone call, which told me Doyle had struggled with his decision as to whether he ever wanted to see me again. But then word had come down through Sarah that he did, and the Amtrak ticket had followed. Doyle liked to avoid commercial air travel as much as possible. Too much scrutiny.

––––––

The Acela train was a good way to travel the East Coast corridor. I had taken it several times for trips to New York when I was still employed at the CIA. I got off at the end of the line, South Station in Boston, and Doyle had a town car and driver waiting for the forty-five-minute drive down I-93 South to his seaside condo in Scituate.

The driver was not from a service, but one of Doyle's men. That was obvious from his countenance and appearance. We drove in silence, which was fine by me. I was nervous, but not in the *oh-shit-I've-been-called-in-to-see-the-big-boss* kind of way. I knew I had done Doyle wrong, going dark on him for five years, but I feared his disapproval, not reprisal. He had been like a father to me when I desperately needed one. We had remained close through my resignation from the army, which, in hindsight, was when the wheels had started to come off my wagon. Our estrangement tracked my withdrawal from the world. I'd learned through Sarah how Doyle had tried to find me, how much I had hurt him. I owed Quinn Doyle and explanation. And an apology. I would offer both. I hoped he would accept them, and that it would be enough.

The large man pulled the town car into the condo's parking lot and motioned for me to get out. He pulled my one duffel from the trunk and dropped it at my feet, then climbed back into the car and drove off without a word. I watched him go.

There was a perfectly manicured golf course at the lot's edge, which made me snicker. Doyle had never picked up a golf club in his life. But I could see what he liked about the place. It was right on the Atlantic Ocean and surrounded by marshland and a state park to the south and west. I grabbed my bag and turned to the water. I breathed deeply; the salty brine stung my nostrils. The muted crash of the surf filled my ears. I'd left Boston in the eighth grade and had been back only sporadically since. I couldn't recall my last visit. But standing there in the parking lot I knew this place was home to me, and always would be. I closed my eyes, took a few more deep breaths of salt air, then hefted my bag and stepped through the building's front doors. I crossed the marble-tiled lobby and took the elevator to Doyle's penthouse condo on the sixth floor.

Doyle opened the door on the second knock, then stood in the doorway and took me in. His eyes widened at the sight of me. I was still getting used to that, the instant shock on the faces of people who had known me before. I guess five years on the streets had aged me. Perhaps it was something I chose not to see in my own mirror. Seeing it in the faces of others was hard to ignore, though.

I stiffened at the sight of him. Pangs of guilt and remorse for what I had done knifed my gut. I smiled feebly. Doyle hadn't changed. I had. I wondered if I would ever be able to set things right between us. Not back to the way things were, that wasn't possible. But a reboot maybe.

Doyle motioned me in. The condo was beautiful, floor-to-ceiling windows offering panoramic ocean views. I recalled Doyle loved his jazz, and he had a smooth playlist going in the background. We sat at a table by the window. Doyle brought us each a cup of black tea. He mostly kept silent, but through his eyes I could see his mind was racing. Calculating. Deliberating. I filled our awkward silence with my apology, then an accounting of my actions. I offered no excuses, just explained my withdrawal and loss of faith as best I could. My homeless vagabond years, wandering around the south, then the southwest, finally ending up in LA before returning to Washington, DC, where I was attacked and left for dead.

I thought I saw Doyle's eyes soften. Maybe it was just the sun's reflection. Doyle held his silence and watched the ocean waves crash ashore. The soft jazz played on.

"You should've told me, Frankie," he said at last, turning his head from the window to face me. "Just disappearing on me like that." Doyle shook his head, held and released a protracted breath. "I thought you were dead, for Christ's sake. I mourned you. Like a father losing a son."

I apologized again. I knew he was right. I wondered how much forgiveness this man had left in his heart.

"If you had just called me, Frankie. You know I would've helped you. Got you out of whatever shit caused you to run."

I had told Doyle of my crumbling marriage and the loss of my job, but had left out the secrets I had recently learned from Nicole and Doug Mitchell. It was too much, too soon.

"What happened in DC?" Doyle asked. "Who did that to you?"

"I don't know. Some homeless guys. Looking for something to steal. I don't remember much of it."

"Sarah said you almost died, Frankie."

I nodded.

"Anything else?"

I saw in his face that Doyle knew of my cancer.

"Sarah already told you, didn't she?"

Doyle nodded. "I'd rather hear it from you, Frankie."

I told him of my diagnosis, the odds, that the leukemia would likely kill me within five years. Doyle grimaced; his lower lip trembled. He looked away for a long moment. He asked me who else knew. I told him Sarah, Nicole, my mother Emily, and now him.

Doyle sipped his tea, thinking. "You know Sarah is taking this pretty hard. She's always loved you, Frankie." He paused. "She's the sister you should've married."

He was right.

"How is Emily? How'd she take it?"

I told him. My mother had taken my return and cancer diagnosis as one would expect. Anger, then hurt, disappointment, then sadness. No understanding or acceptance. She was withholding her forgiveness for the pain I had caused her. I accepted it as my penance.

Doyle pursed his lips. "Emily—she always blamed me for Arthur's death." He went silent at the mention of my father for a long moment, then continued with a wave of his hand. "Emily should've never taken you out of Southie. You two should have stayed—with me. None of this would've have happened."

He was probably right, but if I'd stayed, I would have followed my father into a life of crime. Led one of Doyle's crews. Maybe met the same fate as Arthur: a couple of bullets behind my ear.

Doyle got up, collected our cups and walked back to the galley kitchen across the big open room, where he placed the cups in the sink. He stood there, head down, arms locked, hands gripping the counter. After a moment, he pushed off the counter, walked towards me and pulled up ten feet away.

"What a fucking mess, Frankie," he said, shaking his head. He said it again, trailing off to a whisper. Doyle looked out the window. I kept my eyes on him. "Sarah said you're doing this treatment thing, right?"

I nodded. "Yeah." I could have added the word *eventually*, but didn't.

"Good," he said. He finished crossing the room to my side. "You're sticking around?"

I nodded. Doyle smiled. He left the room, leaving me still sitting at the table by the window. I heard him on the telephone but could not make out what was said. He returned about thirty minutes later with a kite in each hand, said it was a beautiful day to fly a kite.

We left the condo and walked past the eighth-hole green into the state parkland. A short hike through the woods brought us to an open field of wild grass and clover. Doyle's kite took wing effortlessly. He deftly maneuvered it with the strings he held in each hand. I watched the kite dance at his command. It was a beautiful sight.

My own kite defied my efforts. Despite Doyle's instructions, it jerked about, inevitably crashing to earth. After the third such display, I gave up.

"Kiting is all about faith, Frankie," Doyle said, maneuvering his strings like a puppeteer. "Faith and trust. Faith in the winds. Trust in the quality of your equipment and your skill level. Faith and trust. A man needs both in this life, Frankie. You'd do well to remember that."

A gust of wind came off the ocean, putting the kite into a dive. Doyle danced, leaning and dipping his body, hands moving rhythmically, eyes fixed skyward. He put the kite straight and true, then continued.

"You're a lot like your father, Frankie. Art was a good man. But stubborn. And aloof. Liked to do things himself, his own way. Alienated the other guys on his crew. And so, when he needed help, none came."

My gut tightened. My father could be a bastard, true, but hearing Doyle speak of him like this was like chewing beach sand.

"A man is not an island, Frankie. He's got to have trust and faith. It's easy to isolate and destroy the lone warrior. I've seen many badass men take two behind the ear, meeting their maker at the hand of a lesser man. Island men separate themselves from the herd. Make themselves vulnerable to the hyenas of this world—susceptible to treachery and deception, betrayal and intrigue. Present themselves as clean targets to their enemies."

Doyle took his eyes off his kite to make sure I was listening. I was.

"Sun Tzu said 'An army may be likened to water, for just as flowing water avoids the heights and hastens to the lowlands, so an army avoids strength and strikes weakness.' Do you see what this man is saying, Frankie? You must be flexible like water, not hard and immovable like the stone."

"I know."

"Do you? Even as a kid you always attacked things head-on. Frontal assault, Frankie. It won you your Medal of Honor and saved the lives of your men, sure. And you've always been brave; no one who knows you doubts that. But this approach is foolhardy and destined for martyrdom. Do you understand what I'm telling you?"

"Yeah," I said. Doyle had survived decades as a mob boss, a profession that typically had a much shorter lifespan. I had to concede his point.

"'Bravery, without forethought, causes a man to fight blindly and desperately, like a mad bull. Such an opponent must not be encountered with brute force, but may be lured into an ambush and slain.'" More Sun Tzu. Doyle admired the ancient Chinese general and philosopher, and could cite long passages of his opus, *The Art of War*, from memory.

"I know you, Frankie. And I know there's something you're not telling me."

CHAPTER TWENTY-TWO

SEPTEMBER 18, 2016
SCITUATE, MA

DOYLE AND I CIRCLED ONE ANOTHER LIKE BOXERS THE remainder of that first night. He probed and I parried. He grew accustomed to the idea that I was indeed alive and in his living room. The same for me. I broke off around ten, exhausted, and bid him goodnight. He put me in the guest bedroom. I showered and dropped onto the bed. I heard Doyle's muffled voice on his cellphone in the living room. I was asleep in an instant.

We had a late breakfast: fried eggs, blueberry pancakes, and a side of bacon with black coffee. Doyle was a fantastic cook and I emptied my plate twice. We were cordial, better than the day before. Doyle's mood appeared to have bright-ened. I felt more comfortable in his presence. He told me he had to run some errands today, that he'd be back in time for dinner. I wondered if this had anything to do with the tele-phone calls last night.

Doyle tossed me a spare set of keys to the condo. Told me to get outside for some fresh air but to not leave the area. I agreed. He pointed at me with a raised eyebrow. I promised I wasn't going anywhere. He gave me a tight smile and left.

I washed the dishes. Got dressed and went outside. It was overcast and still. The flies were out. I walked past the golf course to the park, then to the field Doyle and I had visited yesterday. I kept going, following the single-track hiking trail wherever it took me. It was still early enough on a Sunday morning. I had the park all to myself.

I walked in the woods all day. The trail turned out to be a three-mile loop. I came around once, got my bearings, and looped it again. I dawdled along, stopping as I pleased. It sprinkled rain for a bit, just enough to cut the flies back some. But mostly I thought and remembered. My trip to the White House. The president telling me how proud he was of me. The faces of the two soldiers who'd died in silence by friendly fire. Resigning from the army and giving it another shot at the CIA. Prisha Baari taking my job and benefits because I wouldn't play her game. Nicole's infidelity and betrayal. My surrender. It was all so surreal, as if I was watching a movie of someone else's life pass before my eyes. Then there was my son Teddy. That was real. That was something I could not ignore.

So I had gone straight at Doug Mitchell. He'd confirmed that Prisha Baari was in the middle of all this, but not much else. I figured he'd told me all he knew about Prisha, but that he'd held out on that secret project we had all been working on. ODYSSEUS. But I now had a name —Prisha Baari. My next plan was to follow Baari from work, catch her at home, and get the truth out of her. Maybe I'd try to reason with her, find some common ground and make my appeal. If that didn't work, I was afraid of how far I might go to get the truth out of her. In the back of my mind I knew this approach would likely fail. If it came down to it, I knew I would not be able to hurt a woman, even one like Prisha Baari. Maybe I needed a new plan.

————

After dinner that night, I cleared the dinner dishes and Doyle joined me in the kitchen, where we made short work of the cleanup. He poured us each two fingers of Irish whiskey, neat, and we went back to the table by the big windows. The skies had cleared just enough to bleed pink and orange over the Atlantic as the sun set. We both held our words until the show was over and twilight brought its darkness.

"You're right," I said, rolling that amber elixir around in my rocks glass. "I can't keep charging the hill alone and expect to get what I want." I took a sip and felt the Irish whiskey bite. "I need a new plan."

"You need a good team," Doyle said. "And you need to trust this team." He flicked a finger at me. "No more of this solo shit, Frankie."

I nodded in agreement. "Will you help me, Quinn?"

"Depends."

"On what?"

"Is your head right, Frankie? Are you back—for good? No more bullshit?"

I told him I was.

Doyle raised his glass. "Do you promise me this, Frankie?"

I knew what this meant. Making a promise over Irish whiskey to a man like Doyle was taking a blood oath. Better than an ironclad signed contract. And more enforceable.

I raised my glass to his. "I promise, Quinn."

With that, we clinked glasses and emptied them in one hard gulp. Our glasses hit the table with a thud. My thoughts went to church bells pealing, birds taking wing.

And just like that, all was forgiven. But not forgotten. Never. Not with a man like Doyle. There would be no second chance with him. All this was unspoken, but known, between us. Such was our bond.

Doyle picked up our glasses and went to pour us another round. I watched his back and tried to steady myself. He returned with a bounce in his step. He had just shed the weight he had carried for the past five years. The load I had put on his shoulders. Doyle placed the two refilled glasses on the table. I immediately grabbed mine and took a deep pull. Doyle observed this with amusement.

"Okay, tell me what's going on."

I fidgeted with my glass. He waited.

I couldn't tell Doyle the truth about Teddy. Not yet, anyway. He and I had just reunited, and I was not sure how he would respond to such news. I had not abandoned my son intentionally, and never would have left had I known. But this fact had been of no use to Teddy, who thought his father dead. For a boy that age, the why didn't matter; it was the what that counted. And what had happened was that I had not been there to raise my son. End of story.

It was best that I leave Teddy out of this for now. I knew it was wrong not telling Doyle the whole truth, but I tried to find some solace in the fact that an omission is not exactly a lie. It sure felt like one, though.

"I have to find out why I got fired from the CIA. Get my pension and reputation restored. Give the money to Nicole and her boy when I die. Put things back together again."

"What happened at the CIA?"

"As best I can tell, I got on the shit list of the deputy director. She's a... piece of work. And she blow-torched me. Fired me. Erased me. Stripped my bones clean."

"Why would she do that, Frankie?"

I told Doyle of that late Friday night on Prisha's office sofa, and what Doug Mitchell had told me at gunpoint.

"And let me guess," Doyle said. "You were going to just bum-rush this Prisha woman and shake the truth right out of her, right?"

"The thought did cross my mind."

Doyle squinted. "How much money we talking about, Frankie? Because I got some money here and there, and I could—"

"No!" I said, too loudly. "I mean, that's very kind of you, Quinn, but no. I need to do this thing right, clear my name and reputation. Make her pay."

"Okay, okay," Doyle responded, hands raised. He rubbed his chin. "So this thing is going to revolve around this Prisha woman. You said she's a deputy director? How high up is that?"

"She's the number two at CIA."

"Fuck," Doyle whispered. "Well, we can't go straight at her, then. That's clearly not going to work." Doyle tilted his head back in thought, eyes on the ceiling. His lips moved in silence, then stopped. His head dropped, a smile on his face.

"We could kidnap her," Doyle offered. "You know—just for a little while."

I shook my head. We both searched for another plan.

I spoke first. "How about we climb the ladder? Map her network, start low and work our way up. People who have placement and access to her and this secret project of hers. People who can get us close to her. We gather evidence, undeniable facts, and then expose her. Or maybe threaten to expose her. Whatever will get me my money the fastest."

"Why would these people, these ladder steps, help us?" Doyle said, thinking out loud. "I know some persuasive people. Maybe I could call them."

"No, Quinn. I don't want to do it like that. Nobody gets hurt. We make it so these people *want* to help. I'm thinking maybe we could help them out with something, and then they'll owe us a favor. Then we just approach them and call in that favor. Win-win."

"Just like that, huh? They're gonna help us out of the goodness of their hearts?"

"Well, like you said, Quinn, you know some very persuasive people. I figure we could get next to her in three, four moves tops. What do you think?"

"What happens when we get close to this woman?" Doyle asked. "What then?"

"Then the gloves come off. We either get what we want or we fucking ruin her. Eye for an eye."

"Ah—talion justice."

I had no idea what Doyle was talking about. The look on my face must have told him as much.

"*Lex talionis*," Doyle responded. "The Law of Retaliation. The punishment should be equivalent to the offense committed. The principle goes back to the early Romans.

We knew a thing or two about this on the streets of South Boston, too, I'll tell you that."

Doyle pondered the proposition for a moment as he sipped his whiskey.

"Okay, Frankie. I'm in."

Loyalty. After all I'd put this man through. I vowed to never disappoint him again.

I leaned in. "You sure, Quinn? I know you're retired. I would hate for any of this to blow back on you. I don't want the feds to come after you because of me."

Quinn Doyle smiled his big Irish smile. "Those bastards haven't got me yet. Let them come."

CHAPTER TWENTY-THREE

Prisha lay silent and still in her bed. She was stretched out on her back, wearing a black silk teddy, and an Egyptian cotton sheet covered her up to the waist. The room was dark. She was alone and had been staring up at her bedroom ceiling, thinking. She rolled to her side and tapped her personal iPhone to check the time. She grabbed the encrypted satellite telephone next to it and hit the button.

"Hello, Prisha," Karlsson said in a gravelly voice.

"Did I wake you?"

Karlsson paused, exhaled into the telephone. "What time is it?"

"One thirty or so."

"What do you want, Prisha?"

"I've been thinking about what Douglas Mitchell said today. I don't like it. I think we should start a package on Frank Luce."

"Silence.

"We already agreed on this," Karlsson responded, the annoyance rising in his voice. "It was just a simple tripwire report. We've got hundreds of tripwires in place for all of the past and present ODYSSEUS employees. Mitchell called in and reported a contact, just like we pay him to do. Nothing to worry about."

"You yourself said you thought Mitchell sounded nervous... that he didn't tell you everything."

"Prisha," Karlsson responded coolly. "Mitchell's a nervous guy. Don't read too much into this."

"I don't know. I—"

"Who is this Luce guy to you, anyway? He's just another notch on your bedpost. And you wiped him. He disappeared for five years and now he's back. So what? He's just a home-less guy. Why should we give a shit?"

Prisha got out of bed and began to pace the floor.

"I don't know, Henrik. I've been thinking about this all day. This guy is different."

"Different to you. Not to me."

Prisha bristled at Karlsson's rebuke. She stopped pacing and took a wide stance near her window, fingered the curtain open and looked out onto the deserted street.

"I want you to start a package on Luce," she repeated. "Put a couple of your best men on him. His return might just be a coincidence, but we've had an uptick in tripwire reports over the past sixty days. Something doesn't feel right. And my gut doesn't lie."

Karlsson again sighed into the phone, which irritated Prisha all the more.

"Luce has nothing to do with the tripwire reports. And I really don't have the men to be chasing him around right now. We've got a lot going on, Prisha. I've got most of my guys working on that other thing. And that thing could become a problem. Another Boone problem."

Prisha paused. Karlsson was right. But she trusted her gut.

"Okay, Henrik, you've been heard. But I'm the boss, and I say we start working on Luce."

"Prisha—"

"Henrik, I'm telling you to start a package on Luce. Now. Do you understand?"

Prisha knew it grated on Karlsson to be spoken to in this manner, so she saved it for special occasions such as this. Every time she had ignored her gut in the past, she had paid the price.

"You're the boss, Prisha." Karlsson hung up.

Satisfied, Prisha went back to bed. Pulled the sheet up to just below her breasts. She replayed the telephone call with Karlsson in her head. Big, strong, Viking Karlsson. She slipped her right hand below the sheet and between her legs.

It was good to be the boss.

CHAPTER TWENTY-FOUR

SEPTEMBER 21, 2016
EDWARD R. MURROW PARK
WASHINGTON, DC

I SHIFTED MY WEIGHT, TRYING TO GET COMFORTABLE ON a wood slat bench in the southwest section of Edward R. Murrow Park, a neighborhood pocket park just south of the Farragut West Metro Station and a half mile from the White House. I suspected President Mo Udell did not visit this place much, despite its proximity. Most of the neighborhood parks in the District, like this one, had become de facto homeless shelters.

And today did not disappoint. I was downwind from the gentleman with whom I shared this bench. His full essence assaulted me with every breeze, making me wince. I wondered if I had ever gotten that bad. I didn't think so, but at the end I suspected the truth was something different.

I sat facing Pennsylvania Avenue, which bisected the park into two equal sections. It was a busy section of road, with two lanes of traffic speeding in each direction amid a jumble of intersections. Large shade trees loomed over the sidewalk and the line of cars parked bumper-to-bumper, tight to the curb.

The homeless man slouched on the bench next to me cackled. "Here we go!" he said.

I turned to look at him. Big gap-toothed smile. He rolled his fat tongue around in his mouth, then smacked his lips shut. He pointed at a dark-skinned Latino man perched in the tight gap between two parked cars. His dark clothing kept him in shadow.

"Time for the show!" said the homeless guy with enough enthusiasm to bring on a coughing fit. A deep, rumbling cough. I remembered that cough.

"What's he doing?" I asked.

"Staging," he said. "You know, accidents." The guy slammed his two hands together in pantomime.

"Car accidents?"

The guy looked at me as if I was half stupid. "Yeah—car accidents. Dummy."

The guy took a couple of sips from his bag, not offering me any. The thought of sharing spit with this guy now made me retch. Six months ago it would have given me no pause.

"See, he waits for the right one, then just walks into it."

I made the sour milk face. "Doesn't he get hurt?"

The guy gives me another look. "No—he don't get hurt! He dodges that car, never hits him square. Nope."

The man shook his head, his hair and long beard a wild mess of snarls. Me six weeks ago.

"The guy just bangs down on the hood and side panel—

pow!" He smacked his fist into his palm. "It's like... um... bullfighting."

I started to respond, but he cut me off.

"... but the car is the bull."

Yeah, thanks. I got that part.

I'd been back in DC less than a week. Took the Amtrak Acela back. Doyle and I had spent much of that last night talking about how we would put our plan into action. We'd agreed on the stair-step strategy, climbing the ladder until we got to someone close enough to Prisha to make her squeal. Our problem, one of many, was that we didn't have any good intelligence to work with. I'd been out of the CIA for five years. I had pushed Doug Mitchell as far as he would go. We needed someone on the inside, with broad access to data. We needed ground truth.

We'd strategized until we settled on network administrators. Who better to gain illicit access to data than the gatekeepers of that data? Edward Snowden had been a contract network administrator when he leaked his classified information. And although that had occurred only three years ago, we were relying on the fact that whatever additional security measures were put in place could be circumvented by a skilled individual with proper placement and access.

Against my better judgment, we had agreed to bring Sarah into our little plan.

We called her late at night from Scituate. She heard us out and said she was in. No hesitation. The three of us had spoken a few more times on secure conference calls, and our plan had begun to come together. Sarah said that her company, White Rogers Young, colloquially known as WRY, had network admins placed all over the intelligence community, but had none at CIA. She thought and pulled up an executive colleague at another firm that did have several network admins placed at CIA. Sarah asked her friend if she could treat one of her admins to lunch, under the guise of gathering lead information.

The friend took the bait, and Sarah had taken the CIA contract network administrator to lunch at one of the best places in town. She'd warmed the guy up with a little flattery (it didn't take much for a woman who looked like Sarah), then deftly pivoted to a discussion of current on-board admins at CIA. She'd hoped for a few names of admins who were failing and could be easily replaced, but no such luck. All were top notch.

Sarah then looked for any of the admins that might have any vulnerabilities we could exploit. Her lunch date had shared some office gossip about a network admin named Chang Li who was going through a hell of a time with a neighbor. It had started as a simple boundary dispute, his neighbor complaining that the canopy of Li's tree had grown into his yard. Li had politely ignored the man's taunts until the lawsuit came. Then another, followed by another. All nuisance lawsuits, all requiring time and money that Li, a young father of two, did not have. Li was terrified that he would have to declare bankruptcy. Lose his house. His CIA security clearance. His wife and family.

It wasn't much, but Li was all we had. He would be the first ladder step on the way to Prisha. Li would have to leave his job, so Sarah and WRY could come in with a low-ball bid to replace him with a hand-picked person who would do their bidding. A trusted person who could map and exploit the CIA computer network for us. Be our inside man.

We disagreed on how to get Li out of CIA. Doyle advocated the simplest way. What Li needed most was money. Simply give him a loan at a usurious rate and turn the screws when he can't pay it back. Sarah didn't come up with anything better and sided with Doyle.

I didn't like it. Li seemed like a nice enough guy. He was early in his marriage with two little kids. He hadn't been at the CIA long but, by all accounts, was doing excellent work. Li hadn't done anything wrong, unlike his asshole neighbor. I knew what injustice felt like. More than most. I just couldn't do it to him. This eye-for-an-eye thing was supposed to be for people who earned it, not innocents like Li. There had to be another way.

And so we were at a stalemate with Li. Both Doyle and Sarah wanted to move on it. I was stalling for more time.

It took forty-five minutes for our Latino street performer to select his victim: a white woman, mid-fifties, approaching in a shiny green Mercedes SUV. He crouched lower, braced his hands on the parked cars on either side of him. He was in the starting blocks. The homeless guy elbowed me, gesticulating at the Latino guy and laughing like an imbecile.

The Latino made his move. Timed it perfectly, with the grace of a ballet dancer. He stepped from behind the parked cars and into the street. I heard the crash and the squeal of the Mercedes' disc brakes. Saw the Latino spin around violently and fall back towards the curb. Away from the other incoming cars. The SUV jerked to a stop. The woman screamed, then panicked, wrestling with her seat belt before she fell out of the vehicle onto the road. She was a short, plump woman, well dressed and made up. Her heels clicked like castanets as she ran to the poor man she had just hit.

The Latino had crawled to the safety of the sidewalk in all the commotion, where he lay moaning. He was very convincing and was putting on quite the performance. The woman bent over him; he pretended to lose consciousness. She shrieked, then bolted back to her Mercedes. She took cover behind the driver's-side door, then flailed about the cabin until she retrieved her cellphone. She furiously pecked at the screen and began to have an animated conversation with whoever was on the other end. Probably her attorney. Certainly not the police, or even 9-1-1.

The Mercedes was off to the side of the road just enough to allow another lane of traffic to eke by, everyone slowing to look and pass judgment.

The idea came to me in a flash, fully formed. I knew how we were going to get Li out of the CIA.

I rushed to the fallen man, kneeled beside him.

"I know what you're doing," I whispered.

The Latino popped one eye open for an instant, took my measure, then slammed it closed. He continued his moaning.

"Look," I said, gently shaking him by the shoulder. "I'm not gonna rat you out. I want in. But if you don't tell me who your boss is, I'll tell the cops."

The Latino's face went slack. He stopped his moaning and opened both his eyes. I repeated my offer.

A couple of vehicles pulled over in front of us. A large man emerged from one of them and began to walk towards us. I could hear the sound of faint sirens approaching. The look on the Latino man's face told me he heard them as well.

"Quick," I said, leaning into the man's face. "Tell me now, or this thing's over. Your boss's name. Now."

The Latino man's eyes shot towards the approaching

man, then back to me. He rolled his eyes and pursed his lips, letting out a low grunt. He slid his hands into his pocket and palmed me something, just as the large man strode up and stood over us. My new Latino friend went right back into victim mode, his wailing more convincing than before.

"You all right? What happened?" the large man said in a deep voice.

"That Mercedes came out of nowhere!" I said, rising to my feet. I pocketed what the Latino had just passed to me. "Hit this poor guy as he was crossing the street. Somebody better call an ambulance. I think he's hurt real bad."

The Latino guy opened his eyes just enough to give me a quick wink. I decided not to stick around and see how this one ended, as I thought it best to not be here when the cops arrived. I passed my homeless friend on the way down Pennsylvania Avenue towards the White House. He was on his feet with excitement now.

"I told ya! I told ya!" He cackled, clapping his hands and dancing a jig.

"Yeah, you called it, all right," I said with a nod. This guy would never know that he'd just saved Chang Li. Such is the mystery of life.

I walked with purpose, head bowed to avoid eye contact. I found an empty bench in Lafayette Square and spread out. Looking around, I fished into my pocket for what the Latino had given me. It was a business card.

Gerardo Gonzalez
"Call Me Gerry!"
I'll fight to get you the justice you deserve.

There was a big scale of justice as a background image

for the card, with one side tipped in favor of the other. The card bore both a local and a 1-800 number, and a NoMa address in NE DC.

I smiled as I fingered the card. "Hello, Gerry. You're just the man I want to see."

CHAPTER TWENTY-FIVE

SEPTEMBER 22, 2016
ATTORNEY GERRY GONZALEZ'S OFFICE
NoMA, NE WDC

"Mr. Gonzalez will see you now," said the gray-haired secretary with a pinched face. She watched me walk across the sparse lobby. I felt her eyes on me as I stepped to the hollow-core door with "GERALDO GONZALEZ, Esquire" emblazoned in gold leaf. I turned the knob to enter. The door felt cheap and lightweight in my hand as I swung it open. I hoped the man behind it was not.

I had taken the Red Line Metro train to NoMa-Gallaudet U Station, in the developing neighborhood known as "NoMa," located north and east of Union Station. It was also the home of Union Market, a restored grocery and specialty food hall that was the epicenter of DC's gourmet food scene. In the second half of the nineteenth and early twentieth centuries, NoMa was known as Swampoodle, which pleased me for some unknown reason.

Gonzalez instantly rose from behind his oversized desk when I entered his office. He appeared to stand no more than five and a half feet tall, but was thick and sturdy as a refrigerator. He strode from behind his desk, hand extended in greeting. I noticed his giant white veneers from clear across the office. They glowed in his tan face, like a jack-o-lantern's grin or that exaggerated smile emoji you never use because it's just too much. We met in front of his desk and shook hands. He had small hands and thick fingers; a gaudy ring adorned the pinkie finger of each hand. The palms were smooth as snakeskin. Strong grip with extended eye contact. Good. He had a full head of matte-black hair, slicked back, and a matching eighties Tom Selleck mustache.

Gonzalez pointed to one of the two yellow upholstered chairs facing his desk. He passed me and walked to his office door. He told his secretary to hold his calls, clicked the door shut, then returned to his desk. It gave me time to give his office a once-over. It looked like a box of crayons had exploded. Bright colors, strangers all, combined to form a jarring palette. I followed Gonzalez as he returned, enjoying his lavender suit and gold tie.

He took his place at his desk, which was so big he appeared to be riding it. I was sure he had boosted the height of his chair so as not to disappear behind it, and wondered if his feet even reached the floor. He laced his fingers on the desk in front of him and smiled again. The wattage pressed me back into my chair.

"Mr. Luce." Gonzalez looked me over good. "I normally do not meet new clients under these circumstances. But for you, I make an exception."

"Me and my one thousand dollars." Sarah had wired the fee to Gonzalez through some bogus LLC she had set up for our little talion adventure. It was Doyle's money. Turns out he had lots of it stashed away from his lifetime of crime.

"Yes, of course," Gonzalez said. "The grand did get my attention. And it let me know you weren't a cop or the feds. They're not gonna walk a grand just for a first meeting with a man such as myself." Gonzalez stroked his black mustache. "First off, that grand is a payment to your attorney—me. Whatever we're about to talk about is protected under attorney–client privilege. I don't talk, you don't talk. Got it?"

I nodded, then looked towards his office door. Gonzalez followed my glance. He paused, and then his large dark eyes grew wide in recognition.

"Silvia?" Gonzalez chuckled. "Don't worry about her. She's been with me forever. I completely trust her. She knows everything going on in my office." He leaned over the desk and whispered, "*Everything.*"

"She didn't seem to like me much."

"Oh, Silvia's just protective of me is all. You came to us under unusual circumstances, Mr. Luce."

"Frank. You can call me Frank."

"Okay, Frank. All my clients call me Gerry."

Gonzalez then explained that he had been reluctant to take this meeting, despite my one-thousand-dollar show of good faith. But he had done his homework on me. Had discovered my military background and that I was a Medal of Honor recipient, which seemed to carry weight with him. He also told me that an attorney he knew and trusted had vouched for me.

"I don't know any lawyers," I said. "Don't like 'em."

Gonzalez laughed at this. A deep, full-bodied laugh. "I

don't like them much either." He paused. "You know a woman named Sarah Reyes?"

I nodded slightly, unsure of where this was going.

"She called my friend. He trusts her. And I trust him. So here you are. It's all about trust in my profession. Do you trust me, Frank?"

"I don't trust anyone, Gerry. Especially someone I just met."

"Well, my friend, you'd better get over that right quick if we are going to work together."

We both allowed that to hang in the air. He seemed to feed on the silence. A confident man. I liked that. I decided to trust him.

"I saw your man yesterday. At Murrow Park. The Latino. Great performance. Whatever you're paying that guy, it's not enough."

A tight grin tugged at the corners of his push-broom mustache. "You want a job, Frank? That's what this is about?"

"Not exactly, Gerry. Tempting, but I'm not interested in getting hit by cars for a living."

I ran through the plan, the first talion ladder step. Gonzalez would stage a car accident just like the one I'd witnessed yesterday, but this time the mark would be Chang Li's asshole neighbor, Kyle Brown. The professional plaintiff who had filed over one hundred frivolous lawsuits over the past decade. This time he would be on the wrong side of the v, see what it felt like to be a defendant for a change. Gonzalez would file a huge civil lawsuit against Brown, throw everything at him. Make him scream. Then dismiss the lawsuit when I told him to. No questions asked. For this, Gonzalez would be paid a flat fee of twenty thousand dollars, five now and fifteen when the lawsuit was dropped.

Gonzalez listened in silence. His eyes blinked rapidly when I got to the money part. He stroked his mustache when I was done.

"Why are you doing this, Frank?"

"Let's just say Chang Li's a good friend of mine, and I want to help him out of a jam."

"Twenty large says he's more than a friend."

"You interested or not?"

"Just the accident? Nothing else?" Gonzalez folded his arms across his chest. He tilted back in his chair, chin raised, as he regarded me through dark, squinted eyes.

"Nothing else. By the book."

Gonzalez thought. I let him, glancing about his office. The diploma behind his desk was from Ave Maria School of Law, which appeared to be a Catholic law school in Naples, Florida. I'd never heard of such a place and made a mental note to confirm whether this school was ABA accredited.

"No one gets hurt, Gerry," I said, breaking our silence. "Push this to the top of your list. Get the lawsuit filed ASAP. It's a lot of money for a little bit of work."

"It's not that simple," Gonzalez responded, sliding his chair back into the desk, the legs scraping against the wood floor. He shook his head. "I don't know. This thing's starting to make my ass itch."

"It's a good payday, Gerry. Take it."

Gonzalez tilted his head back, eyes closed. He only needed a moment to make up his mind.

"Twenty-five K. Ten down, fifteen when we're done. Not a penny less."

"Throw in the Latino guy and we got a deal," I countered.

"Deal!"

Gonzalez shot to his feet. He walked around his desk and shook my hand. I stood a full head taller than he, despite his thick-heeled shoes. His teeth were larger and brighter close up. His big smile did not reach his dark snake eyes.

And that's how I came to trust Geraldo Gonzalez, Esquire.

CHAPTER TWENTY-SIX

SEPTEMBER 30, 2016
CHIPOTLE RESTAURANT BATHROOM
DOWNTOWN, WDC

THE BOY WAS ABOUT TEDDY'S AGE. LAUGHING AND animated. His younger sister sat at his right in a high chair, the parents across the table. All were tucking into a large plate of chips and guacamole at a downtown Chipotle, the one near the National Portrait Gallery. The parents sat close together. They could have been celebrating their child's birthday. But I knew that wasn't the reason for all those smiling faces. No, it wasn't a birthday. It was much better than that.

The boy shrieked in exuberance. His father shushed him, then tousled his hair. The boy giggled. My thoughts drifted to my own son. I swallowed hard, then took a long draw off the straw I'd stuck in my jumbo cup of soda. I pulled the plastic lid off and poked at the ice cubes with the straw. Put the cup to my lips and sucked a few cubes into my mouth, then bit down hard. The chill down my spine brought me back.

It had been a little over a week since I'd paid Gonzalez his ten-grand deposit, and he'd held his word. Things had moved quickly. A lot had been put in place. I hoped it would all pay off tonight.

The father kissed his wife and got up from the table. I followed him at a discreet distance into the bathroom. The man stood at a urinal. I glanced under the bathroom stall doors to ensure they were unoccupied, then stepped up to the urinal directly next to the man, a necessary breach of man etiquette that nonetheless made me uneasy.

I gave the man a quick side-eye and mumbled a greeting. He returned it. We stood in silence for a long moment, eyes forward.

"Is your family enjoying their meal, Chang?" I asked Li.

Li's head shot around. "Excuse me?" Concern rolled across his face.

"I like the guac and chips too. A little high on the calories, but what the hell—you guys are celebrating tonight. Right, Chang?" I turned my head to face him.

"What?" He paused, his eyelids fluttering. "Do I know you? How do you know my name?"

"And Kyle... Can you believe that asshole?" I said. "He actually had the balls to come over to your home last night and apologize to you. Shook your hand and everything."

Li's face went slack. He turned his body toward me, as if in a trance.

"Whoa there, Chang. I don't need to see that. Front forward. Act normal."

Li robotically turned back into the urinal. His breathing became shallow and rapid.

"Listen to me, Chang. We don't have a lot of time here. You're out celebrating with your family tonight, right?"

Li nodded and kept his eyes on the wall in front of him.

"Celebrating the fact that Kyle dropped his lawsuit against you. No more legal fees draining you dry. No more bankruptcy. You're going to keep your house and security clearance. Yes?"

Li turned his head just enough to meet my eyes. "Who are you?" he asked in a whisper.

"I'm the guy who saved you, Chang. Convinced Kyle to do the right thing. I know what it's like to have everything taken from you, to be unable to support your family." I paused. "Do as I ask, and that won't happen to you."

"What? I don't understand." Li looked equal parts confused and miserable.

The door to the bathroom flew open behind us. I hissed "Shhh." The guy gave me a quick look, then made his selection, leaving an empty urinal between us. He took care of business, zipped up quick and left as quickly as he'd arrived, sensing something was afoot that he wanted no part of.

"How did you know I was here?" Li whispered. "Have you been following me?"

"We got a tracker on your car."

"What? No... no." Li shook his head. You're lying..."

"You know I'm not, Chang."

"Leave me alone!"

"I'm here to help you, Chang. Or I can put you back where I found you. Staring into the abyss. Your choice."

I had no intention of bringing Kyle Brown or any other misery back into Chang Li's life. He seemed like a nice guy. I wasn't the kind of man who would step on another to get what I wanted. But right now I needed Li to think that I was.

A man and his little boy came into the bathroom. Li tried to speak and I shook him off. The guy took his son into the stall. The kid took care of his business and they left.

"Look, Chang. Like I said, we don't have a lot of time. I fixed your problem with Kyle. Gave him a little taste of his own medicine. He won't be bothering you again. In fact, I suspect he'll be moving soon. You and your family will never see that asshole again. You can get your life back on track. Put this whole nightmare behind you. Sound good?"

Li nodded.

"Good. Now I need you to do me a small favor in return. That's only fair, isn't it, Chang?"

Li's eyes went wide. His mouth dropped open.

"I need you to say the words, Chang."

Yes," Li mumbled.

"I need you to cowboy up here, Chang. I need you to say the words. *Yes. I will return the favor.*"

Li cleared his throat and repeated the words, this time with more resolve.

"That's better." I looked over his shoulder. The bathroom was still empty. "This is what you're gonna do, Chang. Tomorrow morning you're gonna call a friend of mine, Sarah Reyes, at White Rogers Young. You heard of them?"

"Yeah," Li said. "Everyone knows WRY."

"Tomorrow morning, first thing, you're gonna call Sarah Reyes. You two will have lunch. She will offer you a contract for a job at State—same job you have at the Agency now, but with better pay and benefits. You're gonna thank Sarah and take that job. You understand, Chang?"

"But I already have a job."

"No, you don't. After your lunch with Sarah, you're gonna resign your position at CIA. Give one week's notice. You'll start at State the following week. The first day of the rest of your life. Got it?"

Li looked frightened and forlorn. "But I like my job."

I blew a heavy sigh through pursed lips with enough force to adjust Li's attitude.

"This is your only chance to get out from under this, Chang. To get your life back. Do it for your family. Your kids." I heard my voice catch. "You're lucky to have this chance. Take it, Chang."

"I don't feel so lucky."

"Luck's a funny thing. Sometimes it's Lady Justice balancing her scales. Sometimes it's karma—you know, when the stars align just right, and for the briefest of moments all is right with the world." I zipped up, shrugged my shoulders. "But other times, it's just dumb luck. You know?"

Li remained silent.

"Do you believe in karma, Chang? Dumb luck?"

Li turned away from me and dropped his head. "No. I don't."

"Neither do I. Sometimes Lady Justice is willfully obtuse, her blindfold translucent. In this case, I balanced her scales for you, Chang."

Li made a sound best described as a cross between a sob and a squeal.

"Chang?"

"Okay."

A jolt of electricity flowed through me. Yes! The first step of our talion ladder was in place.

I flushed my urinal. Chang did likewise. We stepped to the sinks in tandem, washed our hands, and then turned and walked towards the door. I handed Chang Sarah's card. He pocketed it, then stopped and gave me a hard look.

"Why are you doing this?"

How could I ever explain it to him? My son. My cancer. Doyle and Sarah back in my life. Prisha. Redemption. Revenge. I was still working it all out myself.

"Go on now, Chang," I told him. "Your family's gonna wonder what happened to you."

Li left the bathroom. I waited a minute then did likewise. Li had rejoined his family at their table. I left Chipotle and walked past the front window. I saw Li gulping his glass of water, his smiling wife tucked into his side. His son bobbing to and fro in his seat, the little girl's hands flapping about.

I had provided Li with a solution to his problem. Put him and his family back on track. Given them another chance. A chance I wished I'd had. Li had taken it, and had returned the favor. We'd have our guy in place at the CIA in a week.

I hunched my head into my shoulders, thrust my hands in my pockets, and bounded down the street towards the Gallery Place-Chinatown Metro Station. Back to my apartment. I'd brief Doyle and Sarah on what had happened, using one of the new burner phones Sarah had purchased for us all. Take a long hot shower, crack a beer. Maybe have a nice chat with Angie.

We were on our way.

CHAPTER TWENTY-SEVEN

OCTOBER 6, 2016
SARAH'S OFFICE AT WHITE ROGERS YOUNG
DUPONT CIRCLE, WDC

SARAH FIDGETED WITH HER MONTBLANC PEN, TWIRLING it between her fingers. She glanced up and checked the time against the giant atomic wall clock at the other end of her cavernous office, which was larger than most apartments in the District. WRY had the top five floors in a modern glass building, one of the tallest in Dupont Circle. As a senior executive vice president, she occupied an office on executive row, which stretched the entire south side of the penthouse floor. All exterior walls had floor-to-ceiling windows, which afforded panoramic views of the city, particularly the White House and the Washington Monument, less than a mile distant. Tinted windows and translucent roller blinds provided privacy as well as protection from the sun. Her office had been decorated in a modern motif, all glass and chrome. She had insisted on bright upholstered sofas and chairs over dark leather, and chose pale rose with gold accents. She was the only executive to stray from the company line with the interior designer, and she suspected her colleagues secretly held this against her.

Sarah had been on edge all week, ever since Frank called her to let her know of his successful recruitment of Li. This meant it was her turn now: she was on the spot to get WRY— more importantly, Frank—the contract for Li's replacement at CIA. She had worked the phones all weekend, calling in favors from across her vast network of business contacts. With difficulty, Sarah had pushed her low-ball bid through her boss, justifying it as a loss leader to catch additional business at the Agency. All the tap dancing and schmoozing had exhausted her, but she wasn't there yet. She had to convince the man about to step into her office that she had an offer he couldn't refuse. Sarah had hand-picked this guy, never even considered another person as their eyes and ears at CIA. If he refused her offer, all her work this week was for naught.

Her heart was racing. She tried to control it with deep breathing and visualization exercises. Sarah opened her eyes and saw she was still playing with her pen. She placed it on the desk and folded her hands. She closed her eyes again.

The knock at her door startled her. Her eyes opened to the sight of Darryl Robinson leaning on a half-opened door.

"Hello, Sarah," Robinson said. "We had a ten o'clock? I could come back later."

Sarah rose from her glass scissor-legged desk and waved him in. She met him across the office in the informal seating area and motioned for him to sit on one of the sofas; she sat opposite him on the other. A low-slung glass table separated them. She asked him if he wanted anything to drink. He first shook his head no, then said maybe water. Sarah went to the door, asked her secretary to fetch water and coffee, and returned to Robinson. His eyes were roaming all over the office, taking in her exalted station at WRY. Robinson was a front-line computer nerd and did not receive many invitations to executive row.

Sarah gracefully crossed her legs at the knee, her skirt revealing just enough thigh to make Robinson take a quick breath. His eyes lingered. Sarah caught his stare. He blushed and smiled awkwardly.

Robinson was a light-skinned second-generation African American, born in New Jersey of Moroccan descent. He stood six foot and had the lean build of an endurance athlete, which he was not. His face was perfectly symmetrical, his features smooth. Bright hazel eyes, specked with green. Intelligent eyes. He was just shy of his twenty-ninth birthday. He was a beautiful creature, like a deer, but lacked the self-awareness of the genetically gifted.

The secretary came in and placed the coffee and water on the low table. Her eyes explored Robinson, but he appeared oblivious of her attention. Sarah thanked her and she left without a word.

"It's good to see you again, Darryl," Sarah said. "What's it been—six months?"

"Eight months, fourteen days."

This made Sarah smile. "How do you like your placement at the FBI?"

"It's okay. Their tech is for shit, but the people are nice enough."

"No problems over there?"

"No," Robinson replied. He looked down at his shoes. "I'm behaving myself, if that's what you mean."

A couple of years ago, when Robinson was placed by WRY at the NSA, he had been caught hacking into the personnel file of a female co-worker he had a crush on. His overtures were misconstrued as stalking by the woman, and she had complained to HR. Robinson was called in and interviewed. HR had found no direct evidence to support the woman's claim, but had contacted WRY and asked for Robinson to be removed.

Sarah's division had placed Robinson at NSA. She had called him in and got his side of the story. She found him socially awkward, sure, and completely obtuse when it came to approaching women, but he was also brilliant and hardworking. And most importantly, she believed him when he professed his innocence.

So Sarah had intervened with NSA on Robinson's behalf and convinced the woman to withdraw her complaint in exchange for a promise that Robinson would have nothing more to do with her. Robinson eventually left NSA for his current contract at the FBI, where he was doing well.

Robinson owed Sarah. They both knew it. It was now time for Sarah to collect. And she always collected on her debts.

"Good. I'm pleased to hear you are doing well at the FBI." Sarah sipped her coffee. "Do you remember your incident at NSA?"

"Some woman at the FBI saying I did something wrong? Because if—"

"No, nothing like that. As far as I know, anyway." Sarah leaned forward on the sofa, closing the distance between them. "No, Darryl. It's time for you to repay the favor I did for you."

"What favor? I lost that NSA gig!"

"Yeah, but I saved your job here at WRY. And kept your record clean, and your security clearance intact. Time to pay up."

"Oh, that's how it is." Robinson's face dropped. "That's why you wanted to see me?" He lunged for his glass of water, almost knocking it over. He took a long draw and placed it back on its coaster. "It's always like that with women." His eyes darted around the room.

"With that kind of charm, Darryl, I just don't see how you can't find a girlfriend," Sarah said with a grin.

Robinson sighed. "What do you want, Sarah?"

"I want to place you at CIA," Sarah said. "As a network admin."

Robinson groaned. "Why? I like the work I'm doing now. And anyone can do admin. Why not get someone else?" He paused. "I told you—I haven't done anything wrong at FBI."

Sarah scooted forward on the sofa, even closer to Robinson.

"You don't understand, Darryl. This is a special assignment. I need you at CIA to gain access to their network, particularly personnel records and such."

"But that's what got me in trouble at NSA."

"This time you'll be doing it at my direction. I'll cover you."

"Why do you need this information?" Robinson asked.

"Let me worry about that," Sarah responded. "You'd report directly to me for this assignment, which means we'll be seeing a lot more of each other over the coming months."

This brought a wide smile to Robinson's face. It was no secret he was infatuated with Sarah. She'd addressed this during their NSA entanglements, and Robinson had accepted her professional rebuke. But it was still there. Sarah saw it in his eyes.

"What would I do there?" Robinson asked.

The hook had been set.

"Well, you'd basically be a network admin. By the book." She gave Robinson a coquettish smile, which found its mark. "And maybe sometimes you'd do special work for me. Data calls, things like that. Mostly personnel stuff; nothing too serious."

Sarah saw Robinson thinking it over, so she continued.

"How are your... *skills*... these days?"

Sarah was referring to Robinson's hacking prowess. He nodded in response. Robinson had an anarchist streak and liked to go right up to, and sometimes over, the line. A risk-taking adrenaline junkie with a keyboard. He was the real deal, too: highly skilled, but difficult to control under the wrong circumstances.

Sarah slowly re-crossed her legs. Robinson fought to keep his eyes steady and lost. Sarah was in control.

Robinson asked specific questions about this CIA contract, which Sarah answered. He would start next Tuesday, October 11th, the day after the Columbus Day holiday. He would work a straight forty-hour week, Monday through Friday, eight a.m. to five p.m., weekends and holidays off. Sarah said they might have to work a few nights together, which interested Robinson more than anything else Sarah told him about this new assignment.

Robinson sat back in the sofa, groaned and wiped his face with both hands.

"I don't know, Sarah." Robinson threw his head back. "I hate the CIA."

Time to close this deal. Sarah rose, gently flattened her dark gray skirt, and joined Robinson on his side of the table. She sat next to him on the sofa, no more than a foot separating them, and canted her body to face him. Robinson seemed to inflate; his eyes widened.

"I would consider this a personal favor, Darryl. It would wipe our debt clean."

Robinson's face again flushed. He started to bounce both legs up and down, pushing off the floor with the balls of his feet.

"What's it going to take to get you to say yes?"

Robinson broke out in nervous laughter. Sarah closed the space between them.

Robinson smiled. Tight-lipped at first, then it spread all over his face.

"What is it, Darryl?"

Robinson cleared his throat. "Uhm... well... How about you and me—"

Sarah barked out a laugh. "Really?" She shook her head, still laughing. "I'm not going to have sex with you, Darryl. Try again."

"How about a date, then?"

"I don't think so."

Robinson retreated. "Set me up with one of your friends?"

"How about I teach you how to be less awkward around women first? Give you a few pointers?"

"Uh, I don't know."

"I did mention, didn't I, that we would be spending a lot

of time together with this assignment? Late nights, shared dinners, that sort of thing?"

Robinson beamed. He nodded his head. WRY had its new CIA network administrator.

"Okay, great!" Sarah said. "I'm sure you'll enjoy your new assignment." She rose from the sofa and looked down at Robinson, who was still smiling.

"And Darryl, here's my first pointer: stop staring at my tits. Women don't like it."

CHAPTER TWENTY-EIGHT

OCTOBER 18, 2016
PRISHA'S CIA OFFICE
LANGLEY, VA

ROBINSON APPROACHED THE SECRETARY SITTING SENTRY outside the boss's office. Robinson had only been at CIAHQ for a full week; he checked the office number. Right above the number was the occupant's name in big, bold letters:

PRISHA VEDA BAARI
Deputy Director

Yup, he had the right office.

Baari's secretary was a man, which surprised Robinson. The guy looked about fifty but could have been much younger. His hair was thinning, his dark eyes unblinking behind large glasses. His face was ashen, thin lips pursed tight. He looked high-strung, as if any sudden noise or move-ment would launch him from his chair.

Robinson introduced himself by first name only, said he was from IT and that he had to do a routine update to DD Baari's computer. The guy's eyes darted about. He said that he had not been informed of such an update, and that he had standing instructions to let no one into Baari's office unan-nounced. Robinson explained that he had been told this update had already been approved, and that it was critical for all senior executives to receive this security patch ASAP.

The secretary again mumbled that he was not supposed to let anyone into her office. Robinson smiled and said that was okay with him; it would be the secretary's ass if the deputy got a virus or caused a network breach because she didn't have the patch. Robinson laced his response with ominous-sounding computer jargon.

It worked. The secretary vapor-locked; sweat beaded on his forehead. Robinson almost felt sorry for the guy. He was a beaten dog. What a joy his boss must be to work for. Robinson waited. The man began to tremble.

"Well?" Robinson asked. The secretary remained mute. Robinson spun around to leave.

"Wait!" the man finally said. "The deputy's in a meet-ing." He stood and scanned the office area in panic. "She's in a SCIF without her phone." He gave Robinson a beseeching look. "Stay here. I'll run and check with her. I'll be right back." He reached down to lock his computer screen, then scampered down the hall.

Robinson didn't know exactly where Baari's meeting was, or how long the secretary would be gone. But judging from how squirrely the guy was, Robinson thought he might be gun-shy enough to equivocate when he got to his boss's meeting, and that maybe this would give him enough time. He decided to risk it.

No one was watching. Except the cameras, of course. Robinson had worn a soft disguise in an attempt to confuse the lens just enough. He kept his eyes down and chin tucked the whole time. That would have to do.

Robinson strode to the office door and tried the knob. Unlocked. He slipped inside and closed the door behind him, leaving it ajar just an inch to better hear anyone approaching. Robinson activated the digital chronograph on his watch. He'd practiced this so many times it had burned into muscle memory. He had gotten it down to under five minutes. He snapped on a thin pair of rubber gloves and ran across Prisha's large office, dodging sofas and chairs, to get to her desktop computer.

0:38

Robinson pressed the power button and willed the computer to boot up. He bounced up and down on his toes as it came to life. He had already hacked Prisha's password (this had been remarkably easy—Ody1975!) and typed it in. Robinson's hands were trembling, and it took him two tries to correctly enter it. *Shit.*

He reached into his front pants pocket and pulled out the thumb drive. He dropped it on the carpet, then dove to the floor to look for it. It had bounced under Prisha's desk. He stretched out and grabbed for it, raking it towards him. He got a grip on it and banged his head on the desk drawer getting up. Cursing, Robinson frantically looked behind the monitor for the USB port. His eyes were having a hard time focusing, his motor skills deteriorating. He grabbed the side of the monitor for stability and forced his eyes to focus. He jammed the drive into the computer, then fumbled through finding and opening the file he needed.

Robinson's fingers flew over the keyboard. The file started to download. *Whew*.

1:41

Robinson's arms were leaden. He shook them out and kept his eyes on the computer monitor.

"Slow is smooth, and smooth is fast." It was how the Navy SEALs did it, and it had been Robinson's mantra in preparation for this little operation. But his nerves were testing him now, now that he was in it. The only way to get smooth was to slow down his careening central nervous system.

He forced some deep breaths. The file downloaded at glacial speed.

Robinson felt naked. Not much he could say if Prisha or her lapdog secretary came in now, with his thumb drive hanging out the back of her monitor. His plan was to feign ignorance, double down on the new guy card, play it up as one big misunderstanding. Turn it into a comic farce. A weak option at best. He figured if he did get caught in the next few minutes with his pants down, the best he could hope for was that he would be fired and walked off campus immediately. But this was the CIA, not Walmart. He expected worse.

2:24

Robinson heard something outside the office. He skulked back to the office door and peered through the opening. His heart was kabooming so loud in his ears he felt certain the whole world could hear it. Two colleagues, a man and woman, walked by talking. They paused as they passed Prisha's office, then turned and pointed. Robinson's heart jumped into his throat. He flattened himself against the wall. The two laughed, then continued to walk down the hall. Robinson dashed back to the computer monitor. Still downloading. Good.

3:51

They had all agreed that this would be their first major operation at CIA, to install software on Prisha's computer to allow remote activation of her camera and microphone, giving them unlimited ability to hear and see everything Prisha did in her office. The software also included keystroke monitoring to track all her computer activity. It was much more difficult and time consuming to try to install this packet remotely, and it had been Robinson who suggested they install it on Prisha's computer the old-fashioned way: human engineering—that is, by duping her secretary. Sarah had never liked the idea but said "her people" did. Robinson had asked about these people, but Sarah refused to elaborate. It was an unresolved friction between them.

Robinson scanned the papers stacked neatly in rows on top of Prisha's desk. His instructions were to photograph anything with the word ODYSSEUS on it. He saw nothing. He slid open her top desk drawer and rooted around. Mostly stray office supplies and keys, of which he took note. A scrap of paper hung down from the top of the drawer. Robinson tugged at it. It was taped in place, so he peeled it off. It was the size of a large yellow Post-it note, and in a feminine hand had the following numbers scrawled on it:

2 - 1 - 5 - 3 - 4

Robinson knew computer users, and knew executives were often the sloppiest when it came to password security.

He didn't know what this number combination meant, but knew it must be important. It was important enough for Prisha to hide it in plain sight, which meant she probably used it frequently. Robinson held it in his hand.

5:02

Robinson checked the monitor and began to breathe again when he saw the download was complete. He got out of the download, removed his thumb drive from the back of the computer and jammed it into his front pocket. His eyes flashed to the office door, then back to the desk and the open drawer. He fished around for a scrap of paper and pen, found what he was looking for and scratched down the five-number sequence.

He heard a voice in the distance. A plaintive voice he had heard before.

The secretary. *Shit!*

Robinson slapped the yellow Post-it back onto the top of the drawer. He threw the pen and the rest of the junk he had pulled out, helter-skelter, back in the drawer and slid it shut. Prisha would of course know someone had been in this drawer, and he hoped she would just blame it on her secretary.

Robinson had to get out of that office *now*. He darted back across the room and, without hesitation, swung the door open and stepped outside. No one grabbed him. Good.

He stepped past the secretary's cubicle and into the hall-way. Voices to his left. He turned and saw Prisha and the secretary in animated conversation. They were about fifty feet away and approaching quickly. Robinson spun and walked down the hall in the opposite direction, at the fastest walking speed he could go short of a trot. He had about seventy feet in front of him before he reached the end of this hallway, where he could take a hard left turn and get out of their line of sight.

Robinson moved forward on heavy legs; white noise filled his ears. He expected to hear "Hey you! Stop!" at any moment. If he did, he would keep going. It was so hard not to break into a run. He dared not turn around, but desperately needed to know what was going on behind him. Finally, a man approached from the opposite direction. He said hello and Robinson nodded, head down. As soon as the man passed, Robinson slid to the other side of the hallway, using the man as a shield to cover the last twenty feet to freedom.

Robinson took a hard left at the end of the hallway. A wave of nausea hit him. He swallowed the stomach bile down and doubled his pace. He passed the elevator and entered the stairwell at the end of the hallway. He pushed his back against the wall and tried to catch his breath.

12:09

Robinson gripped the staircase banister and took the steps two at a time. He needed to be back at his desk ASAP. He needed the secretary's terror of his boss to drive his actions, and by covering for himself cover for Robinson as well. Robinson needed the secretary to tell Prisha that the IT guy must have got tired of waiting and left, without doing the update. And hope it ended there.

12:16—stop.

Back at his desk, Robinson sat still, wiping the sweat from his forehead. His senses acute, as a deer listens for the snap of a twig under the hunter's boot. He stared at his computer monitor, pretending to work, waiting for his world to end.

It didn't. No one came rushing in to tackle him to the ground, flex tie his hands and feet like a steer at a rodeo. His breathing slowed back to normal. He looked around. None of his colleagues were acting suspicious. Robinson got up and walked by his boss's office. His boss said hello and appeared fine as well. Robinson went to the men's room and splashed cold water on his face, sopped it dry with the scratchy brown paper towels from the dispenser. He looked at his reflection in the mirror and smiled. The smile turned into a laugh. *What a rush.*

He couldn't wait to see Sarah tonight and tell her all about it.

CHAPTER TWENTY-NINE

NOVEMBER 5, 2016
HOUSE PARTY
KINGSTOWNE, VA

THE LARGE MAN NEXT TO ME CLEARED HIS THROAT. IT sounded like sandpaper scraping more sandpaper.

"The Pats won last week... you see it? 41-25 over the Bills. They're seven and one. Brady was money—four TDs." He moved the toothpick from one corner of his mouth to the other with a flick of his tongue. "We're going to the Super Bowl again."

The man sitting in the passenger seat of my rented Ford Explorer was named Finn O'Neill. He had a couple of inches and about forty pounds on me and barely fit in his seat. He refused to wear a seat belt, even after I asked him to buckle up. Buzzcut reddish-blond hair, lightened by a few streaks of gray, sat atop his block head and thick neck. His light eyes were flat, expressionless. He had huge meaty hands, the scarred hands of a working man. Doyle had sent him down from Boston to help with tonight's operation. I had seen men such as O'Neill growing up in Southie. Street fighters, men willing to trade with anyone for any reason. Men comfortable with violence. Men like my father, Arthur.

"Didn't see it," I responded. I wasn't much interested in football these days.

The streetlights cast just enough light to put O'Neill in faint shadow. He plucked the chewed toothpick from his mouth, put it in his shirt pocket, and replaced it with another. My attention returned to our target this evening, the house across the street in a residential neighborhood in the upscale master-planned community of Kingstowne, Virginia.

We sat quietly, the silence broken by occasional shouts and the thud of deep bass coming from the high school party raging across the street.

"That Tom Brady... he's a beautiful man."

I turned to face him. A smile creased my face at the incongruity of his statement.

"Yeah, I guess he is," was all I could say.

O'Neill nodded and appeared satisfied with my response. We resumed our silence.

Darryl Robinson had been at CIA for over three weeks now. We had collected eighteen days of data from the bug he had placed on Prisha's computer. It appeared that we had gotten away with it, as Robinson had not been approached and, as best we could tell, was not under suspicion. We'd used all that collected data to map Prisha's network and build profiles on her most important associates. We were looking for vulnerabilities, anything we could exploit.

Looking for our second talion ladder step on the way to Prisha.

Our first ladder step, Chang Li, had proven particularly helpful. Not only had Li kept his word and resigned his position at CIA, he had also provided some valuable tips to Robinson as he shadowed Li during his one-week on-the-job orientation. Li mentioned that Prisha was working on a super-secret project of some sort (I already knew this to be ODYSSEUS from my old boss, Doug Mitchell), and that her project administrator, Linda Webb, was up to her eyeballs in it. Our monitoring of Prisha's computer confirmed this, as the two women corresponded multiple times a day. We opened a file on Linda Webb and struck gold.

Linda Webb was an overweight and bitter woman. In her mid-forties, stuck in a mid-level government job with no prospects for promotion. She had spiraled after her divorce, and blamed her current lot in life on her ex-husband, her co-workers, her daughter—anyone but herself. She was devious and amoral, which was what I suspect had attracted her to her boss, Prisha.

Robinson had begun to monitor Webb's communications, and we quickly learned of her volatile relationship with her daughter Anna, a pretty and popular high school senior. Anna was miserable at home and fought with her mother often. These arguments had grown vicious, and sometimes even physical when her mother drank. They mostly fought about Anna's boyfriend, Ryan Young, a blond-tipped hip-hop drug dealer who pushed oxycontin to schoolkids in Kingstowne. Webb suspected that Ryan had got Anna hooked on drugs. Anna had screamed that she loved Ryan. Her mother had screamed back that all men were pigs, like Anna's father. She told Anna that Ryan was just using her, that he would leave her as soon as something else came along. Linda Webb did not love her daughter so much as she needed her. Anna was all she had left. This need was the hook that would get us one step closer to Prisha.

This need was also what had brought O'Neill and me to this quiet residential street this night. Anna Webb and Ryan Young were among the high schoolers partying across the street. The plan was to catch them leaving the party, then peel Ryan off and persuade him that it would be in his best interests that he not see Anna anymore. That's why O'Neill was here. We figured Linda Webb would be so overjoyed at the demise of Anna and Ryan's relationship that she would be willing to repay the favor. That was the plan, anyway.

Unlike Li, Webb had direct daily contact with Prisha. Great placement and access, although we all knew she was dodgy. A bigger risk than Li, but one we had to take. We hoped she would repay our favor. But hope is not a plan.

We sat motionless in our vehicle, motor off and windows down a crack. The party ebbed and flowed for another hour. Kids straggled in and out. It was overcast, a dark, moonless night. No one paid us any mind. O'Neill occasionally broke the silence with odd proclamations, apropos of nothing. In this manner I learned of his love for cats and Van Morrison. O'Neill was proving to be quite the enigma. I'd have liked to peel his onion sometime, over scotch and a Guinness or two. But not tonight.

Just shy of midnight I saw Anna and Ryan leave the house. Anna stumbled as she walked. Ryan grabbed her hard by the arm, pulled her towards him. She turned on him and yelled something. Ryan slapped her in the face. I flinched. O'Neill grunted low. Anna tried to pull out of Ryan's grasp.

They tussled on the lawn. Anna screamed loud, slapped at Ryan's face with her free hand. Ryan reared back and threw a straight hard jab. I heard the sickening thud of his fist against Anna's face. She dropped like a stone at his feet.

We both leapt from the car and ran across the street towards them. Ryan's eyes went wide at the sight of us approaching. He broke into a sprint across the lawn and down the sidewalk. After a second of hesitation O'Neill gave chase and I went to Anna, still crumpled in a heap on the ground.

I rolled her over and gasped. Her face was awash in blood, her nose bent to one side at a grotesque angle. She moaned and gurgled. I elevated her shoulders and head to ensure her airway was clear. She opened her eyes and stared. It was the vacant stare of an addict. I had seen it enough times on the streets to know. She started choking, then heaving. She turned her head and vomited all over herself. Into her long, beautiful auburn hair. She then started to fight me, trying to stand up. I helped her to her feet, one hand gripped tight around her arm.

O'Neill approached. "Gimme the keys. The guy got to his car and took off."

I tossed O'Neill the keys and he ran to the Explorer. He jumped in and roared off.

I turned back to Anna.

"What? Who... who the hell are you?" She spat and tried to wriggle out of my grip. "Where's Ryan?" she slurred. Her eyes rolled back in her head and her knees buckled. I caught her before she fell. I had watched many men overdose on the streets, but had never intervened. I had no idea what to do. With difficulty, I fished my burner phone out of my pocket with one hand, leaning Anna against me to keep her upright.

Thankfully, she was a small thing. I had my left arm wrapped under her arms, the back of her head tight against my chest. I dialed Sarah with my right hand.

She picked up on the third ring. I told her my predicament. She said she was about twenty minutes out and on her way. I ended the call and slipped the phone back into my pocket. Several kids had gathered on the lawn, watching. A few asked if Anna was all right, none brave enough to approach. I told them all to go back into the house. Most of them did.

I spun her around and gently slapped Anna on the cheeks to revive her. Her eyes fluttered open. I asked her if she was okay. She nodded like a bobblehead doll. I had to get her out of here. The cops were sure to arrive any moment. I asked Anna if she could walk. Another nod. We left the lawn of the house and headed down the sidewalk, me supporting her with a hand under her arm, she shuffling and dragging her feet. We made it about a quarter mile and ducked into a small wooded area between two houses. I called Sarah back and told her my location. She said she had called the ER nurse, Jill Everett, who was en route with Narcan nasal spray to reverse Anna's opioid overdose.

I set Anna down next to me on a big rock fifteen feet into the woods. I held her tight to my side and kept her talking as best I could. Two cop cars flew past us down the street, lights flashing and sirens blaring. I checked my watch and hoped Sarah and Everett would be here soon.

———

Everett arrived a few minutes after Sarah. She rushed out of her car and over to us on our rock in our wooded hiding place. I thanked Everett for coming; she gave me a tight-lipped smile and began to minister to Anna.

"Anna, sweetie, what did you take tonight?" Everett asked, shaking her. Their faces were six inches apart.

Anna said nothing.

"Was it oxy? How many?"

Anna just nodded.

"Was it oxy, Anna?" Everett asked louder, shaking her again.

Anna nodded again.

Everett dug into her coat pocket and pulled out a nasal applicator. "Anna, I'm going to give you a little spray up your nose, okay?"

Without waiting for a response, Everett inserted the Narcan applicator up one nostril and emptied it. Anna came around quickly.

Everett then placed her thumbs on either side of Anna's nose and jiggled. She howled and swiped at Everett. Everett staunched the blood flow from Anna's broken nose and cleaned her face up as best she could.

"She OD'd on oxy. The Narcan worked, but we gotta get her to the ER," Everett said to me and Sarah. "Her nose is broken—bad. She'll need surgery. Sarah and I talked on the way in. Best if I drive her to the ER. I can get her admitted as a Jane Doe for now. Give you both time to get this under control."

We both thanked Everett again. She loaded Anna into her car and left. I told Sarah to go too. Best if she wasn't here. I didn't know if the cops were still at the house, or if they were doing a neighborhood canvass. I hadn't seen them pass by out of the neighborhood. Sarah squeezed my hand, then got in her car and left as well.

Doyle and I had agreed that we would not get Sarah involved operationally in this thing, and I had just broken this vow. Out of necessity, but nonetheless. I didn't look forward to having to explain tonight to Doyle. He was very protective of Sarah. We both were.

I went back to my rock and called O'Neill. He picked up and said it was done. He asked me how Anna was, and I told him. He was relieved. I told him to pick me up in fifteen minutes at the gas station by the main road at the neighborhood entrance. He agreed and hung up.

I slipped out of the woods and looked both ways. The red and blue strobe lights of the cop cars lit the neighborhood to my left. I turned right and strode down the sidewalk towards my ride.

———

O'Neill was already at the gas station waiting for me, engine running. I jumped in and he hit the gas. He weaved the Explorer into traffic. We found the main road and traveled the speed limit. O'Neill even wore his seat belt. One less reason for the cops to stop us. We both checked our mirrors. Nothing behind us.

"How'd it go with Ryan?" I asked.

O'Neill paused before he answered. "I caught him a half mile away. Dumbass jumped the curb and hit a pole. I dragged him out of his car and threw him in the back seat." O'Neill nodded behind him. "A little wet back there now. Sorry about that."

"Wet?"

O'Neill grinned just enough to curl up the corners of his mouth. "Yeah, had to rough the kid up a bit. Get his attention." He changed lanes. "I think he pissed himself." He took an exaggerated sniff, then shook his head. "Yup."

"Jesus." I could smell it too.

"I explained to Ryan that he couldn't see Anna anymore, and you know what that kid said?"

I shrugged, beginning to fear where this was heading.

"Our boy said that he didn't like the bitch much anyway. His words."

I exhaled. "Good."

"Ryan may not have loved his girl, but he sure loved his stash. I asked him for it, and he actually refused—can you believe that?"

Looking at O'Neill, I couldn't believe that, no. I would have given this man anything he asked for. No question.

"Got all indignant. Said he needed to unload them all. Turns out he deals at his high school. Sells to younger kids too. Got Anna high on oxy tonight. He said it wasn't his fault if these kids were all stupid and weak. So I asked him if he used. He laughed, said he's too strong to be a junkie. Believe that?"

O'Neill turned to face me. His eyes were cold. The toothpick danced in his mouth.

"I told our boy Ryan that I'd be taking that wad of cash in his pocket from tonight's take, and he got all squirmy and said he needed that money for spring break. Said he was going to the Bahamas."

O'Neill changed lanes and checked the rearview mirror.

"I've never been to the fucking Bahamas—you?"

"Nope." I pictured Ryan on a tropical beach, strutting around like he owned the island.

"So I busted the kid up some more and took his stash and

his roll." O'Neill withdrew both from his jacket pocket and tossed them at me.

"He's going to break up with Anna, right?"

"Oh, yeah. Don't worry about that. He'll tell her as soon as he's—feeling better."

I did not like the look of the smile on O'Neill's face. So I asked.

"What do you mean?"

"I was thinking about what we were talking about earlier tonight, Frank. What was it? Tralion justice?"

"Talion. It's talion justice."

"Yeah, that's it. Eye for an eye. Code of the streets. So I'm looking at this sack of fuck Ryan, slinging these pills, getting all these kids addicted to this shit. And I'm thinking, that's no way for these kids to start a life, you know? I mean, in my day we drank, smoked some weed, maybe did a little coke, but this oxy shit will ruin you. And Ryan's attitude about it all. How he was so much better than all these kids he got hooked. So I thought—"

"Finn, what'd you do?"

"Well, like I said, I took his pills." O'Neill chuckled. "And so did he."

"What?"

"I jammed a handful of his oxys down his throat. Don't know how many. Don't care. He was tripping balls when I left him."

"Damn it, Finn! That wasn't part of the plan." I ran my hand through my hair, scratched the back of my neck.

"Eye for an eye, Frank. Just like you said."

"Is he going to be all right?" I asked. "He's not going to OD, is he? We've already had one tonight."

"I don't know," O'Neill said, rubbing his stubbled chin.

"Don't think so." He paused. "I liked the kid better when he was tripping, though," he said with a smirk.

———

And so Ryan Young had his first opiate trip that night at O'Neill's hand. More followed. By the time he graduated high school, he was hopelessly addicted to opioids like millions of other American kids. Ryan got sloppy. Got behind with his supplier and couldn't pay his frontage back. The supplier sent muscle after Ryan to collect his debt. Ryan fled Virginia. No one ever heard from him again. Rumor was he graduated to shooting heroin and was shot and killed in a pissant street-level drug dispute somewhere in Florida before he was old enough to legally buy a beer.

CHAPTER THIRTY

NOVEMBER 7, 2016
KINGSTOWNE LAKE
KINGSTOWNE, VA

I LOOKED AT MY WATCH FOR THE THIRD TIME IN FIVE minutes.

"She'll be here," Sarah said.

Sarah and I sat on a bench at the perimeter of Kingstowne Lake, situated off South Van Dorn Street and Kingstowne Village Parkway just across from Kingstowne Towne Center. The three-quarter-mile path that ran around the lake was popular with local joggers and elderly residents who liked to amble and feed the ducks.

Sarah asked me how I was feeling, which was code for cancer talk. I told her I felt fine, which at the moment was true. She gave me a quick update on her and Jill Everett's efforts to find me a treatment facility. The VA was dragging its feet, as was the public health resource in the District. Sarah told me not to worry, they'd find something.

I wasn't worried either way. We had agreed that I would seek treatment as soon we wrapped our talion project up. Sarah had made me promise I'd start treatment early in the new year. I'd agreed to go as soon as my benefits were restored, with Nicole and Teddy as beneficiaries. Sarah didn't like this but came around to it.

A cancer diagnosis is a funny thing. Like living in a haunted house. Every ache or twinge an ominous noise in the dark. Was that a ghost, or just the house creaking? Just another nosebleed, or the onset of my leukemia? I kept these thoughts to myself.

We were waiting on this bench for Anna's mother, Linda Webb. It'd been two days since the clock fell back to standard time, which meant it got dark an hour earlier. It was 5:15 p.m. now, and dusk was settling in. We figured it was best to meet Webb in shadow.

Anna and Sarah had bonded two nights ago. Sarah and Everett had covered for her at the ER, and her mother Linda had no idea she'd OD'd on oxy. Anna said her mother knew Ryan got her high sometimes, but had no idea how deep her addiction was, and that she would go ballistic if she found out.

Anna told Sarah that her mother was a duplicitous woman. She snooped in Anna's room and interrogated her girlfriends. Anna explained that her mother drank on occasion, and the vodka made her mean and violent. These were the nights Anna packed an overnight bag and slept at a girlfriend's house. Anna said her mother hadn't always been this way, but had only become a bitch after her father left them.

"I don't know, Sarah," I said. "I don't feel good about you being here. Quinn and I wanted to keep you out of this."

"I'm already in it, Frank." Sarah patted my leg. "Besides, I'm the one who talked to Anna most of the night before Linda showed up. And the way Anna described her mother, she would never have agreed to meet with a man she didn't know about something that couldn't be discussed over the phone."

"I don't know. I can be very persuasive sometimes."

Sarah shook her head. "Trust me, this was the only way to get her here."

Sarah had called Webb this morning at work and told her she was the one who had found Anna and taken her to the hospital. The cover story Sarah and Anna had agreed to was that she and Ryan had gotten into a car accident, that Anna had briefly lost consciousness and that she had a broken nose and mild concussion but was otherwise okay. Sarah was the good Samaritan who had happened upon the accident and rushed Anna to the hospital. Webb never asked about Ryan.

Sarah told Webb she had to speak with her tonight about her daughter, that it was important. Webb had got belligerent, demanding Sarah tell her what she had to say over the phone now. Sarah had resisted, and Webb had reluctantly agreed to stop by the lake on her way home. The Webbs' townhouse was less than a mile away.

We sat in silence. I watched the ducks gliding around the lake. Sarah fiddled with her phone.

A squat woman approached us, cigarette hanging from her lips. She walked heavy-footed, stamping her feet against the cement path with the clop-clop of horse trot. Her shoulder-length hair, a mixture of bottle blonde and wiry gray, framed a plump, fleshy face. She wore a pinched expression, like a rat on its hind legs.

"That's gotta be her, right?"

"Yup." Sarah sighed. "It's her."

Sarah had told Webb at which bench they would meet. She'd failed to tell her about me.

Webb stopped in front of us. Took a wide stance. Sarah greeted her politely, thanked her for coming. Webb took a long look at Sarah, then at me, then back to Sarah. She took a long final drag off her cigarette, exhaled a plume of smoke, then flicked the butt in a long, wide arc past my head and to the woods beyond.

Webb pointed a crooked finger at me. "Who's this?"

Sarah introduced me as a friend.

"What he's doing here?" Webb asked with a sneer. "Did he do something to my daughter?"

Sarah laughed and said no, but that I had something important to tell her, and that she ought to listen very carefully to what I was about to say.

Webb squinted at me, then took a step backward.

"Hello, Linda," I said with a smile meant to put her at ease. "My name's Frank."

Webb ignored my smile and addressed Sarah. "You lied to me—you bitch! This isn't about Anna. What the hell do you want?"

I stood. Sarah silently followed my lead.

"C'mon, Linda, let's all take a walk." I gestured towards the walking path.

It was getting darker and a chill had come into the air.

"I'm not going anywhere with you." Webb turned to Sarah. "And fuck you." Webb began to leave.

"What'd you spend the money on, Linda?" I called after her.

Webb spun back around. "What?"

"The money you embezzled from ODYSSEUS. What did you spend it all on?"

The color drained from Webb's face. She blinked rapidly, her squinty eyes widened. Dark eyes swimming in rash pink sclera.

"You want to take that walk with us now, Linda?" I asked, serving her up the same smile she had refused a moment ago.

I took a few steps down the path, then looked over my shoulder, still smiling. I waved at her to join me. Webb stood frozen, then slowly shuffled forward. Sarah flanked her. I waited for them to catch up, and we began our sojourn around the lake three abreast.

I waited her out. Listened to Webb's breathing increase and become labored. She wheezed under the exertion and stress.

Webb finally broke the silence. "Who are you? How do you know who I am?"

"You strike me as a no-nonsense kind of woman, Linda," I said, ignoring her question. "So let me get right to it. I've already done you a great service, and now I simply ask that you return the favor."

"What the hell have you done for me?"

"Has Ryan been in contact with Anna since the night she went to the hospital?"

Webb stopped in her tracks. She started to speak as a jogger approached. Sarah stood aside to give him room to pass.

"How do you..." Webb stared at me, incredulous. She

took a moment to regroup. "No, as a matter of fact, he hasn't. He's not returning any of her calls, either. Ghosting her, she says," Webb responded in a thin voice.

Webb pulled out another cigarette, lit up, took a big draw. She held the smoke in her lungs as long as she could, then exhaled. With that done, we started walking again.

Webb spoke again. "I hate that fucker Ryan! Thinks he's a little gangster or something. Got my Anna on the wrong path."

"Ryan won't be bothering Anna again," I said. "He'll break up with her, and she'll never see him again. I promise you that."

Webb faced me, her mouth agape. I thought her cigarette would fall out. Confusion all over her rat face.

"I know about your animosity towards Ryan, that you wanted him out of Anna's life forever," I continued. "I've done that for you." I looked at Sarah and corrected myself. "We've done that. Our favor to you."

"Anna's a great kid," Sarah interjected. "She's got a good shot to get her life back on track. But she's still a teenager, and this is her first major heartbreak. She needs support right now. Do you understand?"

Webb nodded. She kept on stomping doggedly along the path, her flat sensible shoes slapping the pavement in contrast to Sarah's graceful, gliding steps.

"It's your turn, Linda," I said. "I need you to tell me all you know about Prisha Baari and Project ODYSSEUS."

Webb stopped cold. I motioned for her to keep walking, and she stumbled forward again, more slowly this time. She began to tremble, and took another deep drag on her cigarette before she cleared her throat and began to speak. Her voice wavered, the words coming with difficulty. At first, she wouldn't even admit she worked for the CIA. Then she took a long look at my face.

"Wait a minute," Webb said. She fell silent, squinting. Suddenly, she jabbed a finger at me. "Don't I know you? Didn't you used to—"

"Work at the CIA?" I finished her sentence. "Yeah, I did. I got fired for no good reason. Remember me now, Linda?"

That cut through some of her bullshit. I had not known her in my relatively short stint with the Agency, but she clearly knew me.

"What are you doing?" Webb stammered. "What do you want?"

"Just information, Linda," I said. "I helped you, you help me. Quid pro quo." I leaned into her, taking away her personal space. "If you don't want to help me, Linda, that's okay. But I'll make sure Anna patches things up with Ryan, and that the CIA learns all about your embezzlement."

Webb's eyes darted between me and Sarah. I thought she might try and make a run for it.

"You're a smart woman, Linda," I said. "You know what the right play is here. What do you say?"

Webb looked like she had just seen a ghost. And in a way she had. If Prisha was the one responsible for my demise, as Doug Mitchell claimed, and Webb was one of her lieutenants, which she was, then Webb likely knew something about my firing and defrocking. She had clearly never expected to see me again. Had not thought of me once in the past five years.

I didn't like Linda Webb. I did, however, like Anna, and would never endanger her by bringing Ryan back into her life. But if Webb didn't see fit to return our favor, I sure as hell would make sure her embezzlement came to light. I had no problem doing that.

We continued our walk. Webb clung to her claim that she knew nothing about Prisha Baari or any project called ODYSSEUS. There were many statements and denials, thrusts and parries, during that first lap around the lake. Webb was not a stupid woman, not even close. The more we talked, the more lies I caught her in. I told her things about herself she couldn't refute. The color drained from her face. I kept at her. Sarah joined in. It was like landing a marlin or other big game fish. Give her enough line, be patient, let her tire herself out.

It wasn't until the end of the second lap around the lake that Webb finally showed signs of surrender. We took one more lap before she finally broke. We finished up on a bench, a different one on the opposite side of the lake. Webb couldn't walk anymore. Her face was flushed, and she was sweating despite the chill night air. Webb sat between Sarah and me. We each gave her space, leaning away from her.

We sat on that bench for the next forty minutes. Webb chain-smoked and answered our questions. She admitted her role as project administrator for ODYSSEUS. She said it was some secret government project having something to do with sound waves or something, but feigned ignorance about any further details. Webb had no problem, however, giving us three people who she claimed knew much more than her. She said these three were much closer to Prisha than she was, and that they, not her, were the ones we should be after.

The first name was Khabir Ahmad, the Arab computer whiz who handled all of the project technology. Webb said she thought Ahmad stored ODYSSEUS data offsite somewhere. She said she didn't know where.

Webb told us Prisha had a private security guy called the Viking. She said she didn't know his name or what he looked like, but that he was dangerous. He was an off-the-books guy, not officially affiliated with ODYSSEUS. He never came to the office.

The last name she gave us was Charles Hewitt. Webb was adamant that this was Prisha's number two, her closest associate. He was an older white guy, a big shot at CIA. She said Hewitt's close connection to Prisha was not widely known, that he had been a benefactor to her at some point. Webb said she wouldn't be surprised if Prisha had screwed Hewitt to get her job as deputy. Said Prisha was a sociopath. I thought of Prisha and our shared night on her office couch and winced. It felt worse to relive this memory in Sarah's company.

Webb's mood lightened as she spoke. She had snitched out her colleagues in an attempt to put us off her scent. Minimized what she claimed to know while pointing us elsewhere. Treachery came easily to her, it turned out. A slithering snake.

It was late. Webb had smoked the last of her cigarettes and was getting fidgety, almost manic. We were all exhausted. I looked past Webb to Sarah on the far side of our bench. She nodded. We had gotten everything we could out of Webb tonight. I had hoped to press her on the details of my firing but knew this would go nowhere right now. Webb had given us three good leads—Ahmad, Hewitt, and the Viking—and we would run those to ground. I decided to give Webb a few days before I took another crack at her. Besides, Hewitt felt like a good next step on our talion ladder.

I told Webb to go home, that Sarah or I would be in touch. Sarah told her to take care of Anna, be good to her.

Webb just sighed, rose off the bench, and slumped off towards the parking lot. We both watched her disappear into the darkness. A chill wind blew some fallen leaves over our feet. Sarah wrapped her arms around her chest.

We sat on that bench in the dark for a while, saying nothing. The space between us still smelled of cigarettes and noxious perfume. We held our mutual silence, each of us deep in our own thoughts. Neither one of us made any move to close the space between us. We sat there for what felt like a long time.

CHAPTER THIRTY-ONE

November 10, 2016
Parkview Market
Petworth, NW WDC

"Hey, Frankie, what do you think Emily would say about this?" Doyle asked. "You and me, out here in the streets, working?"

I chuckled at the thought of that.

"How is your mother, anyway?"

"Good," I responded tentatively.

I'd been up to see her several times in the three months since I resurfaced. She still lived in Maryland, less than a mile from the Silver Spring neighborhood we moved to when I was a kid. My second act had stirred a multitude of emotions in my mother. Shock and relief had morphed into a low-grade anger and resentment. I couldn't blame her. She was part of my mea culpa tour, my road to redemption. My disappearing act had wounded her and others I cared about. Including the man seated next to me in this beat-up Chevy. No one's fault but my own. I hoped to earn their forgiveness. One step at a time.

"You tell Emily I was in town?" Doyle asked.

I shook my head no.

"Probably for the best," he said. "She blames me for your father's death... Has carried a grudge ever since." Doyle sighed. "Shame, really."

Doyle had arrived in the city the day after Sarah and I met with Linda Webb. Things were heating up down here, and Doyle said he would be of more use on site. I think he just wanted to be part of the action. After all, he certainly had the pedigree for this kind of work, and we could use his expertise going forward. The closer we got to Prisha, the tougher things were going to get.

Sarah had insisted that Doyle stay in her Dupont Circle townhouse, which she had surreptitiously purchased in preparation for her divorce from her husband, Victor the cop. Doyle thanked her but declined, thinking it best that he book a month at one of those extended-stay hotels just outside the Beltway. He found one near a Metro station and also purchased—with cash—the beater car we now sat in.

Doyle had also upgraded our comms. He'd asked around Boston and got us the latest in cellphone skullduggery. We still used burner phones, but now purchased them randomly in different high-volume retail outlets. We also switched out these new phones and SIM cards weekly, sometimes daily. It proved to be a low-tech but effective way to secure our comms. Doyle also taught us to be more observant and aware of our surroundings. Particularly Sarah.

Doyle and I had squabbled over this. He detested Sarah

being operational in any way. I agreed, but accepted that at times it was unavoidable. Plus, Sarah felt strongly that she should be involved, and she was a woman who usually got what she wanted. Doyle and I came to the understanding that we would use Sarah only when necessary, and as long as we could keep her out of harm's way. I feared that this would be a hard pledge to keep.

Sarah had been hard at work with Robinson, doing background on two of the names Webb had given us: Khabir Ahmad and Charles Albert Hewitt. It had taken him a while, but Robinson had identified Ahmad through the take from Prisha's computer. Ahmad had a distinctive Middle Eastern accent and spoke with Prisha daily. Robinson had scrutinized these recent conversations and made the contextual identification. Some more sleuthing revealed the car Ahmad drove, a leased silver Acura RLX sedan. I slapped a tracker on it the next night at o-dark-thirty.

We had been monitoring all communications between Prisha and Ahmad for a few days now. They spoke of a place they called "the shop." It appeared that they met there frequently after hours. Two days ago at noon, I'd got an urgent call from Sarah saying that Ahmad was now headed over to the shop, alone. I'd jumped in my car and, using the tracker, found Ahmad at a bodega in the Petworth section of the District, northwest of downtown near Rock Creek Park. I got only a fleeting look at him as he hustled into the bodega, named Parkview Market.

Doyle and I sat outside the Parkview Market now. Doyle had asked to come along on Ahmad's next lunchtime visit to the bodega, saying he had just arrived from Boston and wanted to "get his feet wet."

This time I had plenty of notice from Sarah, and Doyle

and I got to the bodega early, which afforded us enough time to have our awkward chat about my mother.

Ahmad arrived and parked down the block as before. I got a few good photos of him this time. He was a dark-skinned Pakistani, tall and thin. He wore khaki pants and a dark button jacket. Ahmad emerged from his car with a cigarette, and lit another right before he entered the bodega. Doyle asked me if that was him. I said it was.

A shiny new Lexus passed us and turned right at the end of the block. I suspect I only noticed it because it was spotless and cost well over six figures, unusual for this part of town.

I saw her minutes later. On foot, emerging from where that Lexus had just turned. My stomach clenched and I fought for breath. I leaned forward, stuck my head over the dashboard up close to the windshield. Tunnel vision. Long raven hair, pulled back into a perfect ponytail. Expensive heels and long cashmere coat. Erect posture and elegant gait. It was her. Prisha Baari.

I hadn't expected her to be here. Sarah had said nothing of it. Only Ahmad had been mentioned. But here she was. Gliding down the sidewalk, head slightly downcast, hands tucked in the side pockets of her coat. Heading straight my way. My mind flashed back to that late night in her office. Me on top of her. Her nails on my back. How one moment of weakness had changed everything. And now this woman was blithely sauntering down the sidewalk. Her world hadn't changed like mine had. A rage, like a dragon, arose in my gut. I wanted to breathe fire, incinerate her and her cashmere coat. My hands trembled on the steering wheel.

Doyle was shaking me by the shoulder. "Frankie! What is it?" He followed my eyes to her. "Who's that? Is it—"

"Yes," I whispered.

"That's her? The woman? Prisha?"

I nodded.

We both watched in silence as Prisha entered the bodega.

I reached for the door handle and opened my door a crack.

"No!" Doyle hissed, grabbing me by the arm. "You're not going in there, Frankie. You rush her now and it'll ruin everything. All that we've done."

I pulled my arm out of his grasp, fire in my eyes.

"Sorry, Frankie. Now's not the time. Get back in the car. I'll go in."

I slammed the car door shut. Doyle exhaled loudly.

"You all right?"

I nodded. My eyes fixed on the front door of the bodega.

"Okay, I'm going in to take a look around. You stay here. Nothing stupid. Promise me, Frank."

I nodded without looking at him. Doyle took me at my word, got out of the car, crossed the street and walked into the bodega.

My mind raced. Still photograph flashbacks. Prisha under me on the sofa. Nicole yelling, me waving her off. My first night on the streets. And my last one, the night I was almost beaten to death. The look on Sarah's face when she saw me at the hospital. And Teddy. Most of all him.

My hands milked the steering wheel with enough force to turn my knuckles white. Nervous energy rocked me back and forth in my seat. I closed my eyes and forced some deep breaths. Then some more.

When I opened my eyes, they were fixed on a second-floor window above the bodega. A young Arab boy was looking directly at me through the gap in the lace curtain. We made eye contact. I slouched down, pulled the lid of my Redskins cap low on my face. I looked up through my eyebrows and the kid was still watching. I pulled out my cell-phone and pretended to make a call. The kid lingered a minute more, then closed the curtains tight and disappeared. There was something about the kid. Like he somehow knew why I was there. It spooked me.

I checked my watch. *Damn, Doyle, let's go.* I checked my side mirror and saw a guy approaching the passenger side of the car. He was a homeless guy, or appeared to be. The kid had made me a little paranoid. The guy stopped at the front passenger window, bent down. His lips were flap-ping, trying to get my attention. I turned the key and lowered the window. He leaned in. He was homeless, all right.

"Any spare change? Help a brother out?"

I had never panhandled, out of stubborn pride, but knew what this felt like. I reached into my pocket, pulled out a five and extended it to him. Then a thought flashed in my head and I pulled the bill back before he had a chance to grab it.

"You in this neighborhood?" I asked.

The man looked confused. He nodded yes.

"I'll tell you what, brother. There's another ten in it for you if you tell me who lives above that market," I said, pointing to the bodega.

The guy looked across the street, stroked his matted beard. "There?" He pointed a filthy finger.

"Yeah, the market."

He leaned back into the window of my car. I leaned against my door. His breath was awful.

"A family of ragheads live there. The ones that run that

market. Fuckers always run me outta there too." He turned his head and spat.

"What about the kid?"

"What kid?"

"The kid at the market?" I asked.

"I dunno. He lives there with 'em. Got big eyes, but don't say shit." The guy snorted. "Okay? Now give me my money, man."

I handed him a five, and then his ten.

"All right, then," he said and walked on, folding and pocketing his cash.

I looked back towards the bodega and saw Doyle crossing the street at a brisk pace. He approached the car with a small smile on his face, opened the door and got in.

"See anything?" I asked.

"Plenty."

"This street is hot. I think the kid above the market might've made me."

"Let's go, then," Doyle said.

I pulled out past the bodega and drove down the street. I checked my rearview as I left. Prisha and Ahmad were still in there, as best I could tell. I held my questions until after we cleared the first traffic light and a few cars had pulled in behind me.

"Well, what did you see?"

"I didn't see Prisha or the Arab at all. There was a Muslim guy at the register. Smiled at me when I walked in. Older guy. Short gray hair and a beard. Neatly dressed. He watched me like a hawk. I walked through, pretending to look for something. The place was cluttered. Shit everywhere. Food, diapers, office supplies, everything. All crammed together."

"Was there anyone else in the market?" I asked.

"No. Just me and the guy behind the register. I asked him if he had any Pepto. He didn't understand, so I explained that I had cramps. Still a blank. He did understand the word *diarrhea*, apparently, because he pointed me to the right aisle."

Doyle pulled the pink Pepto-Bismol bottle out of the small paper bag. Then reached in, retrieved something and tossed it in my lap.

"Got you something."

I looked down. A bag of peanut M&Ms.

"Pepto's for you?"

"Don't mock your elders, young man."

We both needed to laugh.

"The register guy," Doyle said, taking a swig of Pepto straight from the bottle. "His English was good. Not as heavy an accent as the call you played me."

I told Doyle about my conversation with the homeless guy. We both agreed the register guy probably lived upstairs, and that the kid checking me out was his son. Doyle said this was common with the mob. They put an old stay-at-home couple from the neighborhood above their social clubs to keep the feds away, like garlic and vampires.

I pulled into Rock Creek Park and looked for a shaded parking spot. It didn't take long. I parked under a towering oak in the far corner, away from the other vehicles.

"Anything else, Quinn?"

Doyle thought a long moment.

"What?"

"I don't know," Doyle said, scratching his chin. "It might be nothing, but I thought it a little strange." He paused. "Behind the register guy was a passageway, packed with boxes and such. And to the right, against the wall, was a door. A big fortified steel door."

"A walk-in cooler?"

"No, I don't think so," Doyle said. "It had a big combo door lock and a security keypad on the wall just to the right of the door. Just looked strange. Out of place."

"What kind of combo lock?" I asked.

"The kind you punch a numerical combo into. Right above the doorknob."

The thought hit me with a thud. The five-digit numerical code Robinson had found taped to the top of Prisha's desk drawer. I shared this with Doyle. He smiled broadly.

"We've got to see what's behind that door," he said.

"Yes, we do," I agreed.

We toasted our discovery. I popped a fistful of peanut M&Ms into my mouth, and Doyle took another swig of his pink Pepto.

CHAPTER THIRTY-TWO

NOVEMBER 10, 2016
PARKVIEW MARKET
PETWORTH, NW WDC

"So old Mo Udell got his second term, just as we wanted," Prisha said.

The presidential election had been held two days ago, and Udell had won with fifty-six percent of the popular vote. Not the mandate he had hoped for, but it put him in the driver's seat when ODYSSEUS was scheduled to go online in eighteen months. Or so he thought.

Prisha shared the crowded basement space with Khabir Ahmad and Henrik Karlsson. Frank and Doyle had not seen Karlsson enter the market; he had arrived early, as was his custom.

Prisha focused her attention on Ahmad. She again pushed him to accelerate ODYSSEUS, reminded him she needed it to be fully tested and operational well before mid-terms. Prisha planned to run for a senate seat in New York and joked that ODYSSEUS would be her campaign manager.

Ahmad scoffed at democracy and the tyranny of fifty-one percent. He said ODYSSEUS would be ready, and that one day, *Inshallah*, it would be instrumental in establishing the caliphate right here in the heart of the great Satan.

Ahmad's American Caliphate proclamation drew a loud, guttural laugh from Karlsson.

"I don't care about this country," Karlsson said, "nor my own, for that matter. It's all just arbitrary lines drawn on a map as far as I'm concerned. But you're crazy, Khabir, if you think Americans are going to embrace Allah and let you wipe your ass with their Constitution."

Ahmad bristled every time Karlsson spoke the word *Allah*. His face reddened.

"Hey, Khabir, how's your team doing?" Karlsson continued, unconcerned.

"What business is that of yours?"

"Because I know your team of geniuses are growing mutinous. You're pushing them too hard. And they're sick and tired of all your Islamic bullshit."

"And what of you, Henrik?" Ahmad said, raising his voice. "We've had a twenty-five percent rise in tripwires in the past month, a spike in unauthorized access to ODYSSEUS personnel files, and the homeless guy is back in the picture, talking to his old supervisor. What are you doing to address all this?"

Karlsson stepped towards Ahmad, who retreated.

Prisha stepped between the two men, much to Ahmad's relief. She chastised them to keep their voices down.

Prisha tolerated Ahmad's religious extremism because he was an effective team lead and his loyalty was unquestioning, as it was with many religious zealots. She strung him along, placating him and his dream of an American Caliphate. But Prisha had no interest in such things. She would not share power with anyone—including Allah. Karlsson was well aware of Prisha's secularism, of her many illicit behaviors that would result in a death sentence in her Wahhabi faith.

Prisha and Karlsson had already agreed that Ahmad would be disposed of once ODYSSEUS went operational. But for now, she needed him. Ahmad was no tech genius, but he was good enough to wrangle the real geniuses who worked in the shadows. Ahmad kept the project moving forward, and so she dripped enough Islam his way to keep him placated.

Ahmad did have a point about the tripwires, though. There had been too many for her liking. And Frank Luce was back. Prisha was not sure what to make of that yet, but it made her anxious. She would speak to Karlsson about this, have him step up his efforts against Luce.

Silence filled the basement as the argument waned. Suddenly Karlsson looked up at the ceiling towards the head of the basement steps. He placed a thick finger over his lips, then pointed. Prisha and Ahmad followed his gaze.

Prisha heard the doorknob jiggle. Then stop. Then jiggle again. All three of them tiptoed across the basement to a computer monitor. Prisha saw a teenage boy standing outside the basement door, wide-eyed.

Ahmad broke for the staircase. Karlsson grabbed hold of Ahmad's arm and jerked him back with enough force to pull him off his feet. They watched the boy try the knob one more time and then flee.

Prisha turned to face Ahmad. Her narrowed eyes bored into him.

"I told you to handle Yazid," she scolded. "Speak with the boy's father tomorrow. See to it that he fixes this problem —or Henrik will. Understood?"

Ahmad broke eye contact with Prisha. He nodded yes with downcast eyes.

Yazid's family was from Saudi Arabia and had been hand-picked by Prisha's Saudi benefactors to mind the bodega. They were instructed to keep their eyes open and mouths shut, and were to contact Ahmad if they saw or heard anything suspicious. Their family back in Saudi were being heavily monitored. It was unsaid but clearly understood what fate would befall them if anything went wrong at the bodega. Yet despite this very real threat, curiosity had gotten the better of Yazid. Ahmad thought him a good but precocious teenage boy, already too Western for Ahmad's liking. He had already spoken sternly to the boy, but apparently to no effect. And now he had lost face in front of Karlsson.

Ahmad would fix this. Once and for all.

CHAPTER THIRTY-THREE

November 15, 2016
Tysons Corner Marriott
Tysons Corner, VA

THE MAN SLUMPED AT THE EDGE OF THE BED, SHEETS balled up in tumult. He wore a thin hotel robe, hanging open at the sash knotted under his slight paunch. His gray eyes were several shades darker than the sparse hair that haloed his pale, bald pate. Deep red indents sat on either side of his nose from the square eyeglasses on the nightstand behind him.

I sat in a chair pulled up tight to the bed, my knees inches from his. Doyle sat next to me.

"I'm glad it's over," the man said, looking down at his chest. "God help me."

It had been a little over a week since we had learned of Charles Hewitt and Khabir Ahmad from Linda Webb.

Robinson's research supported Webb's claim that both men were close to Prisha and critical to ODYSSEUS. We had chosen Hewitt as our next talion ladder step, believing Ahmad to be too much of a zealot and not worth the risk.

And so it was Charles Hewitt that now slouched in front of Quinn and me, avoiding our eyes and muttering to himself.

The honey trap had been Doyle's idea. A time-tested espionage tactic that was highly successful with the right target. A target like Hewitt. Doyle had started working on this scheme several months ago, well before either one of us had heard the name Charles Hewitt. Sex never fails. Doyle had used his criminal contacts with the Russian mob in Boston to find a beautiful Russian woman with just enough dirt in her background to blackmail any unsuspecting male with a government security clearance.

The blonde and blue Russian had first bumped Hewitt two days ago at the local sports bar where he liked to watch his beloved Redskins. They'd beat the Vikings 26–20, which put him in a rare good mood. The Russian was a pro, Hewitt lonely and vulnerable, and she'd quickly closed the deal.

The Russian had finished Hewitt less than thirty minutes ago. The pungent smell of sex still filled the room. Doyle and I had rented a room identical to Hewitt's down the hall. We had a camera and microphone installed in a lamp from our room, then swapped it with an identical lamp in Hewitt's room while the Russian distracted Hewitt down in the lobby bar. So Doyle and I got to watch and listen to Hewitt's performance. The perfect placement of the lamp ensured we didn't miss a thing. I felt dirty watching this man's life circle the drain. Hewitt was different from the other two, Li and Webb. He had no problems we could solve, no favors to barter. So Hewitt would get all stick and no carrot. It was the most expedient way to bring him to heel, the only viable option we could play. But that truth didn't make me feel any better about this.

The beautiful Russian had just left our hotel room moments ago. She'd given us her version of what happened in the room, as well as the spare key card she'd swiped from the nightstand while Hewitt was in the bathroom. It was how we'd entered Hewitt's room so casually.

Hewitt was in the bathroom when we entered. He must have thought we were the Russian, but his smile quickly faded when he realized his mistake. He was a squat man, unremarkable in a crowd. A tangle of coarse white chest hair sprang forth from the opening in his cheap terrycloth robe. He had the bloated face and thick unruly eyebrows of a man who had already surrendered to time. In sharp contrast to Doyle, Hewitt looked every bit his age.

We sat Hewitt down on the bed. He didn't act surprised or overly concerned. He was robotic and appeared resigned to his fate. He followed our instructions without protest. Both Doyle and I had pistols tucked into our waistbands. Neither one of us brandished them. Hewitt gave us no reason to.

I started our negotiation. "Charles, let me tell you what's going on here—"

"I know what this is," Hewitt said, shaking his head. "Vasya. Such a beautiful name." He sighed. "How could I be so stupid?"

"Let us walk you through this, Charles," Doyle said.

"Who sent you? The Russians?" Hewitt straightened himself at the side of the bed, planting his feet on the floor.

"I'll not betray my country to the Russians, or any other foreign government."

I told him no, we were not with the Russians, that we were true Americans, just like him. I told him we needed his help.

"What do you want?" Hewitt asked, looking between me and Doyle. I started to answer, and he cut me off. "You know what? I don't care. I'm not interested in helping anyone. Do whatever you're going to do." He mumbled "I don't care" several more times, slowly, enunciating every word.

I told Hewitt his country needed him. That America now faced a great threat. This got his attention. He stopped muttering and locked eyes with me.

"ODYSSEUS," I said.

Hewitt shot to his feet, his face a mask of confusion and fear. He loomed over me. Doyle, also now standing, eased Hewitt back onto the bed.

"What do you know about ODYSSEUS?" Hewitt asked, both hands gripping the side of the bed.

"We know you've been a part of it from the start. You and Prisha Baari," I said.

Hewitt recoiled at my mention of Prisha, then gathered himself. "That woman ruined my life."

"You and I have that in common, Charles," I responded.

Hewitt cocked his head to one side and studied me. I saw the recognition cross his face.

"Wait," Hewitt exclaimed. "You're that homeless guy. The Medal of Honor guy that used to work on ODYSSEUS."

"I never worked on ODYSSEUS," I said.

Hewitt guffawed. "Yes, you did. You just never knew it. We had many intel analysts across the CIA and the USIC

working on various parts of ODYSSEUS. Your supervisor—
Mitchell, right? He knew all along what he was doing."

I thought of Mitchell and me in the parking lot at Walter
Reed. *Bastard.* I bit down hard.

"I know about you and Prisha having sex in her office.
She told me all about it. In detail," Hewitt said with an
empty chuckle. "Yet another thing we both have in
common."

I felt my face get hot. "It was one night. A big mistake."

"Prisha and I shared many nights, I'm afraid," Hewitt
said. "At first—many years ago. That all stopped once she
hooked me, of course. She played the long game with me."

"Not me," I said. "I was fired within a month of my one
night with that black widow."

"Yes, I remember now," Hewitt continued, nodding his
head. "About five years ago, wasn't it? Yeah, I remember she
was pissed that you blew her off. No one *ignores* that
woman. She took great satisfaction in scorching you. Had
you fired. Took your TS security clearance... called around
the USIC, made you unemployable. Salted the earth."

I thought of her now. Saw her face. My nostrils flared.

"She bragged about it to me. How she took down an
American hero. Medal of Honor winner. She's destroyed
many, but you and I were her highest achievements. Her
magnum opus, as it were."

There it was. It was Prisha. Mitchell hadn't lied about
that. Now all I needed was proof. Proof that I had been
improperly fired. Proof to get my benefits restored. Proof that
would put a proper roof over Teddy's head. Proof to show
my son I was an honorable man, not a traitor. Proof that
Hewitt could provide, should he choose to do so.

I fell silent, my mind racing. I now knew the truth. I

believed this man. One night. One mistake. The wrong woman. Prisha had knocked me to the canvas, and for the first time in my life I had taken the count. Chosen not to rise and keep fighting. My entire life had pivoted on that one night.

Doyle jumped in.

"He had his night," Doyle said, nodding at me, "but you —you stayed in that woman's bed."

"What do you want of me?" Hewitt asked Doyle.

"We want to help you, Charles," Doyle responded. "Tell us how it happened."

Our courtship lasted several hours. Hewitt went from silent, to sullen, to suicidal, then back to silent again. He whimpered and wept and wailed. He swung from self-right-eousness to self-loathing, and everything in between. He cursed us, then Prisha, his life, and finally himself. We hung on for the ride, patiently closing doors and opening others as we led him down the path to his redemption. It was impor-tant he came to it himself, not pushed into it by Doyle or me. We watched as Hewitt danced around it, flirted with the idea. *Why not do it? Fuck Prisha, she had this coming. Do the right thing, Charles. It's time to do the right thing.*

It was well past midnight now. Doyle once again probed Hewitt, asked him to tell us how it had all happened. This time he was ready. Hewitt hung his head, then told us his story from the beginning.

Hewitt had been a major political force in his day, heavily networked on Capitol Hill and at the White House. He was a Senior Executive Service political appointment. Prisha was an ambitious, vivacious middle manager when Hewitt landed at CIA. She instantly saw his value and targeted Hewitt as her tool for advancement. This was the early years, when the sex started. Hewitt was smitten with Prisha and had secretly advanced her career from the shadows. She pestered Hewitt for an assignment to ODYSSEUS, and he made it happen. She rapidly became *the* rising star at CIA.

Prisha's seduction ended as her and Hewitt's power reached equilibrium. That's when the sex ended and the blackmail began.

Hewitt was married at the time he first got involved with Prisha. A marriage he stayed in for the sake of his two young daughters, whom he loved above all else. By the time they had grown to an age where they might perhaps have accepted his infidelity, it was too late. Prisha had set her hooks in deep and he was fully compromised. By that time, he had done enough damage for her to put him in prison. Hewitt's wife had passed away three years ago. He said she was a good woman who deserved better. Hewitt, formerly a gregarious man, grew despondent. And lonely.

Hewitt then gave us the basics of ODYSSEUS. How mind control could be established by attaching hidden suggestive messages to sound waves, and delivering these sound waves, as benign streaming music and such, through various consumer goods like iPhones and the smart speakers that had begun to hit the market.

Doyle and I both gasped at this revelation. We had heard only the codename ODYSSEUS, never what the project entailed. *Mass mind control.* So this was what Prisha was plotting. Hiding. Protecting at all costs. This explained the fear on Doug Mitchell's face when I'd pressed him for answers.

Doyle and I asked lots of questions. Hewitt had answers. We challenged him, pushed him hard, but he stuck to his story. This was ODYSSEUS. He swore it was true. Said the technology was not quite there yet, but it would be soon. When, he knew not.

Hewitt told us that soon after Prisha had taken control of ODYSSEUS, she'd created a secret cell—a project within the project—that worked offsite to explore asymmetrical uses for ODYSSEUS technology. Prisha kept this sub-project close hold. She hand-picked all cell members and purchased their loyalty. Prisha kept two sets of books: one she shared with the CIA director and the president, and a true set only certain members of her cell were privy to. Hewitt confirmed Khabir Ahmad as her trusted tech advisor, and put a name to the Viking: Henrik Karlsson, her Swedish head of security. It was clear that Hewitt feared Karlsson and gave up his name only after some prodding by Doyle.

I went into the bathroom and poured Hewitt a glass of water. I noted the spent condom lying in the trash beside the sink. In the moment I felt bad for Hewitt, worse about myself. Wanted to jump in the shower and scrub all this off me. I walked back out to the bed and handed the glass to Hewitt.

"Anything else, Charles?" Doyle said, leaning in.

The two men seemed to have developed a rapport. Same generation. Very different men. One a politician, one a criminal. Which was which depended on one's perspective.

Hewitt put his face in his hands, rubbed his eyes, then ran his palms over his bald head. He thought long before he spoke.

"Prisha's going to use ODYSSEUS messages to brainwash the electorate into putting her in the White House in 2020. She plans to succeed Mo Udell as POTUS 46."

That sucked the air out of the room. Silence. The drip of the bathroom sink resounded like the toll of a church bell.

"The presidency is just the start with that woman," Hewitt said. "Her appetite for power and dominance is unquenchable. She'll stop at nothing to get what she wants."

Both Doyle and I began to pace the room. Hewitt rose to his feet and re-cinched his robe closed. Doyle had one arm wrapped around his torso, the other hand rubbing his chin. I leaned against the wall by the window, watching them.

Doyle leveled Hewitt with a stare that lingered. "You sure about this?" he asked. "I mean, really sure?"

Hewitt nodded.

"And you're on the inside now?"

Hewitt scoffed. "Prisha doesn't trust me anymore. She still uses me when she needs me to run interference for her, keep people out of her business. I still know a lot of people."

"Then how do you know what she's up to with ODYSSEUS?" I asked from across the room.

"I got a woman who's close to Prisha now, at least close enough to tell me what I need to know to keep me—alive."

"Who?" Doyle asked.

Hewitt shook him off. He had gone as far as he would go.

It was time for the pitch. Through Robinson we had learned that Hewitt's world had begun to crumble completely last year, after his beloved nineteen-year-old daughter had taken her own life, distraught over a breakup with her boyfriend.

Doyle pulled the lever: "Charles. Tell us about your daughter Allyson."

Hewitt began to sob. Softly at first, then harder. It was difficult to watch. I looked to Doyle for reprieve. He held up a hand and watched Hewitt closely. Hewitt started to speak, then choked up again. We waited him out.

Hewitt finally regained control of himself and faced us squarely. He spoke softly now, barely above a whisper. About how Allyson's death had hollowed him out to the point that nothing really mattered anymore. He told us he had begun drinking again, breaking thirty years of sobriety. He'd started seeing escorts, first discreetly and tentatively, lately much less so. There was other high-risk behavior as well. He said most of him just didn't care anymore. He confessed to having suicidal thoughts. Hewitt said he was actually glad that he'd got caught, relieved it was now all over.

I jumped in and told Hewitt what we needed from him, to work with us against Prisha. To stop her before she ruined the country. Hewitt equivocated. Told me he was not up to the job, that he was a tired old man at the end of his rope. I tried to buck him up but got nothing.

Doyle tried a different approach. He closed on Hewitt slowly. Placed a hand on his shoulder.

"Allyson," Doyle said. "Make her proud. Do it for her, Charles."

That did it. Hewitt's face hardened to grit. He asked us what we needed him to do.

By now it was closing in on two a.m. Hewitt said he had an ODYSSEUS staff meeting with Prisha that morning, but that he would call in sick. We told him no. Instructed him to go home, grab few hours' sleep, and go to work like nothing had happened.

I gave Hewitt his first official tasking: find out when Prisha intended to go live with ODYSSEUS. Hewitt accepted my direction without rebuttal.

Hewitt got dressed and prepared to leave the hotel room. Doyle and I stood aside, by the door, careful not to touch anything.

We said our goodbyes. Hewitt was again on the edge of emotion. I took a step back and patted him on the shoulder. Told him not to worry, everything would work out. Doyle swooped in and, without words, wrapped Hewitt in a big bear hug. He patted Hewitt's back gently, whispered something in his ear. Hewitt nodded and broke their embrace dry-eyed and resolved. He turned and left the room.

Doyle and I watched him walk down the hall.

Allyson would've been proud of the old man.

CHAPTER THIRTY-FOUR

"Isn't that right, Charles?"

Hewitt sat across from Prisha, in his usual spot. His elbows were on the conference table, head in hands, downcast eyes fixed on the six inches of mahogany directly in front of him.

"Charles?" Prisha asked again, her voice rising.

A colleague next to Charles nudged him. He stirred, pulled his head up. His eyes darted around the room as if he had just awoken from a bad dream. His gaze settled on Prisha.

"Pardon?" Hewitt asked in a wavering voice.

"I asked if you were still scheduled to meet with the

Speaker next week on the Hill. We need his support on the budget enhancement for ODYSSEUS."

Hewitt saw a drop splash to the table, then realized his forehead was covered in sweat. He brushed his brow with the back of his shirt sleeve.

"Oh... yeah. Sure," Hewitt stammered. He kept nodding his head. "Yeah."

"Everything all right, Charles?" Prisha asked, now concerned. "You look peaked."

"Yeah. No. I mean, yeah. I'm fine. I'm just not feeling quite right."

Prisha squinted at Hewitt. She felt a stone in the pit of her stomach. Prisha had feared this day might come. Hewitt had been acting strangely this past year, something she had chalked up to the death of his daughter. But he hadn't bounced back, and his odd behavior had continued. Prisha thought of the all the security issues that had plagued ODYSSEUS over the past month. And now Hewitt, who knew enough to sink both her and her ambitions, sat catatonic across from her. Something dramatic had clearly happened to Hewitt in the past twenty-four hours. No, Prisha didn't like this at all.

She rushed through the rest of the meeting. Wrapped it up and dismissed everyone.

Hewitt haphazardly gathered his things and bolted for the door. A colleague blocked his escape by engaging him in small talk, just long enough for Prisha to catch up to them.

Prisha and Hewitt now stood alone outside the conference room door.

"You sure you're okay, Charles? You look like you've seen a ghost."

Hewitt squirmed. Prisha stepped closer. He stepped

back into the wall behind him and hit it with a thud. Prisha smiled at this.

"I'm not feeling well," Hewitt croaked. "I think I'll go home early today."

"Anything wrong, Charles? Anything you'd like to tell me?"

Hewitt's face turned crimson. He was hiding something. Prisha pressed him some more, but Hewitt held out, stammering again that he wasn't feeling well. Prisha had seen enough. She held up a hand, stopping him in mid-sentence.

"Would you excuse me just for a moment, Charles? This will only take a minute."

Prisha pulled her encrypted satellite phone from her bag. Not her CIA-issued phone for official business, but the other one. Hewitt went silent.

"Oh no, please keep talking, Charles," Prisha said as she pecked out a quick text message. "I'm listening." She gave Hewitt the big open smile that she knew he liked so much.

Prisha: *something's wrong. hewitt's got a secret. find out what it is. he's going home early today. pay him a visit. do what you have 2 do.*

Prisha hit send and looked up. She told Hewitt to go home, that she hoped he felt better. Hewitt was all twitchy, like a cornered animal. Prisha let the moment linger until Hewitt spun off the wall and excused himself.

Prisha looked down at her phone.

Karlsson: *k*

CHAPTER THIRTY-FIVE

NOVEMBER 16, 2016
HEWITT RESIDENCE
McLEAN, VA

I LIKED THE FEEL OF THIS MERCEDES; IT WAS SO MUCH
better than that beater Chevy we took to surveil the bodega.
Fine German engineering. Doyle said that we needed an
upgrade now that we were working Hewitt, as the bodega
Chevy would raise suspicions in this neighborhood. We were
to meet with Hewitt after work at his home in McLean,
Virginia, to pick up where we'd left off last night. Posh
McLean, home to congressional bigwigs and diplomats, and
now the hollowed husk of a hero who would save the country
from the villainy of Prisha Baari.

I glided the Mercedes off the 495 Beltway Loop and
onto Route 123 heading east. McLean was beautiful. I
thought of what might have been, had I played my cards

differently. Accepted my Medal of Honor with a smile. Cultivated the network of powerful people that came with that medal. Looked the other way and keep my mouth shut. Maybe I could be living here now, next to some ambassador or big-money lobbyist. Teddy would have loved it here, making little powerful and privileged friends. Friends that would be his own network of gatekeepers when he graduated from the Ivy League. All that could have been, and wasn't. All because I couldn't keep my mouth shut and look the other way. I wondered what Teddy would do when his moment came.

"Hey, Frankie," Doyle said, snapping his fingers. "Frankie."

"Yeah?"

"How are you doing these days?"

"Huh?"

"How are you feeling?"

Doyle looked me up and down. Oh, the cancer. He didn't like to say the word. Truth was, my bones ached and the night sweats had started, but I would keep this all to myself. I had extracted a promise from both Doyle and Sarah that we would see our talion project through to completion, and then I would seek treatment. I figured that would be a couple more months max, beginning of the new year. I would postpone my fight against cancer until my forty-first year.

I told Doyle I was fine and spun the question back on him. He responded in kind. Two stoic Boston Yanks. He did say he missed flying his kites in Scituate, and something about the Capitol being a swamp. I agreed. We talked about Sarah, our mutual concern for her well-being. We both despised her philandering husband Victor, but felt she'd be safest under the roof of this cop bastard a little longer. Sarah would leave him come the new year. It was setting up to be a big year for all of us.

I pulled into Hewitt's neighborhood and onto his street. One magnificent home after another—multi-story brick colonials, on manicured one-acre lots dotted with old oaks and beech. Glistening foreign cars filled the motor courts and circular driveways of sprawling manors tucked behind ten-foot iron gates, fenced in to keep the world out. The world these people shaped every day.

We had to be careful in a neighborhood such as this, even in the Mercedes. Neighbors had sharp eyes and quick 9-1-1 fingers. And unlike my neighborhood, the response time for cops here was lightning fast. Shit, here they'd pull a cat out of a tree faster than I could get a dead body removed from the front of my apartment building. I thought of Angie. She would like McLean as well.

I parked at the curb on the opposite side of the street from Hewitt's brick manor, about three houses down. We'd got here over an hour early to look for any activity or visitors at the house leading up to our visit. Activity that would indicate that Hewitt had sold us out. Doyle and I didn't think he would, but caution was required. Doyle would watch the neighborhood, I the house. We would move the Mercedes up and down the street as needed, depending on how hot we got. I figured two strange men sitting in an unknown car on this street (albeit a gleaming Mercedes) had only an hour before the cops showed up, no matter what we did.

I was pulling away from the curb, preparing to loop around the block to find another fixed surveillance spot, when Doyle looked down at his phone. His face darkened.

"What is it?" I asked.

Doyle stayed silent while he read.

"Hewitt says something came up at work and that he won't be able to meet with us tonight."

I made a face at Doyle. I could see he was thinking the same thing.

"Something's not right," Doyle said. "There were typos in his text. Does Hewitt strike you as someone who sends text messages filled with typos?"

No, he didn't.

Doyle sent Hewitt a return text, seeking clarification. I parked the Mercedes in a different spot, in front of another neighbor's house but still within view of Hewitt's place. We waited for a response. Time slowed. I looked at my watch, Doyle at his phone. This spot was worse than the last. An old guy in crisp trousers and shirt gave us a long look as he walked past. I smiled at him (more suspicious to look away), but knew we were now on the clock. I watched him toddle down the sidewalk past a few homes then turn around to look back at us for another long moment.

"We're heating up this street," I said.

Doyle had his head tilted back against the seat's headrest, thinking. "Maybe Hewitt's gonna run on us."

"Yeah, maybe."

"We should stay on the house a little longer. See what happens."

I nodded. "We don't have much time left on this street. Fifteen, twenty minutes tops."

I knew the old man would double back to our spot and call the cops if we were still here. I rolled around the block and carefully selected our last stand. I checked the street in the mirrors. No one was out. And I had a clear view of Hewitt's house. Good.

Doyle watched the neighborhood, I the house. Street vehicular traffic picked up; people coming home from work, I guessed. Cars slowed as they passed, their drivers turning to look our way. Hard to stave off paranoia when you're in the fishbowl.

We passed the minutes guessing what might be wrong with Hewitt. Doyle was concerned, said his street smarts were shouting that something bad had happened. Or was about to. I tried to take the other side and played devil's advocate. I said Hewitt was probably fine, just overwhelmed or, at worst, waffling a bit. We would buck him up and get him back into the fight. My words rang hollow, even to me. Doyle was shaking his head, picking at his fingers and glancing at the side and rearview mirrors. I spoke without taking my eyes off Hewitt's house.

All we needed was for Hewitt to get us some incontrovertible evidence, enough to blackmail Prisha, and we were home free. She would choose herself over all else and accept my reinstatement as a business cost. I would address any fallout from this after my benefits were restored and sitting in a retirement account, with Nicole and Teddy as primary beneficiaries. We had reached the final talion ladder step. We were so close.

But hope can blind as easily as it illuminates.

A man emerged from the back of Hewitt's house, walking quickly and with purpose. He headed in our direction, striding down the driveway with the grace of an athlete, past Hewitt's BMW and through the front iron gate, which he slammed shut but didn't take the time to latch. He was a large man, young and broad shouldered. The black ball cap pulled down low over his face failed to fully conceal his light blond hair and alabaster skin.

The man checked up and down the street, careful not to lift his chin and reveal his features. He then looked across the street, right at our Mercedes. I pushed hard against the back of my seat to avoid his scrutiny. He stood at the gate for a long beat, raising his head just enough for me to catch a glimpse of what was hiding below that cap. I knew in an instant who this man was. A tremor ran through me. I watched him fast-walk to a waiting SUV parked a few houses down.

"It's the Viking!" I said, low and urgent. "Quinn—the Viking!" I repeated, pointing.

Doyle had been watching our rearview mirror for nosy neighbors and apparently hadn't seen him.

"What?"

"It's the fucking Viking! Getting into that SUV!" I said, still pointing.

The Viking was already in the SUV by the time Doyle was on target. We watched him pull away.

"Viking?" Doyle asked. "You mean Karlsson? The security guy?"

"Yeah."

"You sure?"

I paused. "Yeah. I'm sure."

We both looked at Hewitt's house. Silent. No activity.

"Shit!" Doyle exclaimed.

"We gotta go in," I said.

Doyle nodded, and in an instant, we were both out of the car and rushing across the street. I reached the iron front gate first, Doyle two steps behind. The gate was still rocking from Karlsson's touch. I opened it and raced up the length of the driveway, keeping my eyes fixed on the front windows and door. Expecting to see muzzle flash. We reached the back of the house and posted up by the rear door, backs flat against the brick wall. A small pane of glass by the knob had been shattered. I tried the knob and the door swung open. I drew the 9mm pistol from my waistband. Doyle did the same, then stacked behind me. I had cleared my share of houses in Afghanistan, looking for high-value targets hiding in urban areas. I knew the risk. Two men could not safely clear a house of this size. Not even close. But we had to get in there and find Hewitt.

We stepped into the kitchen, trying not to crunch the broken glass. The house was quiet. Too quiet, eerie. Doyle was tight at my back. I saw he had his gun up by his ear. I reached behind me with one arm and lowered his weapon to belt height, muzzle depressed. I knew Doyle was well acquainted with guns, but I'd seen plenty of accidental discharges in Afghanistan. Better I take an errant round in the ass than in my head.

We moved through the first floor, creeping around corners and moving as silently as possible. I used hand signals that Doyle could understand. We did only cursory checks, putting partially cleared rooms at our back. A necessity that sent chills down my spine. All we could do was move fast and quiet, and take whatever we found.

I heard muffled noise as we approached the staircase to the second floor. It sounded like moaning and heavy breathing. *Not good.* I pointed up the stairs and Doyle nodded. We pressed our backs against the wall and raised our weapons up the staircase. We started up. The wooden steps creaked under our feet, no matter how slowly we went. Whoever was up here now knew they had company. I slid my finger from the side frame of my SIG Sauer and placed it on the trigger. A breach of tactics, but I did it anyway. I quickened our pace and we got to the second-floor landing alive. I pressed my back against the wall and took a few deep breaths. I raised a single finger to my lips. Doyle nodded.

I heard it again, louder now. The sound was definitely human. Gasping, labored breathing. Choking. Coming from the last room down the long hallway in front of us. I feared it was Hewitt. He sounded bad. I also figured anyone else who might be with him already knew we were here.

I did a quick peek down the hall, then pulled back behind the wall. Nothing. One more. Same thing. I took a deep breath, hung my head out in the hall and called out.

"Charles? Is that you?"

No response. No gunfire.

"Charles! It's us. Frank and Quinn. You all right?"

He tried to speak but choked. Silence followed.

I whispered instructions to Quinn, and we began to creep down the open hall, guns raised. No cover or concealment. Naked. Anyone could pop out from behind any of the closed doors we were passing up and shoot us in the back. Dead. Nothing we could do about that now. Tunnel vision. All I saw was the open door at the end of the hall. The hall seemed to lengthen as we walked, the open door growing more distant, like something you would see in a carnival house of mirrors. Our footfalls creaked over the hardwood floor. The moaning and choking intensified.

We walked back-to-back down the hallway, pressed against each other. What went unsaid was that we had always had each other's backs, Doyle and I, and that we would both live or die together in this hallway. This gave me strength. Kept me moving towards that open door.

I posted up outside the door and did a quick peek inside. My stomach dropped. Hewitt was on the floor in a pool of blood at the foot of large four-poster bed. Lying on his back, his head turned away from me. The room looked empty.

"Charles!" I shouted.

I felt Doyle spin around and look over my shoulder. He cursed, and I told him to stay at the door and watch the hallway. I stuck my SIG into my waistband and rushed to Hewitt's side. I knelt over him. His face was beaten raw and swollen. Blood oozed from his nostrils and mouth. It trickled from both ears and down the sides of his neck. I turned his head towards me, elevating his shoulders off the floor. I shook him until his eyes fluttered open halfway. It took Hewitt a long moment to register who I was. He grabbed hold of my arm, tight. Tried to speak, but choked. He spat up a gurgle of blood, which dribbled down his chin. I raised him higher. He was surprisingly heavy.

"I'm sorry, Frank," Hewitt rasped. "I'm an old man." He paused for a coughing fit. "Not as strong as I used to be."

"Who did this to you? The Viking—Karlsson?"

Hewitt nodded. Spat something out of his mouth. "He knows everything now..."

"Does he know about us?"

Hewitt's eyes closed.

I shook him awake. "Charles! Does Karlsson know about us?"

Hewitt nodded. His eyes welled up. A tear rolled down his face, mingled with the blood.

"I'm so sorry, Frank," he whispered.

Quinn called into the room. "Frank! How is he?"

Hewitt turned his head towards the door. "That you, Quinn?" He flicked his eyes towards Doyle.

Doyle alternated frantic looks into the room and down

the hall. He chose the room and ran to Hewitt's side. Hewitt grabbed hold of Doyle's hand. Doyle leaned over him, close.

"They got me, Quinn. I didn't want to talk..." He coughed more blood. Tears flowed freely from his tired old eyes now.

"I know you didn't, Charles. I know you did your best."

Hewitt blinked back his tears, struggling to raise himself off the floor. He groaned.

"She'll come for you now, both of you," Hewitt said, his voice suddenly strong. "Run," he mumbled, then caught his breath. "RUN!" He collapsed back into my arms.

"Don't talk," Doyle said. "We need to get you to a hospital."

Hewitt shook his head. His eyes fluttered wide open. "Tell my girls I thought of them in the end." A smile crossed his face, then faded. "Now go." He released Doyle's hand. "It may already be too late..."

Hewitt closed his eyes. His head rolled to one side and he went slack in my arms. I knew he was dead. Doyle knew it too. He reached over and gently closed Hewitt's eyes with a swipe of his hand. I placed him back down on the floor.

We both knelt in silence around Hewitt's body. I felt the rage rising within me. The guilt would come later, and would stay with me until my own death. Only one way this thing was going to end now. I was all in. Pot committed. This was no longer just about me putting things right for my family. It was about Quinn and Sarah. Robinson and Chang Li. And now Hewitt. Charles Albert Hewitt.

Doyle finally looked up, cleared his throat and said we had to get out of there, that the cops would be here soon. We both stood, paid our last respects to Hewitt, then hastened out of the room. I failed to notice the faint footprints I left in

Hewitt's blood on the hardwood floor, or the microscopic hair and fibers I deposited all over this crime scene as I knelt over the now deceased Charles Hewitt. Or even the partial fingerprint I had left on the front iron gate.

It was not much, but would be more than enough for Prisha Baari to work with.

CHAPTER THIRTY-SIX

NOVEMBER 22, 2016
PRISHA'S CIA OFFICE
LANGLEY, VA

PRISHA WAS FAST-TALKING THE JOB CANDIDATE SITTING across the desk from her in her office. Hewitt had been dead for six days and she needed a new deputy for ODYSSEUS. The woman candidate was a senior staffer to the chair of the House Intelligence Committee. Before that, she had done a stint at the White House. She was a slick thirty-something careerist and reminded Prisha of herself at her age. Prim and polished, with sharp fangs. The candidate smiled when she was supposed to, displayed the proper balance between deference and cockiness. Prisha thought she would make a fine dance partner.

Prisha charmed the woman right out of her Jimmy Choos. Telling her what she wanted to hear, giving her just enough of what she needed. Told her that as deputy, she would be her second-in-command on Project ODYSSEUS, the most important clandestine project in the entire U.S. government. Told her the work was groundbreaking, how it was America's best defense against both internal and external threats around the globe. Prisha spoke of career advancement and five-figure cash bonuses. Hinted that the candidate herself could one day succeed her at the helm.

Prisha thought the woman bought most of it, at least enough of it to seriously consider the job. If she demurred, Prisha would take another run at her. Try out some other fables. She wasn't concerned. She figured she'd have Hewitt's replacement in place right after Thanksgiving break.

Prisha had left Hewitt's fate to Karlsson, and she was not displeased with his results. They now knew with certainty they had a Frank Luce problem, but Prisha was not overly concerned about him. Who would believe the rantings of a homeless man? A thoroughly discredited one at that. Besides, Luce would meet Hewitt's fate soon enough, and no one would miss him or bat an eye. This guy Quinn Doyle, however, posed a different problem, given his mobster past. But it was too early to tell. Luce appeared to be the head of the snake. She would cut this head off quickly and sweep up the pieces later.

Karlsson had covered his tracks well. The cops saw Hewitt as the victim of a home burglary gone bad. Hewitt had surprised the thieves by returning home early, and they'd shot him dead. The beating was harder to explain, but Prisha and Karlsson had seen to it that the cops chose not to dwell on that anomaly. Hewitt was a prominent government official, a quasi-famous man in USIC circles. The media loved the story, a story made for click bait. *Rich white guy killed in mansion in rich neighborhood. If it could happen to him, here, it could happen to any of us.* Fear. Fear was the commodity, and the media sold it hard. The Hewitt story lasted a news cycle or two, then faded. The media moved off the carcass, found other things for people to be scared of.

Prisha saw Charles Hewitt's face as she finished up her spiel. She smiled, which the eager candidate misinterpreted as the end of her interview. Both women rose. Prisha came around her desk and shook the woman's hand, grasping her elbow with her left hand. She said she would be in touch soon, and directed her across her office to the door, telling the candidate that her driver would take her back to Capitol Hill.

Prisha opened her door and grimaced at the sight of her program administrator, Linda Webb, sitting in her waiting area. Prisha had a distaste for Webb, with her slovenly appearance and rat face. But she was good at her job, which was to say she was treacherous and cruel. Attributes Prisha prized in a dutiful subordinate. Prisha intentionally kept Webb in fear, just off-balance enough to keep her in line.

Prisha locked eyes with Webb, who returned a twitchy, tight-lipped smile. Webb looked more disheveled than usual, which was saying something. She had a sallow, cadaver-gray complexion, puffy bags under her eyes. Prisha could smell the cigarettes on her wrinkled clothes from across the room.

Prisha asked her secretary to escort the woman candidate to her ride, and he jumped to her command. Prisha watched the woman go, letting Webb stew. She turned to face her when she was ready.

"Do we have a meeting, Linda?" Prisha asked, keeping her distance.

Webb stood, brushed at her tan below-the-knee skirt that was hopelessly creased. "Um, no, ma'am. But I... I have something I need to talk to you about."

What? Pissant admins don't just waltz in and demand time with deputy directors. Prisha's face held, but she resolved to make Webb's life miserable this week, ruin her Thanksgiving.

"I'm quite busy today, Linda. When my secretary gets back, you may schedule a time with him and get on my—"

"Ahem... ma'am?" Webb interrupted. Prisha saw Webb's hands were trembling as she clutched her bag. "It's really important that I speak with you. It won't be long. Please."

Prisha smiled, intrigued despite herself. *This might be interesting.* She invited Webb into her office, closing the door behind them. Webb shuffled in and plopped onto the first chair she came to. Prisha marveled at this woman, who had the sophistication and manners of a barnyard animal. The senior always sits before the subordinate. Prisha smiled at this lapse of etiquette, her big open smile meant to put Webb at ease, to lull her and loosen her tongue. Prisha took her seat across from Webb and motioned for her to begin.

"So, was that one of the candidates to replace Charles?" Webb asked, up-talking in an attempt to soften the mood.

Prisha ignored the question. She fixed Webb with her dark brown eyes.

Webb's tremors began anew. She cleared her throat. "Well, this is about Charles, anyway."

Prisha switched effortlessly into sadness mode, and for the next few moments she put on a performance worthy of her background in theater. She spoke of what a tragedy it all was. How some deranged person had broken into Hewitt's home and killed the poor man in broad daylight. How the police thought it was a home burglary, and that Hewitt had simply been in the wrong place at the wrong time.

And poor Charles—he had become so despondent before this dreadful incident. If only he had reached out to her. If only she had seen the signs. But his death had made her reflect on how valuable life truly was, and wouldn't Webb agree? Prisha ended her performance with a flourish, asking Webb to bow her head and join her in a moment of silence for Charles Hewitt. Webb did.

Prisha looked up through her eyebrows and watched Webb squirm. She allowed herself a tiny smile, which she carefully erased before raising her head again.

"Okay, Linda," Prisha said, breaking the silence. "Why are you here?"

Webb fought her emotion. "I'm scared," she said in a thin voice. "Charles's death has frightened me. It's keeping me up at night."

"Whatever for, Linda? His death had nothing to do with you."

"It... it might have had something to do with me." Webb began to sob.

"What are you talking about, Linda?" Prisha leaned forward. The woman now had her full attention.

Webb avoided the question, but instead began to blather on about ODYSSEUS, how maybe it was a cursed project. How there had been other mysterious deaths in the past. She questioned whether they should continue, and offered that maybe they should just shut ODYSSEUS down.

Prisha felt her anger rise. "What are you trying to say, Linda?"

"It's just that... I may have done... a bad thing. And now Hewitt's dead. I'm afraid."

"What did you do, Linda?" Prisha said, sounding out each word.

More sobs.

Prisha got up and fetched a box of tissues from her credenza. It gave her a moment to focus her thoughts. *Stay in character and find out what this bitch did.*

Prisha handed Webb a tissue, placed the box on the low table. Prisha now sat down next to Webb on the sofa, invading her personal space. Another big open smile and a reassuring pat on the shoulder.

"It's okay, Linda. You can tell me." She looked into Webb's cloudy, yellowed rat eyes. Webb's shoulders relaxed. She leaned back into the sofa.

"Well," Webb began, "I met with some people two weeks ago. A man and a woman. I didn't want to, but they threatened my daughter." She paused. "I had to!" Webb scanned Prisha's face for any sign of acceptance of this lie.

"Who did you meet with, Linda?" Prisha asked, in the tone of an elementary school teacher trying to tease a tale out of an eight-year-old.

"They said they'd harm my daughter if I didn't cooperate." Another lie.

"Linda, who—?"

"They assaulted my daughter's boyfriend. They're dangerous. And now Charles is dead. I'm afraid I may be next. Me and my daughter. Will you help me, Prisha? Please!"

Prisha knew Webb was lying. Time to tell this woman what she needed to hear to loosen her tongue.

"Of course I'll help you, Linda," Prisha said. She reached over and placed her hand on Webb's leg, gave her a reassuring squeeze. "But you've got to tell me what's going on.

You're not only a valued colleague, but I consider you a friend as well. You're a brave woman, Linda. You can tell me. What happened?"

The story started to tumble out. Slow at first, then faster.

"I didn't want to do it!" Webb said, her words spilling out now. "These people are dangerous. First Ryan and now Charles. Help me!"

Prisha told Webb to calm down, take a few deep breaths. She told Webb she would help her, but that Webb had to tell her who'd threatened her.

"I don't know!" She lied. "A man and a woman. A guy with dark hair. The woman was a blonde."

"You don't know their names?"

"No." Webb's eyes went high right. Deception.

"I want to help you, Linda. But I can't unless you tell me the truth."

Prisha slid right alongside Webb now. Cigarettes and body odor filled her nostrils. Prisha hid her revulsion.

"Don't be afraid, Linda. I'll protect you. I know a top-notch security guy. I've used him myself in the past. But you have to trust me." Prisha waited for Webb's eyes to find hers. "Do you trust me, Linda?"

Webb nodded and smiled. "Okay," she began. "It was that Medal of Honor guy. Frank Luce."

Prisha feigned ignorance. "Who?"

"You know. The guy we fired five years ago. I'd forgotten all about him too. Had to look him up in our database."

"What did you tell him, Linda?"

"Nothing! He already knew all about ODYSSEUS. The blonde knows too."

Prisha's eyes narrowed. That's how they'd found Hewitt. Webb had told them. Karlsson had said he couldn't get an answer from Hewitt as to how he had been selected by Frank and Doyle. Prisha now knew why. Hewitt hadn't known that Webb had betrayed him.

"What else did you tell them, Linda?"

"Nothing!"

"What else, Linda?" Prisha said in a cold voice. She was about to let her volcanic temper flow.

Webb blinked rapidly, wiped at her face.

"I..." She lowered her voice. "I told them about Charles. They said they needed the name of the person closest to you. I gave them Charles." Webb jolted upright in her chair. "I didn't want to! They threatened my daughter!"

"And what did they say about me?"

"I think they're coming after you. Us." Webb's rat face pinched, but no tears came.

Prisha waited.

"I didn't do anything wrong! I just had this guy fired like you told me to. I was just doing my job."

Prisha thought for a long moment, and then it came to her. Of course. She could use this. It would be easy to have Karlsson kill Luce. But that still left Hewitt's unsolved murder lingering, which could prove to be a much bigger threat to her in the long term. Better to pin Hewitt's murder on Luce, then have him killed in prison for a carton of smokes. A smile crossed her lips.

"Don't you mean Charles?"

"Huh?"

"As I recall, it was Charles who fired Luce, not you. Fired him for cause, then stripped his TS clearance. Those two never got along. It got ugly, remember?"

Webb was clearly confused.

"You remember, don't you, Linda? You were right here in

this office with me when Charles fired Luce. They exchanged words, almost came to blows. I had to threaten to call security to get him out of my office. You remember now, right?"

Prisha saw the realization wash over Webb's face when she finally understood the story her boss was spinning.

"Yes! That's right," Webb said with relief. "Now I remember. It was Charles who fired him."

"Good, Linda. So that puts Luce at the top of the suspect list in Charles's murder. A disgruntled employee who hated his boss enough to kill him. Regrettably common these days. And Luce fell apart after his firing, as I understand it. He's a homeless guy now. Pathetic. He must have thought about killing poor Charles for five years before he manned up enough to do it. Sad."

Webb beamed. "Yes. That's it," she said, and shook her head. "Thank you for helping me, Prisha."

Prisha reached out and clutched Webb's hand. "That's what friends are for, Linda." She paused. "And I know a detective with Metro PD. I'm going to pass along the information you just shared with me, see if we can get justice for Charles."

Webb's eyes grew wide. She tried to pull her hand away but Prisha held tight.

"I don't want to get involved," Webb squealed. "Please don't mention my name."

Prisha brought her big smile back. "Don't worry, Linda. You can trust me. I'll take care of this."

Webb sighed deeply. The color was beginning to return to her face.

"But Linda," Prisha said, "tell me more about this blonde woman."

CHAPTER THIRTY-SEVEN

November 24, 2016
Doyle's Hotel Room
Outside Beltway, WDC

Thanksgiving Day. I was eating takeout with Doyle in his hotel room. I'd rather have been by myself, having a beer with Angie at my place, but Doyle had insisted I come over. Didn't want me to be alone today, I guess. Truth was, I wasn't feeling very thankful these days.

It had been eight days since Hewitt died in my arms, and nothing had gone right since. I felt like shit, couldn't shake the thought that it was all my fault he was dead. Doyle and Sarah had both tried to convince me otherwise, but it didn't stick. I had passed the days since his death in a stupor, going through the motions. We tried to step back to Linda Webb, reboot our plan, but she was evasive and non-responsive. She had stopped returning my calls completely, only replying back to Sarah sporadically. The three of us discussed making another hard approach against Webb, but my heart was not in it. Not now. We had come so close with Hewitt. I felt we could have had Prisha with some luck and a little more time. But now we were pretty much back where we'd started.

I'd thought a lot about things this past week. How my plan had put Doyle and Sarah at risk, how it had gotten Hewitt killed. All three were grown adults, adults who made their own choices for their own reasons. Doyle and Sarah out of love for me. Hewitt because I'd blackmailed him into it. At least that was how I saw things now, but I still didn't feel good. Maybe I should have stayed on my own. Maybe everyone would have been better off.

"Eat up, Frankie," Doyle said. "You haven't touched your turkey."

I had ordered a turkey sandwich at a local deli. Doyle worked on his pastrami on rye. I poked at the turkey, tore off a piece and stuck it in my mouth. It was cold. It didn't taste like much.

"It's our fault, you know," I said.

Doyle sighed. We had been through this before.

"Hewitt was a fundamentally decent man who got in over his head," Doyle said. He wiped mustard off his hands with a paper napkin, then balled it up and tossed it back into the takeout bag. "He sat by and did nothing as Prisha bent ODYSSEUS to her will. He was already deep into this by the time we came along."

I shrugged. Picked another piece of cold turkey off my sandwich and started chewing.

"We gave him the chance I think he'd been waiting for, for a long time. We gave him his shot at redemption."

"We got him killed, Quinn."

"That's not how I see it. We all thought we'd have more time. If I'd thought Prisha would strike that fast, we would never have left him alone like that." Quinn rubbed his eyes with his fingertips. "I really thought we'd have a little more time," he said, more to himself than me.

I turned my head and looked out the window. Doyle had a corner room on the third floor. My mind drifted to my last Thanksgiving, at a homeless shelter outside Albuquerque. Then to Nicole and Teddy, having turkey in their shitty apartment. I thought of Sarah and Victor, in their beautiful home and loveless marriage. I had somehow believed I could fix all this. Set the world right again. I wasn't so sure now. The harder I tried, the more the universe tittered.

Prisha held all the cards now. All the resources of the U.S. government were at her disposal. Hewitt had told Karlsson everything, and he had undoubtedly told her. Hewitt's death proved Prisha had no problem using Karlsson to play outside the lines. And she must have access to hundreds of Karlssons. I would never get to her now. Never get my pension and government benefits restored. Or my good name. What the hell had I been thinking?

Time for a new plan. One I could do alone, without jeopardizing anyone else. One that would pay out before the cancer got me. I'd been thinking about it all week. Angie and I had worked the idea out together. She approved.

"Hey, Quinn, you know anyone who could help me make some quick money?"

"Frankie, you know that—"

"I mean it," I said.

Quinn saw I was serious. He folded his hands on his lap and studied me for a moment.

"What kind of money you talking about?"

"Seven hundred fifty large," I said.

Quinn snickered. "I can tell you one thing, Frankie. You don't want to get involved with that. Those people swim in the deep end of the pool."

"How about armored cars?' I asked. This was what Angie and I had come up with. "You know any guys that do armored car work?"

"Why you asking me these questions, Frankie?" He looked at me quizzically.

I explained to Doyle my realization that I would never get my money from Prisha. We had given it our best shot and failed. Got a man killed, too. I told Doyle I'd given it a lot of thought this past week and had decided on armored cars. I would rob an armored car. One dare-to-be-great moment for all the marbles. Catch the right load and I'd have the money I needed to set up Nicole and Teddy. Course I might need a second gun, and maybe someone to help me wash the money. I was counting on Doyle to help me with that.

Instead, he just laughed. "You can't rob an armored car, Frankie. What—you just going to walk up and bang on the back door? *Open up and give me all your money.* It's not trick-or-treat, Frankie."

I persisted.

Doyle said he had known a few crews back in the day who did armored cars. Most of them had someone helping on the inside. All the guys he knew were dead or in prison now. Sometimes they got a big payday, but it was dangerous. Unlike bank tellers, those guards were armed and would shoot back. And those trucks were like tanks, twenty-five thousand pounds of hardened steel and bulletproof glass. Doyle said it took a lot of training, skill, and luck to pull off an armored car job. He'd never got involved in it. Too much heat and too much risk. It was a federal crime, and he didn't need any more feds up his ass. He told me I was stupid for even bringing it up.

"I could learn. With my military background. Train hard and just hit it."

"Oh, so old Frontal Assault Frank is back now?" Doyle asked.

"I think I could do it. The hell with all this ladder-stepping shit. We tried it—it didn't work. So, yeah, I'd rather just walk up to an armored car and take my chances."

"And what if those guards don't see it that way?" Doyle asked, rising to his feet. "What are you prepared to do?" He stood behind his chair, hands braced on the backrest. "Are you going to shoot them? Kill them?"

We both knew I wouldn't kill anyone like that.

"Maybe just in the leg, you know?" I said weakly. "Just enough to get them to do what I ask."

Doyle laughed at me again, this time with a bite.

"Did you hear what you just said right now?" he asked rhetorically. "Stop talking nonsense, Frankie. I know our plan's not perfect, and that Hewitt was a setback, but we have to stay the course here. Regroup. We'll find another way to get to Prisha. Trust me."

I really wanted to trust Doyle on this. But I just couldn't see how we were going to get to Prisha now.

I looked past him to the clock on the wall, its sweeping second hand ever moving. Time was relentless, and it was running out for me. I did not have the luxury of patience. Cancer had robbed me of that.

It was time for a new plan. And I would go it alone this time. Again.

CHAPTER THIRTY-EIGHT

November 26, 2016
Frank's Apartment
Fort Totten, Upper NE WDC

"An armored car robbery, Frank? Are you fucking crazy?"

It was a blustery Saturday morning, two days after Thanksgiving. Pewter-gray skies threatened rain. Sarah had arrived at my apartment unannounced. She hadn't even bothered to sit down before she started in on me. Apparently, Quinn had told her about my new plan. She was not a fan.

"It's suicide, Frank. I'm not gonna let you do it."

I took a seat at my rickety table, motioned for Sarah to do the same. She scowled and stayed standing. I patted the tabletop. She unzipped her fleece top, hung it on the back of the other chair. Sarah wore tight black yoga pants, running shoes, and a thick baggy sweatshirt. Her hair pulled back from her face. No makeup. She looked beautiful, even in that scowl.

"Come over here for a workout?" I asked, my attempt at levity.

"Told Victor I was going to the gym."

"How was your Thanksgiving?"

"Sucked," Sarah said. "That'll be our last one together."

I offered an apology, which she waved off. She accepted my offer of coffee, though. I went to the kitchen, fired up the hotplate and put the kettle on. Two cups were all I had. I filled them both with two fingers of Folgers Instant and headed back to the table to wait for the kettle to boil.

I glanced out the window as I went. Angie's smile told me to hold my ground. We had already talked this through. The new plan could work. It would have to work.

I rejoined Sarah back at the table. She studied my face, tight-lipped and still pissed.

"Quinn shouldn't have told you," I said.

"Shouldn't have told me?" Sarah shouted, incredulous. "You've decided—without telling me—that you're going to run off, stick up an armored car and get yourself killed? Quinn's not supposed to tell me that?"

It sounded dumber in my ears than it had in my head. I looked at my hands. Sarah waited for me to explain myself. I didn't know what to say to her. I chose silence. It seemed to be the right choice. Her storm was starting to pass. Sarah took a few deep breaths. I looked up and watched tentatively as her face relaxed and her eyes softened.

"You're not alone anymore, Frank. Quinn and I love you. We're all in this thing together now."

She reached across the table and grabbed both my hands

in hers. The table teetered and squeaked. She offered a faint smile, her eyes misty. Her hands were soft and warm. Her hair had the scent of flowers after a summer rain. I wanted to go back to a time when there were no Victors or Nicoles. Back to when the world was not my enemy. Back to when everything made more sense. I felt myself sliding away. I gripped her hands harder.

We both were startled by the whistle of the kettle. I went back into the kitchen, poured the hot water over the Folgers, stirred, and brought our two coffees back to the table.

Sarah raised her cup and drank. Her eyes widened, then she gave a little head shake. Serving this woman instant coffee was like taking her to an all-you-can-eat discount lobster joint. But she dutifully took another sip, accepting my offering with grace.

"I don't want to put you and Quinn at any more risk," I said.

"Let us decide that, Frank. We're not going to leave you."

"It's not gonna work. Hewitt's dead. Webb's bugged out on us," I said, slugging back a gulp of Folgers. "It's over."

We talked about Hewitt's murder. Sarah was as aggrieved about it as I was. But it had also steeled her spine to this talion plan of ours. Realizing its dangers had paradoxically drawn her closer to it. *Sarah had chosen me and Doyle over all else.* Her will was now resolute.

Sarah tried her best to bring me back around. "I'll call Webb again. Go over to her house. Get her back on plan. We'll start over with her."

"Webb's done," I said. "All we can do is threaten her embezzlement again." I paused. "We can't trust her. And I don't think she'll go with us anyway."

"Then we'll come up with something else."

"I already have." I drained my cup. Sarah wasn't touching hers anymore. "If Quinn can get me an AK, I can do this. I'll just take a guard hostage. Make the driver open up the truck. Quick loot and scoot."

Sarah just sighed and closed her eyes.

I got up, collected our cups, and took them back to the kitchen, where I rinsed them out and put them on the counter to air dry. Gave her time to chew on what I had said. I returned to the table, but the expression on Sarah's face hadn't changed. She leaned back in her chair, away from me.

"So what if you survived... and even got the money?" she asked. "What then? This doesn't restore your reputation or your honor, Frank. It just makes you a felon. And what if the guards don't play along? You going to kill them?"

The question hung in the air.

"And how are you going to get the money to Nicole and Teddy? What are you going to do? Just show up and hand them big bags of bills and coins? Or are you a money launderer now too?"

"I'm still working on it," I mumbled. I glanced toward the window, but Angie had nothing to offer.

"Think, Frank!" Sarah shouted, startling me. She tapped her temple with a forefinger. "Broad daylight. Wild West style. You don't even know how much money would be on the truck. What about witnesses? Maybe a mom and kids going grocery shopping. What are you going to do about them? And forget about you shooting the guards. They have guns too, Frank. What if they shoot *you*?"

She was making too much sense. I pushed my plastic chair back away from the table; the legs screeched against the floor. I got to my feet, causing the chair to rock back. I caught it before it toppled over, set it upright, and walked to the window. I leaned my shoulder against the wall and turned to face Sarah again. She remained seated, glaring at me from across the room. Angie loomed above me from her billboard perch. I looked to Sarah first, then turned my eyes to the billboard.

I thought Angie and I had this all worked out. I felt comfortable going it alone. Like falling back into a well-worn groove. But Sarah saw my withdrawal as a betrayal of her trust. I was just trying to protect her, shield her from the wreckage of my life. What remained of it, anyway. I'd rather take my long shot alone than drag the three of us down together. If I got the money, good. Nicole and Teddy won. If not, I'd die trying. That was good with me as well. Angie smiled back at me. She was good with it too.

"Look at me, Frank."

I turned from the window to face Sarah.

"The money's not your problem," she said. "Your problem is you're running again. Running from the people who love you."

"It's not that simple, Sarah."

"No? Then explain it to me, Frank."

I started to answer, then stopped. I felt Angie's stare boring into my back.

"We stuck our necks out for you, Frank. Quinn. Darryl. Chang Li. Anna Webb." She paused. "Charles Hewitt too. We all trusted you. We need to finish what we started here. Take this bitch Prisha down and make you the man you used to be. The man you can be again."

I lowered my head and blew out a loud breath. Sarah awaited an answer that never came. A long moment passed as the silence between us grew to a crescendo.

"God damn you, Frank!" Sarah exploded. She shot to her

feet, and the plastic chair flew backward, skidding across the floor. "Quinn and I will not help you with this. You're on your own."

I didn't respond. Just stared at her. My silence seemed to enrage her more.

"I'll turn you in, Frank! You keep this up, I'll call the cops."

"Go ahead."

Sarah's eyes narrowed. Her face contorted in fury. She flew across the room and was on me in an instant. Her right hand came up fast. The slap stung my face; the sound ricocheted off the walls like a gunshot. Sarah howled, deep and guttural. The wail of a wounded animal. She had kept it to herself for five years. The ferocity of it startled me. Sorrow and rage battled within her. Rage won.

She balled up her fists and reared back. I caught the punch before it landed. Up came the other hand. I ducked as it sailed by my ear. I grabbed this one too, before she could reload. I spun her around, leaned her against the wall, holding her by both wrists, chest high. She screamed and flailed. I held on.

Sarah slumped against the wall; her eyes bored into mine. She was searching for the boy she had known in high school. The man who had worn the Medal of Honor around his neck. Right now, I was searching for that man too.

"God damn you, Frank," she said again, then repeated it in a voice barely above a whisper. "God damn you."

Her body sagged, and she began to weep. Softly. Tears streamed down her face. Her whimpering felt like a sword thrust into my heart. I released her wrists, and her arms dropped to her sides. I reached down and held her hands. She wept harder. I wrapped my arms around her, our faces close now. Neither of us looked away. Her floodgate opened and she began to sob; five years of pain and grief and loss wracked her as we stood clinging to each other. She tucked her head into my shoulder. Our embrace tightened. I leaned into her, basked in the floral bouquet of her silken blonde hair. She heaved in my arms. I held her like this for a long time. I could have done it for eternity.

Our entire life together flashed through my mind. How we had met and fallen in love. My prom. Hers. Trips to DC and the Delaware shore. Her visits to the Point. The good times. Neither one of us spoke, words mere ornaments in this moment.

Finally, Sarah drew a quivering breath and pulled away from me just enough to meet my eyes again. It was only then that I realized I was crying as well.

"I won't lose you again, Frank," she said. "It was the biggest mistake of my life. My heart can't take that again."

I stroked her hair, kissed the top of her head. Then again. My lips lingered longer this time. Oh, she smelled so good.

Our eyes met again. Hers widened, then mine. She leaned in and kissed me gently on the lips. I felt her warm tears on my cheek. We separated, exchanged shy smiles. I kissed her back. A soft, exploratory kiss. Sarah returned it, tinged with a hint of passion this time. A tremor shook my body, bells tolling in my head. More kisses followed, each more ardent than the last. My tongue found hers, and she tightened her arms around me.

We had found each other again.

In this moment, I realized it had been me all along. I'd lost my way. My faith. Failed to trust the people who loved me when I'd needed them most. Failed to see what my withdrawal from the world would do to them. How I had punished only them and not myself. The armored car, with its impenetrable steel and glass, was but a metaphor for my retreat back into myself.

I would not do this again. I would place my faith in Sarah. And Quinn. And we would stop Prisha and make me whole again. Somehow. Together.

I pulled away to catch my breath. Sarah was breathing hard as well. Our smiles turned to laughter.

"What time is Victor expecting you home?"

PART III

He that wrestles with us strengthens our nerves and sharpens our skill. Our antagonist is our helper.
    — Edmund Burke

CHAPTER THIRTY-NINE

December 3, 2016
National Zoo
Washington, DC

"I wanna see the elephants," said the small boy in a low voice and head of unruly dark hair. He turned and tucked himself tight into Sarah.

"We already saw the elephants, Teddy," I said. "Remember?"

"I wanna see 'em again," he pleaded.

"After the show, okay?" Sarah said. "Then we'll go back and see the elephants. You wanna see the wolves, don't you?"

Teddy shrugged. "I don't know."

"C'mon," Sarah said. "It'll be fun."

Sarah and I exchanged smiles. Our eyes lingered. It had been eight days since we'd reclaimed our love at my apartment, and I wanted to spend every moment with her now. Ached when we were apart. It felt good to be alive again.

Nicole's babysitter had cancelled on short notice, and she couldn't afford to give up her lucrative Saturday night shift at the bar. Sarah had agreed to take Teddy for the overnight, and cleared it with Nicole for Doyle and me to join her and Teddy for an afternoon outing at the National Zoo. I'd only met my son the one time at the WWII Memorial. Doyle not at all. Teddy had been shy with Doyle and me much of the day, but he was loosening up a bit. Doyle had a way with small children that was endearing to watch.

Teddy loved the National Zoo. Located in the heart of Rock Creek Park, its one hundred sixty-three acres was home to over twenty-seven hundred animals, representing more than three hundred and ninety different species.

We had arrived at the zoo early this morning and had been all over the place, including trips to Amazonia, the Panda House, the Great Cats, and the Primates. And of course, by special request, we would be making a return visit to Elephant Trails.

Teddy loved seeing all the animals, and had clung to Aunt Sarah for the most part while we made our way around the grounds. We had already eaten lunch and were now headed to the American Trail exhibit to settle in for the twenty-minute Keepers Choice Event, where animal handlers introduce visitors to one selected species featured in the American Trail exhibit. Today's animal: the gray wolf.

We all took our seats in the raised bleacher area. The handler arrived and began the talk in front of the gray wolf enclosure. Sarah told Teddy he could change seats to sit closer to the enclosure, as long as he stayed right in front of

us. He bounded forward four rows and sat down, stealing a
quick look back at us.

We three adults huddled together, Sarah in the middle,
and took advantage of our twenty minutes of privacy to talk
over our new plan. We had worked on it all week, most
evenings at the secret Dupont Circle townhouse Sarah
intended to move to after her divorce from Victor was final-
ized. The townhouse was three stories. Four thousand square
feet. Two garaged parking spots. Real swank. Sarah stopped
by each night after work with takeout, and we worked late
into the evenings. Sarah had told Victor she had to work late
all week on a big project with a tight deadline. This was
actually true, but of course disingenuous. Doyle had guessed
our secret by the second night. We'd thought we were being
coy, but true love shines bright, I guess. He was very happy
for us. Our little family was reunited.

We all agreed that something was going on at Parkview
Market, behind the big steel door with the numeric lock.
Further inquiry indicated that the door led to the bodega's
basement. Our new plan was simple: we would break into
the bodega after hours and use the combo Darryl Robinson
had found in Prisha's desk to get down into the basement.
Once there, we would snoop around and take anything
damning enough to blackmail Prisha with. Same objective as
before.

This plan had many unknown variables. Could we get in
and out of the bodega undetected? Robinson had discovered
a standard alarm system (easily defeated), but we were still
vulnerable to any other high-tech systems that might be
hidden in the place. Then there was the door combo. Did
that scrap of paper say what we thought it did? Had the

combo been changed? And what exactly would we find down in that basement?

We puzzled over these and many other questions all week, with all discussion eventually leading back to the same conclusion: we had to get eyes on that basement. Sarah had sought Robinson's input on some of these variables, and he had proven himself a valuable resource. He said it was highly likely that we would encounter computer and digital media. He recommended we attempt to introduce malware into their network, as well as the same tracking software we had been using to great effect on Prisha's office computer. Robinson said the malware would be another lever against Prisha, that it would give him the ability to torch much of whatever we found down there. Maybe not put Prisha out of commission, Robinson opined, but inflict enough pain to get her attention.

We came to realize we needed Robinson with us in the basement. None of us had anywhere near his expertise. And it was out of the question that Sarah was going anywhere near Parkview Market. So that left me and Doyle. We asked Sarah about Robinson, a man neither of us had yet met. She vouched for him. And that was good enough for us. Sarah approached him and he agreed. Robinson would join us in the basement.

Doyle did most of the talking. I nodded and agreed where I was supposed to, but my attention was on the little boy sitting four rows in front of me. I loved the slump of his little shoulders. The swirl of his hair in the back, the little cowlick in front. I had a son that I longed to know. I wanted the whole world to know I was his father, Sarah most of all. And Doyle. Keeping this final secret from them was killing me.

We were breaking into the basement this Tuesday night, three days hence. I knew the risks. We all did. There was a chance I wouldn't come out of that basement alive, which I'd accepted straightaway. What I was struggling with was the fact that if I didn't make it out alive, my secret would likely die with me. I suspected Nicole would take it to her grave, not sharing it with Teddy, or Sarah, or anyone else. Not being Teddy's dad bothered me more than the prospect of my own basement death. Or my death from cancer, which was even more of a certainty. It was a weight I chose to carry, at least until I got Teddy and Nicole back on their feet in our old neighborhood.

I grabbed hold of Sarah's hand and squeezed hard. She squeezed back. Her smile faded when she saw my face. I dismissed her "What's up?" look with a nod. She cocked her head.

I noticed Teddy start to turn around and I quickly released Sarah's hand. She followed my eyes as Teddy got to his feet and approached us. I slid over to make room, and he plopped down between Sarah and me. She wrapped an arm around him, and he leaned into her. It might well have been the happiest moment of my life.

We all sat together on this crisp, clear day at the zoo, bathed in the radiant heat of a December sun, and listened to the handler as she finished her presentation.

"Also called the timber wolf, gray wolves are the largest members of the canine family. Devoted parents, they are also among the most social carnivores."

She paused as she looked over her audience. Teddy stared past her, entranced by the wolves in the enclosure.

"A 'lonesome howl' is a shortened call that rises in pitch and is used by a wolf that is separated from its pack," the woman continued. "If answered, the wolf switches to a deep, even howl to inform the pack of its location so that it may be found."

I beheld Teddy, Sarah, and Quinn.

I had been found.

CHAPTER FORTY

DECEMBER 6, 2016
PARKVIEW MARKET
PETWORTH, NW WDC

According to the FBI, the most common method of entry in a burglary was still forcible entry, such as kicking in a door. A method used in almost sixty percent of the burglaries at the time I'd committed my first burglary. But this low-tech method was not available to us on that pitch-dark night, four days into a new moon, at the back door to the Parkview Market.

We had caught a break of sorts, however. The market had a commercial wireless DIY security system. Doyle had seen the control panel by the big steel door, and based on his description we were able to figure out the manufacturer and model. We all figured Prisha had gone with this unsophisticated solution for its anonymity and privacy. It was certainly effective to keep out all the neighborhood amateurs and door-kicking bandits. And it also kept curious snooping teenage boys upstairs at night.

Luckily for us, Doyle had added a pro to our team tonight. Some guy who knew a guy Doyle trusted. He was from Philly and never gave us his name. A thin, high-strung guy who barely said a word. But he was Irish and an expert B&E man, which was enough. His job was to get us into the market undetected, and get us out of there alive. The guy would do the break-in, defeat the steel door lock, then wait in the white panel van outside. It sounded simple and easy. It never was.

The DIY system was vulnerable to a pro, like our guy from Philly, because all wireless alarm systems rely on radio frequency signals, sent from door and window sensors to the control panel, that trigger an alarm when any of these entry-ways are breached.

Using a cheap wireless remote available on Amazon, these radio signals could be jammed by sending radio noise to prevent the signal from the sensor to the control panel. That was what we intended to do.

We all wore black head to toe and stood stacked and silent by the back door of the market. It was me, Doyle, Darryl Robinson, and the Philly guy. I shivered at the biting wind that occasionally whipped around the back of the market. At least I hoped it was the wind that was giving me the shakes.

Doyle gave Philly guy the go sign, and he got to work with the Amazon remote. Blind trust was not my nature, but he certainly seemed to know what he was doing. Smooth, no hesitation. We gave him room to operate. He put the remote away and picked the back-door lock in minutes. He turned to

Doyle and nodded. Doyle gave him the thumbs-up sign. The guy reached for the doorknob. I held my breath. The door opened and—silence. I exhaled, switching from flight to fight mode. We were going in.

We crept into the bodega, tiptoeing around all the clutter. Philly guy was in the lead, followed by Doyle and Robinson, with me at rear guard. Doyle guided Philly guy to the big steel door. He pulled out a scrap of paper and entered Prisha's five-digit numerical code into the door lock. A tinny metallic click for each number entered. My senses were acute and everything sounded loud. I looked up at the ceiling. The boy's light had been on tonight, as it had been every night we'd surveilled the market in the run-up to this operation. One of the many risks we had to live with this night.

On Doyle's go-ahead, Philly guy turned the door latch and gently tugged. We had no way of knowing if this door was independently wired. I braced myself for a loud siren and got ready to run back to the van. The door swung open silently. Another victory. Doyle patted Philly guy on the shoulder. He turned and casually walked back through the bodega and out the back door. Mission accomplished. He was just our getaway driver now.

I took first position at the door. I drew my pistol, then took my mini-flashlight in my weak hand. I popped the dead man's button at the butt of my flashlight and saw that this fortified door did indeed lead down into a basement, as we thought it would. I started down the stairs. My first step caused the ancient wooden staircase to groan. I held up my hand to halt Robinson and Doyle. I stood in place for a long moment, listening. Hearing nothing, we continued to descend the stairs in a slow, exaggerated fashion. Stepping as lightly as possible. Doyle closed the steel door behind us. It took us over two minutes to get to the landing at the bottom of the stairs. I raised my weapon upon reaching the landing. I was ready to use it.

My flashlight pierced the darkness, sweeping left to right across the space. It was crowded and crammed with stuff, but different stuff than upstairs. Instead of food and beer and diapers, the basement had workbenches, computers and loads of electronic gadgets strewn about. And unlike the chaos upstairs, everything down here was organized and orderly, arranged precisely by someone who took great care to do so.

I entered the basement space. Doyle came up from behind and joined me. He held his gun and flashlight as I did. We passed through the lab to a ten-foot wall opening that led to a back supply room, which was also packed with equipment. My eyes fell upon a neon green curtain at the far corner of the room that appeared to be covering a closet. My stomach clenched when I noticed a pair of shoes, toes out, behind the curtain in the one-foot gap between the bottom of the curtain and the floor. I turned and looked at Doyle over my shoulder, jabbing my finger towards the curtain. His eyes widened when he saw the shoes.

I hand-signaled us into place, both of us stacked to the left of the curtain. I held three fingers up to Doyle, then gave myself the count. *One, two, three.* I whipped the curtain aside, gun up and finger sliding to trigger. No legs in those shoes. Just a large oversized closet, with some hanging clothes and a roll-away cot tucked against the wall. Someone was pulling some late nights down here. I paused a few beats for the adrenaline dump to dissipate. I turned to Doyle; his face was pale, and he was breathing heavily. We smiled. We had cheated death—for now, anyway. We were in the basement, undetected. So far, all was to plan. I checked my watch: 12:19 a.m. I activated the chronograph stopwatch. Time to get to work.

Doyle and I hustled back to Robinson, still stone still at the foot of the basement stairs. He wore a thick canvas vest covered in pockets, like a fisherman's vest, and carried his laptop in a soft case under his arm. He also had a large LED hiker headlamp strapped to his forehead. I motioned him into the basement and whispered for him to make it quick. I had only met Robinson a few days ago, in preparation for tonight, but I liked him enough so far. Mostly I respected his skill. He was the real deal. He went to work. Like Philly guy, it was all blind trust with Robinson too.

Robinson pulled a bunch of thumb drives and tools out of his vest pockets and set upon the electronic equipment. He rushed from computer to computer, carrying his laptop everywhere. Doyle and I stood at ready gun at the foot of the stairs, the only way in and out of the basement. We alternated looking up into the darkness of the stairwell, then to the jerky circles of light from Robinson's headlamp as he flitted from workbench to workbench.

After a few minutes, I noticed the light had stopped moving, that Robinson had been working on the same computer for an inordinate amount of time. He flipped his headlamp up on his head and approached me and Doyle.

"We got a bit of a problem," Robinson whispered. He explained that he had been able to copy plenty of good evidence of Prisha's criminality with ODYSSEUS, but that he couldn't get his tracking virus software to load. I told him to try again. He shook his head no; he'd already tried it twice. It wasn't going to load tonight. He said maybe he could patch the software and we could try to load it another night. Doyle and I said no, that we had only one bite at this apple. It was too risky to do a second entry.

I pressed Robinson for a Plan B. He thought a moment and pulled another thumb drive from his vest. He said it contained a doomsday virus, that it would torch the ODYSSEUS local network set up in the basement. The bad news was that we would also lose our ability to monitor or retrieve any further data. Robinson assured me we already had enough good evidence secured on his laptop. He gave me and Doyle a few examples. I liked what I heard. We decided that nuking the basement network was our best available option. Robinson said it would take about ten minutes to load the virus. I told him to do it. He rushed back to the workbench and got started.

As he worked, I turned my head towards the top of the basement steps, listening. I had heard the faint murmur of voices when we'd made entry into the bodega. They came from upstairs, and from their cadence I'd surmised the boy was watching late night television at low volume. I now heard that faint murmur again, but different voices and cadence. I closed my eyes to listen more intently. I definitely heard voices, and they appeared to be getting louder. Approaching.

I grabbed Doyle by the arm and pointed up the stairs. I rushed to Robinson. Grabbed his arm, whispered for him to be absolutely quiet. I strode back to Doyle, careful to not make a sound. I stood stiff, straining to hear, blood pulsing in my ears. The voices had stopped. I began to think maybe I was hearing things, paranoia creeping in. Then the unmistakable sound of the market's front door being unlocked and opened. Multiple voices. *Upstairs in the market.*

The squeak of footfalls tracked across the basement

ceiling and towards the basement door. I heard a woman's laughter, coming closer now. I tapped Doyle and pointed to the supply room, pushing him ahead of me. We collected Robinson as we ran, careful to make no sound. *The metal clicks of the numeric lock.* We rushed into the supply room. *The sound of the steel door opening.* I pushed open the neon green curtain and we crowded in behind it. Closed it tight again. *The creak of the first staircase step.* I swatted at Robinson to turn off his headlamp.

The voices were loud now; they were making no attempt to hide their presence. They switched on all the basement lights, which cast a spotlight under the curtain and into our closet hideaway. We shuffled away from the curtain and stood shoulder to shoulder, backs pressed up against the wall.

I fingered back the curtain a sliver. Two men and a woman. They were in the basement now. I got a good look at them. The curtain shook in my hand. I dropped my hand to my side. *Fuck.* It was Khabir Ahmad, the tech. And Henrik Karlsson, Hewitt's killer. And Prisha Baari. My brain wouldn't believe what my eyes had seen. I checked again. I saw the same thing.

I whispered it in Doyle's ear; he in turn relayed the news to Robinson. I saw with dismay that Robinson's eyes were watering, and feared the man would start crying and give us all away. I reached across Doyle and shook Robinson's arm, then held a finger to my lips. He nodded, unconvincingly.

I watched and listened. I saw and heard Karlsson best, as he sat directly opposite me, not fifteen feet away in my line of sight through the opening to the supply room. Prisha and Ahmad chose seats out of my view behind the wall. Their voices were casual as they spoke amongst themselves, but their words came to me mostly garbled, too low to be made out. I did hear ODYSSEUS mentioned a lot, and President Mo Udell's name as well. Prisha dictated to Ahmad, as an exasperated boss does to a subordinate. Ahmad's replies were short and brusque through his pronounced Arabic accent. Karlsson didn't speak much. Twice he looked through the supply room directly at our curtain. Twice my sphincter puckered tighter than a snare drum. Thankfully, Karlsson made no move to get off his seat to investigate. Maybe, just maybe, we might all survive this yet. Maybe what I was watching would be a quick visit. It was well past midnight. Tomorrow was a workday. Maybe we'd get lucky. We stood dead still and quiet in the darkness behind the neon green curtain. Waiting for Lady Luck to roll her dice.

———

But luck would not be a lady tonight. Instead, it was an obstinate man named Murphy, whose law defies the best-laid plans of mice and men: *Whatever can go wrong will go wrong.* Our old friend Murphy was kin to something I was all too familiar with from my army days: *FUBAR—fucked up beyond all recognition.* I was the one who had done our ops plan for this bodega basement break-in. It was me who was responsible for searching the shadowy corners where Murphy liked to lurk. It was my job to keep FUBAR on the sidelines. This was what I'd excelled at in the army. Why they'd given me that big medal. I had beaten Murphy many times at his own game. He picked the worst night to settle the score.

I had planned for everything. Everything but allergies, that is.

I didn't plan for the three of us to be huddled together in a cramped closet for twenty minutes. I didn't know that Robinson was allergic to wool. I didn't notice that the neon green curtain that shielded us from our enemy was made of *one hundred percent wool*.

I saw it all. His head jerk triggered my peripheral vision. His eyes slammed shut; his mouth gaped wide. My hand clamped around his mouth, but it was too late. Robinson let loose a full sneeze, the sound loud and unmistakable. I knew instantly we were done.

I whipped back to the curtain and looked out. All conversation had stopped. Karlsson was now most definitely looking directly at us, eyes squinted. He slowly rose and walked into the storage room, hitting the light switch on. My eyes fought to adjust to the brightness as he crept closer. Karlsson was three steps away. I let go of the curtain and pushed Doyle and Robinson back a step. I raised my gun high to ready position and waited.

The curtain flew open in a blur. I raised my gun on target.

"Hands up!" I heard myself shout.

Karlsson's eyes went wide but he quickly recovered. I took a step forward, he backwards. We did it again. I was out of the closet now. I sensed Doyle at my side, gun drawn. I told Karlsson to keep going. I heard shouting coming from the other room. In this way, Karlsson walked backwards, hands up, into the main room of the basement. Doyle swung his weapon on Prisha and Ahmad. There was a lot of shouting. With difficulty, I got everyone quiet again.

I put Karlsson on his knees, then flat on the floor on his belly, feet crossed at the ankle. He smirked the whole time, never taking his piercing eyes off me. I then told Doyle to cover him while I put Prisha and Ahmad on their bellies too. Told Doyle to kill Karlsson if he moved, which was performance art for Karlsson's benefit, as I already knew Doyle would kill him.

All three were now on the floor, heads straining upward to see us standing in front of them. I told Doyle to disarm Karlsson and then motioned for him to pass me his weapon, which he did. Then he approached Karlsson from my opposite side, leaving me a shooting angle. Doyle bent down and frisked Karlsson's waist, finding big-caliber Ruger tucked into the front of his pants. Doyle tucked it away and rejoined me. I gave him back his gun.

"Hello, Frank," Prisha said with a smile. "I am oh so happy to see you after all these years."

Prisha's lilting voice made me retch. I saw the pistol shake in my hand. I really, *really* wanted to shoot her in the head. I forced my thoughts back to the mission. We had made a lot of noise down here, and I had no idea whether the kid and his parents would come down and investigate. Or if Prisha had sent the bat signal already. Either way, we had precious little time.

"Shut up and listen, Prisha," I said evenly. "I'm only gonna say this once. You're through. ODYSSEUS is over. Your network is toast, all your data corrupted. But not before we copied what we need to put you in prison for a long time."

This wiped the smile off Prisha's face. Her dark shark eyes darted back and forth, seeking a card to play.

"So here's the deal. You're—"

"You need to think this through, Frank," she said. "You may think you have the upper hand here, but I assure you, you are mistaken."

"You're gonna write me a letter," I continued, ignoring her, "saying my termination was a mistake. That I should be put back in good standing—"

"You did all this for an *apology*, Frank?" Prisha laughed. "Okay. I apologize," she said mockingly. "Now stop pointing that gun at me and get the hell out of here."

"You'll have my full benefits package restored—"

"You want your old job back?" she said, incredulity creeping into her voice now.

"—and you resign from CIA."

Ahmad tried to respond. Doyle told him to shut up or he'd put a bullet in his leg.

Karlsson was calm as ice, still wearing the same smirk. It was unnerving. Our eyes locked.

"I assume there's a 'but' in here somewhere?" Karlsson asked me. "Get to it. I'm not lying on this floor all night."

I turned back to Prisha. "I get my money and reputation back, you resign from CIA, and I won't tell anyone what I know about you and ODYSSEUS." I took a half-step closer to her, leaned down to give her a good look at my face. "You fail to do this, and I'll expose everything. I'll ruin you, Prisha, as you did me. Eye for an eye. You'll go to prison. And we both know that's no place for woman like you."

"You're actually serious," Prisha said with a dismissive shake of her head.

Ahmad shouted something in Arabic that sounded like cursing. Karlsson told him to shut up.

Prisha tried charm now, stalling for time. I repeated my demand. She feigned ignorance, tried the *this-is-all-one-big-mistake* thing. Then made excuses and shifted blame. I got terse; she grew emboldened. Doyle tapped the face of his watch. Robinson spoke up and shared a few key pieces of evidence he had copied off the server. Prisha's face dropped. I pressed for her answer. She agreed to my demands but argued for time. I gave her one week, which she said was impossible, that I should know that the government doesn't move that fast. We agreed on two weeks. I would have my money and CIA letter by December 20. My Christmas present, she said.

I told Robinson to cut some lengths of CAT-6 wire and motioned for Doyle to tie up Prisha and Ahmad. Prisha stayed silent while Ahmad again cursed in Arabic.

Without instruction, Doyle slid over to Karlsson. He approached from behind and grabbed at his hands. Fast as a cobra, the big man spun to his feet, grabbed his ankle knife and pressed it to Doyle's neck. He had his left arm wrapped around Doyle's chest. His right hand held a six-inch blade.

Karlsson was smiling now. A wide-open smile that displayed his big white teeth.

"Your move," Karlsson said.

"Shoot the bastard, Frankie," Doyle shouted. "Shoot him!"

Karlsson had the knife hard against Doyle's neck, enough that a slow trickle of blood was already running down his neck. One slice and his carotid artery would go, spewing like a fire hose. He'd be dead in minutes. I had my gun sights trained on Karlsson; he was so much larger than Doyle that there was enough of him showing to provide a good target picture.

Doyle drew my attention to him by repeatedly flashing his eyes to his side, the side opposite the knife. I flashed back to when I was a child and Doyle and I would play street football with the neighborhood kids in Southie. Doyle was always quarterback, me his favorite receiver. We got so attuned to one another that we could change pass plays at the line of scrimmage with a look. Like the look he was giving me now.

Doyle had just changed the play. I backed more slack off the trigger and waited.

Doyle slammed the heel of his shoe into Karlsson's instep while spinning his body away from the knife.

I saw it all in slow motion. My vision tunneled to the left half of Karlsson's chest, which lay open now. That's where I put the three rounds. He fell like a tree.

Doyle grabbed at his neck. I saw the blood through his fingers. He said, "I'm all right" or something to that effect. I saw his mouth moving but didn't hear the words. I heard Prisha and Ahmad screaming, saw them writhing around on the floor. I shook myself back into real time.

I screamed "Let's go!" and Robinson raced ahead of me towards the staircase. I put an arm around Doyle, and we followed. We raced up the basement stairs and flung the steel door open. The Arab family were on the other side of it. I raised my gun to them, shouted for them to back up. They did. At least the mother and father did. The teenage boy, the one I had seen in the window, held his ground, saucer-eyed. His face was cut and bruised.

Robinson raced through the bodega, knocking boxes over in his wake. I pushed through to the back door, Doyle pinned to my side. We raced to the white panel van and jumped in. Philly was a stand-up guy and had waited for us through the gunshots.

We rolled down the street. Lights and sirens approached in the opposite direction.

CHAPTER FORTY-ONE

DECEMBER 9, 2016
MEDSTAR TRAUMA CENTER
WASHINGTON, DC

PRISHA HEARD HER PHONE VIBRATE AND FISHED INTO her Gucci bag. It was her secret encrypted sat phone, not her CIA work phone. She flinched. She hadn't gotten more than a few hours of sleep in the past three days and was on edge. It was a text from Ahmad. More bad news. Robinson had inflicted grave damage on ODYSSEUS. His virus had ruined their network and corrupted most of the data. Much of it would eventually be recoverable, but some key pieces were gone forever. Ahmad boasted that he would soon have a patch to fix the devastation Robinson had wrought, but Ahmad's bluster was well known to her. Prisha knew this would set her and ODYSSEUS back for many months.

The waiting room at MedStar, the level-one trauma

center where Karlsson had been taken, was nondescript. Off-white walls dotted with watercolor landscapes. The steady hum of the vending machine in the corner. Prisha ignored the others waiting for news of their loved ones and kept her eyes down. Karlsson's false identity had held up to scrutiny. The bodega family had untied Prisha and Ahmad, then helped drag Karlsson out to the street. They made good police witnesses. Just another random, senseless mugging in the neighborhood.

Karlsson had been admitted with life-threatening injuries. One of the bullets had nicked his aorta, and he had lost a lot of blood. The surgeons had patched him up good. Karlsson was strong as a bull, and he would make a full recovery in a week or so. This was not Prisha's pressing problem at the moment.

Frank Luce was. And now Prisha had only eleven days left in which to maneuver. Luce was sending her a count-down clock text message every day at eight a.m. to remind her. She'd tolerate him in her life for the time being. But her time was running out, and she knew it.

Prisha was unaccustomed to holding the shit end of the stick. She had to find a way to spin this the other way, to reverse gravity. She had no intention of submitting to Luce's demands, his bumbling attempt at blackmail. She would play chess to his checkers. Her biggest problem was the criminal ODYSSEUS data they had downloaded. Her fingerprints were all over it. If they released it now, it would ruin her. She had to find a way to neutralize that data. She knew she could not simply retrieve it, as Robinson would have a million copies hidden in a million different places. This was what had kept her up the past three nights and put those dark shadows under her eyes.

Prisha could discredit Luce to such a degree that anything he said would be ridiculed as paranoid conspiracy theory. This was a tried-and-true CIA tactic that had worked well in the past. And Prisha already had a nice head start with this, her ongoing effort with Linda Webb and some corrupt cop friends of hers to frame Luce for the murder of Charles Hewitt. And Luce did have that five years of home-lessness. A good start, perhaps, but not the mortal wound she needed. She wanted more.

Prisha happened to look up as a fit blonde approached the reception desk to her left. Of course—the blonde! Frank Luce's blonde. Sarah Reyes was her name. Linda Webb had said she and Frank had acted like a married couple. Prisha knew Luce to be unmarried, but maybe there was enough between these two to leverage. Luce and his sidekick Doyle had gone underground; Karlsson's men could not find them anywhere. But Prisha bet Sarah Reyes had not. For the first time in three days, a smile crossed Prisha's face.

The receptionist called Prisha to her desk. She said the doctor had cleared her visit with Karlsson, but only for a moment. He was still weak and needed his rest.

Karlsson looked much better than he did two days ago. He was sitting up in bed and the color had returned to his face. He was still hooked up to machines and monitors, tubes in his arms.

"How you doing, Henrik?"

He shrugged. "They say I'll be out in a week." He motioned Prisha closer to his bedside and regarded her with a blank, impassive expression. She pushed a chair against his bed and sat down.

"Did they find him?" Karlsson asked.

"No," Prisha responded. "They're still looking."

"I'll find him. And kill him."

"No!" Prisha said, more loudly than she intended. She leaned into Karlsson and lowered her voice. "We kill him now, and they release their ODYSSEUS files. They do that, we all go down."

"So we're just gonna submit to this guy?"

"No, of course not. I ruined this guy once, and he resurrected. Time to finish the job."

"I don't understand."

"We frame him for Hewitt's murder. Discredit him for good. And get rid of this unsolved case before it can come back to bite us in the ass."

"Discredited isn't dead," Karlsson said, rising up in his bed with difficulty. "And how the hell's that going to help us? If we can't find the guy, what chance do the cops have?"

"I'm still working on that," Prisha said. "But he's got a blonde that may be more than a friend. I might be able to use that to smoke him out."

"Then I kill him."

"No!" Prisha said. "You're not following, Henrik. We slap a life sentence on Luce for Hewitt's murder, and he dies in prison. Happens all the time. No one will notice or care. Then we take out his sidekick, the old guy. I think that will be the end of it. You'll kill the sidekick, okay?"

Karlsson didn't agree with this plan and said so. He said they should try to lure Luce to a meeting and he would kill him there. Prisha now saw this for what it was: pride. Karlsson had never been bested on the battlefield, and he wanted revenge. A simple matter of testosterone and misguided honor.

Karlsson, too, played checkers. Prisha would stick to chess.

CHAPTER FORTY-TWO

DECEMBER 19, 2016
SARAH'S WRY OFFICE
DUPONT CIRCLE, WDC

"TOMORROW'S THE BIG DAY," SARAH SAID TO FRANK over their burner phones. She was between meetings in her office at WRY. "What do you think she'll do?"

Not sure," Frank responded. "Hoping she goes our way on this. I haven't talked to her in almost two weeks."

"How's Karlsson?" Sarah asked in a whisper.

"He'll be all right. He's out of the hospital now. Got out a couple of days ago."

"And you and Quinn are safe?"

"Yeah," Frank said. "They won't find us. Quinn's been through this kind of thing before. He knows what to do."

Sarah fell silent. She had her hair up the way she always wore it for work. She twirled the wisps that hung down and framed her face. She wore a finely cut navy jacket and skirt with red lipstick and light eye makeup. To anyone who knew her, she looked a touch haggard, not her usual radiant self.

"What's wrong?" Frank asked her.

"I don't know..." Her voice trailed off. "I'm scared, Frank. What if Prisha doesn't do what we want her to do? What then?"

"You've got nothing to worry about, Sarah. We're going to—"

Sarah was distracted by a commotion outside her office. Rough voices, the shuffling of feet. The protestations of Sarah's secretary. Her office door flew open, slamming against the wall with a bang that to Sarah, in her current frame of mind, sounded like the report of a gun. The loud noise caused a spasmodic jerk of her hand. The burner phone dropped to her desk. Her nerves had been taut for two weeks, ever since Frank and Doyle had told her of the events that transpired in the bodega basement. She started to shake.

Two cops marched across her office and stood in front of her desk. One was a young Hispanic guy in uniform, the other a squat guy in beige pants and an ill-fitting sports jacket, tie undone at the neck.

"Sarah Reyes?" The squat guy held out his Washington Metro PD detective shield at arm's length.

Sarah rose to her feet behind her desk, too dumbfounded to speak. The detective repeated his question. All she could muster was a nod.

"My name is Detective Macias, and I'm here to place you under arrest for the murder of Charles Hewitt."

Sarah felt herself grow light-headed, like the floor had tilted and would swallow her up whole. She gripped the desktop. This could not be happening.

"Ma'am, what I'm going to have to ask you to do is walk out from behind the desk and keep your hands where I can see them. Officer Cruz here will handcuff you."

"No!" Sarah's secretary screamed. She had followed the cops into the office and was being wrangled by Officer Cruz.

"Julian," Macias said, turning to address him. "Get her out of here."

Officer Cruz escorted Sarah's secretary out of the office. She was in tears now. She looked back at Sarah and tried to speak, but could not.

Now alone, Macias took a step closer to Sarah's desk. Beads of sweat dotted his shaved head. He smiled, revealing jagged yellow teeth. He smelled like potato salad that had spoiled in the sun.

Macias leered at Sarah; his eyes ran over her body. Up and down, slowly. Then again.

"Sarah Reyes." He paused. "I know your husband, Victor. He's an asshole." Macias laughed himself into a coughing jag. "I sure respect his taste in women, though." Macias looked over his shoulder for Officer Cruz. They were still alone. "I'll tell you, sweetheart, you're in a world of hurt. This is big girl shit—felony murder."

"What?" Sarah stammered. "What are you talking about? I didn't do anything!"

"Save it, sweetheart. We got a witness puts you in the getaway car outside Hewitt's house at the time of his murder. All we gotta do is prove the killers broke into Hewitt's house with intent to steal, and pow! We got burglary. Now you're part of a burglary that went bad. Now we got you for murder. Don't matter if you didn't pull the trigger. Hell, we don't even have to prove you went into the house. And because this Hewitt guy was such a big shot, DA's gonna file this as first-degree murder."

"I wasn't there!" Sarah shouted. "This is bullshit!" She studied Macias's face and saw the blunt arrogance. He wasn't kidding. Sarah's field of vision began to narrow and darken at the edges. Her knees buckled. She splayed her fingers on the desktop for balance.

"The DA's got a hard-on for this case," Macias said, his eyes roaming again. He stepped closer. "Me too."

Officer Cruz returned and stepped up next to the detective. Macias's eyes didn't leave Sarah.

"Book her, Julian."

Officer Cruz issued his commands, which Sarah followed robotically. He walked her to him, hands up, and had her turn around. She was cuffed in the back, like the felon she now was. Cruz was professional and apologetic. Macias was not. He insisted on searching Sarah himself, and did so with open palms, not the backs of his hand. Macias's hand shot between Sarah's legs, lingered over her breasts. His fingers kneading, exploring. Sarah retched stomach bile into her mouth. She felt tears threatening but caught herself. She would not give Macias that gift.

The groping search complete, Macias stepped in close behind her. "This is my favorite part," he said, his breath moist in her ear. "The perp walk." His right hand gripped the handcuffs, pulling down slightly to alter Sarah's balance. Macias turned her towards the door, then pushed her forward. Sarah began to move, Macias pressed tight against her back. Officer Cruz fell in behind them, a look of disgust on his face.

Sarah's secretary was standing right outside her office

door, her face pale and blotchy. Her eyes went wide at the sight of her boss in handcuffs.

"Call Victor," Sarah said in a steady voice. "Tell him I've been arrested."

Macias jerked Sarah forward, preventing this conversation from continuing any further.

The long hallway was filled with Sarah's co-workers. Her CEO, Peter Smith, pushed through the crowd and strode forward. He had the look and comportment of a well-dressed mannequin. A silver fox, with not a hair out of place.

Macias whispered in Sarah's ear. "The show's about to start." He chuckled, exhaling his warm, fetid breath on the nape of Sarah's neck. She recoiled from him.

"What is the meaning of this?" Smith demanded.

"Sarah Reyes is under arrest for the murder of Charles Hewitt," Macias announced in the voice of a carnival barker.

This stopped Smith in his tracks. As it was intended to. He swallowed hard.

"This must be some mistake," Smith said with less vigor. He glanced around the hall at his staff. All eyes were on him.

"I'm gonna ask you to stand aside, sir, and not interfere in official police business," Macias said.

Smith silently did as he was told. Two more paces and Sarah was now beside Smith, less than eighteen inches from her boss of over a decade. Their eyes met. Sarah had expected to see fire or defiance, or, lacking that, compassion at least. But all she saw behind Smith's eyes was deliberation and calculation. It was as though a mask had been peeled away, showing him for what he was, had been all along: the CEO of a multi-billion-dollar consulting firm, not Sarah's longtime mentor and friend.

"You know me, Peter!" Sarah shouted, her voice cracking. "You know I didn't do this." She looked wildly around at her co-workers, who shifted uneasily and looked at their feet. "You all know me! This is a mistake."

CEO Peter Smith straightened his tie and leapt into damage control.

"WRY will fully cooperate with law enforcement in this matter," he told Macias in his level CEO voice. "Our lawyers will be in touch, Detective. Anything you need."

Sarah gasped. "Peter! No, please!"

Macias yanked up on her handcuffs again and pushed Sarah past Smith and forward through the gauntlet of co-workers. Most gave her the dead-eye. Their boss had chosen a side, and they would follow.

Their indifference struck Sarah almost like a physical blow. It knocked the air from her lungs. She shrieked and struggled to regain her breath. This beautiful office. These beautiful, accomplished people. None of it ever mattered. Sarah saw that now. How false and fleeting it all had been. She had given everything to her career, this company. And in the end, it had shown her no loyalty whatsoever. The promotions, the coffee clatches, the Friday lunches; congratulating each other on milestones and mourning each other's losses—it had all been an illusion. Her colleagues—her *friends*. She'd been at their homes for cookouts and cocktail parties. Attended children's birthday parties and parents' funerals. And when it all mattered most, it mattered not at all. Not one goddamned bit. Sarah choked back a sob.

Macias marched her into the elevator and placed her tight in the corner, eyes facing the wall. The three people already in the car immediately looked away, staring at the floor numbers as they descended to the lobby.

Sarah tried to focus. Life as she knew it was over, that

much was clear. Peter Smith would fire her by day's end, she was sure, in a succinct statement written by the lawyers and approved by the WRY board of directors. She was going to jail now. Sarah had never even visited a jail before. The thought of being behind bars with real criminals terrified her. She had to contact Doyle as soon as possible. He had a lifetime of experience with this sort of thing and would know what to do. And she desperately needed to see Frank. Needed to be tight in his arms. Needed to hear him say everything would be all right.

The elevator doors opened at the main floor, and Sarah was led through the lobby of her building, past the gaping faces of WRY colleagues and visitors. The security guard sprang from his station and held open the door. Sarah saw the awaiting police cruiser and froze like a mule in the doorway.

Macias heaved her forward into the brilliant sunshine. Sarah squinted and dropped her head. She thought of how long it would be until she was in sunshine again. She went limp. Macias jerked up on the handcuffs. A bolt of pain shot between Sarah's shoulder blades and made her gasp. Macias tucked her head roughly to one side and dropped her into the rear passenger seat of the cruiser. Officer Cruz belted her in and shut the door.

Macias drove and Cruz rode shotgun. He screeched the tires as he pulled out, then lit up the light bar, its red and blue flashes parading Sarah out of the WRY parking lot. She would never return.

———

It was as quiet as a wake back on the floor where Sarah had

once held court. Colleagues huddled in tight clumps, whispering. No doubt a few were already scheming to take possession of Sarah's now vacated office, with its panoramic view and close proximity to Peter Smith. Power, like nature, abhors a vacuum.

No one paid any attention to the muffled shouts coming from Sarah's office, faint exhortations from the phone on Sarah's desk. Right where she'd dropped it when the cops rushed into her office. The call had remained open throughout her entire arrest.

Frank Luce had heard everything.

CHAPTER FORTY-THREE

DECEMBER 22, 2016
ATTORNEY GERRY GONZALEZ'S OFFICE
NoMA, NE WDC

SARAH WAS NOW BOOKED INTO THE CUSTODY OF THE DC Department of Corrections. She had spent the past three nights at its Correctional Treatment Facility, in a six- by eight-foot cinder block cell, one of thirty-two identical cells in the housing unit on the sixth floor of the brick tower facility. Each unit had a television and access to the recreation yard. These were privileges Sarah no longer enjoyed, however; she had fought with an inmate soon after her arrival and had been isolated into a single room, segregated from the general population.

I had barely slept since Sarah's arrest. My first call was to Doyle, my second to the only attorney I knew, Gerry Gonzalez. I convinced Gerry to take Sarah's case, and he had visited her in jail the morning after her arrest. Nicole had visited her as well, bringing messages from Doyle and me with her. It killed me not to visit Sarah, to not be there to comfort her. But this was impossible. Doyle and I both knew Prisha was using Sarah as bait to lure us out into the open. I hated her even more for it. It took me to a whole new level of rage I promised myself I would rain down upon her at first opportunity.

Doyle simmered as well. He had been on the phone nonstop, contacting old friends and calling in old debts. We were getting ready to go to war.

———

Silvia stood up from her desk and motioned Doyle and me through the door with the gaudy gold "GERALDO GONZALEZ, Esquire" stencil. Doyle paused and gave me a questioning look before entering the office. Same bright, retina-burning color scheme. Same Gerry too. All slicked-back hair, eighties mustache, and pinkie rings. He came around the desk, shook our hands, and motioned for us to sit down.

This was the first time that Doyle and I had been out in public together since I'd shot Karlsson. We had immediately changed burner phones and vehicles; Doyle had bought another beater, a Ford this time, off some guy on Craigslist for twelve hundred dollars cash. He checked out of his hotel room, I abandoned my apartment under the overpass, and we rented a little two-bedroom outside Baltimore from a landlord that liked cash and didn't ask any questions. This was where we'd been holed up for the past two weeks. It felt good to be out of that apartment. I wished it were under better circumstances.

I watched Gonzalez size up Doyle, saw the glint of recognition in his eyes. He knew a made guy when he saw one. A serious guy. It made Gonzalez less flashy, more deferential. More matter-of-fact than when I'd first met him, three months ago to the day. Everything was different now.

"This case against Sarah is bullshit," Doyle said. "What do you intend to do about it?"

"She didn't kill anyone, Gerry," I added. "And neither did we."

"I don't want to know if you did it or not," Gonzalez said. "I don't even *care* if you did it."

"We didn't do this, Gerry!" I shouted.

"Okay, okay," Gerry said, hands raised. "Do either one of you know anyone who would set you all up like this?"

Doyle and I said nothing. Gonzalez stared at us through steepled fingers.

"Okay, so you do know," he correctly surmised. "Does it have anything to do with that twenty-five K you gave me, for that little kiss-and-fall lawsuit?"

I looked at Doyle, then started to mumble a response.

Gonzalez interrupted me, hands again raised. "Wait! Don't answer that. I don't want to know that either."

"What are we gonna do to get Sarah out of jail—now?" Doyle deadpanned.

Gonzalez said that was not going to be easy. He'd been in touch with the DA's office, some young assistant district attorney, last name of Calderon.

"This Calderon bitch, he's coming after you two hard," Gonzalez said. "I don't know what you two did to spill his milk, but he wants to put you up under the jail, Frank."

I asked Gonzalez when he'd visited Sarah last. He said he'd seen her again yesterday afternoon, had told her every-thing he was about to tell us. We asked how Sarah was holding up. He answered tactfully, I think in deference to Doyle. Sarah was doing better now that she had been placed in a single cell, he said. Her first night there she had been labeled "Princess," and a couple of women had taken a particular interest in her. Sarah had rebuffed her suitors. They'd insisted. The princess had punched back.

"Is she okay?" I asked.

"Fine," Gonzalez assured me, eyes on Doyle, whose silence was beginning to unnerve Gonzalez a bit. "She's got a bruise on her face and such, but she'll be fine." He paused. "She's tough, but jail is no place for a woman like her."

Doyle finally spoke. "So what are we looking at here?"

Gonzalez explained that I had been charged with first-degree murder, Sarah with first-degree felony murder. The government had me as the trigger man, Sarah the getaway driver. We were both facing life imprisonment. I had a felony warrant out for my arrest, and, based on false infor-mant information that I had fled back to Boston, the locals had convinced the FBI to file an "unlawful flight to avoid prosecution" felony warrant on me as well. That made me an FBI fugitive now too.

Sarah's bail had been set at ten million dollars, an outra-geous amount given Sarah's lack of criminal record and her ties to the community. Gonzalez had argued hard but failed to budge the magistrate to lower it to a more reasonable amount. Something didn't smell right at the bail hearing, he told us now, like he had been left out of something between Calderon and the magistrate. Gonzalez could spot a fix when he saw one.

Sarah couldn't get her hands on one million cash. She wasn't that fluid, and it was too rich for the local bail bondsman's blood. Doyle had put his feelers out, but it's not that easy to get your hands on one million cash overnight. He would keep trying.

"We can beat this case, right?" Doyle asked.

Gonzalez explained that it wouldn't be that easy. They had a DNA match for my hair at the crime scene, and my skin cells were under Hewitt's fingernails. They had pulled my fingerprints from Hewitt's front gate, and they had boot prints matching my size (11W) in Hewitt's blood in his bedroom.

I exhaled hard and raked my palms over my face.

"Yeah, I know, Frank," Gonzalez said. "And that's not all. Calderon says he has a rock-solid eyewitness who saw you running out of Hewitt's residence, with what appeared to be a gun in your hand, then jump in a car and speed away."

"But nothing on Sarah?" I asked.

"The witness will testify that Sarah was driving the car."

"Bullshit!" Doyle said.

Gonzalez explained that Calderon was clubbing him with this witness, but that he thought he was bluffing. Gonzalez had called a few friends in the DA's office, and these friends had done some checking around on his behalf.

"Do you know a woman by the name of Linda Webb?" he asked me.

A bomb went off in my head. I slammed my fist on the arm of my chair. "Linda Webb?"

Gonzalez nodded.

"She's lying," I said. "She must be working with... them."

I exchanged looks with Doyle.

"You've managed to piss off some powerful people, Frank," Gonzalez said. "I don't understand it. You seem like a nice enough guy to me. But then, I really don't know you, do I, Frank?"

I got out of my chair and began to pace the room.

"So you're a Medal of Honor winner? Big-time war hero?" Gonzalez said, his voice rising. "And then on to the CIA, where you're fired by a boss who just turned up dead—with your hair and skin all over him?" Gonzalez's face was turning crimson. His voice was no longer friendly. "This is the kind of shit you're supposed to tell your lawyer, Frank, so the DA doesn't jam it up my ass. You made me look like some fucking amateur."

"I'm sorry, Gerry," was all I could say. "But it's not like that."

"No? Then tell me—what is it like?"

I walked back to the desk, stood behind my chair, hands jammed into my pockets.

"Hewitt wasn't my boss," I said. "They're lying." I paused to check my rising anger. "They had no good reason to fire me, and now they're trying to ruin me again. Finish the job."

"Well, as your lawyer, I'd say they're doing a pretty good job of it." Gonzalez spun his pinkie ring once, then again. "You got a problem, Frank. A big problem. Sarah too." More ring play. "In my experience, once the government turns on you like this, puts you in its crosshairs..." He shook his head and puckered his lips. "*No Bueno*, my friend."

"What are our chances of beating this?" Doyle asked.

Gonzalez blew out a protracted breath. He sat back in his chair, swiveled around a bit, eyes upturned to the ceiling. He drew another long breath and then regarded us both.

"Not good," Gonzalez said evenly. "They got a lot stronger case against you, Frank, than they do Sarah. I might be able to bargain a bit for her, but you, my friend—they want you bad. I think they're gonna go to the wall on you. Calderon's not bluffing on that score."

Doyle pressed. "What are the odds?"

I sat for his answer. Gonzalez stroked his bushy mustache in thought.

"Now, don't hold me to this—because trials can be a crapshoot, and you never know what those jury puppets are going to do—but I see it as eighty-twenty for acquittal for Sarah... and the opposite for you, Frank."

Twenty percent? A twenty percent chance Sarah would be convicted of first-degree felony murder and sentenced to life in prison? This beautiful woman. A woman I had never stopped loving, and had only recently learned still felt like-wise. They were now trying to ruin her, as they had me. And for what? So Prisha could get to me.

Twenty percent? Two chances in ten? No! Sarah had returned my faith, given me hope that I could be the man I knew I was. She had trusted me, joined me in this fight without reservation. Now it was my turn to fight for her. My number for Sarah was zero. She would not spend another day in jail, not as long as I had the power to do something about it.

It's never too late to become what you might have been.

"Call Calderon. Cut a deal," I said. "Tell him I'll surrender on my warrant if he drops all charges against Sarah."

"No! You surrender and they'll kill you in prison, Frankie," Doyle said. "I can't protect you in there." He was shaking his head vigorously. "No, we will find another way."

"No, Quinn. I can't live another day with Sarah in jail because of me." I whirled back to Gonzalez. "Tell him I'll plead guilty to everything. All of it. And in exchange, I want Sarah out of jail and home by Christmas. Call him. You've got three days. Can you do it?"

"You sure you want to do this, Frank?"

I nodded.

"They got no case on her. It's you they want. I think he'd go for it."

"Then do it."

"I'll call Calderon today. See if he bites. I'll ask for a bail reduction. If Calderon doesn't fight me on it, yeah—I can have Sarah home for Christmas. But you—"

"Do it."

"Now, Frank, you really need to think this through. You plead guilty to first-degree murder, the way they're looking at you..." Gonzalez whistled low, "... they're gonna put a life sentence on you."

I stood. "They already gave me a life sentence. Five years ago. I won't let it happen again."

Doyle stood as well. Stepped over to me. Took my face in his hands. Tears filled his eyes. He rested his forehead against mine. He gathered himself, then pulled away to arm's length.

"You sure about this, Frankie?"

"Let me do this, Quinn."

The old mobster nodded.

I turned to Gonzalez.

"Call him."

CHAPTER FORTY-FOUR

DECEMBER 28, 2016
CDF/DC JAIL
WASHINGTON, DC

"HOW WAS YOUR CHRISTMAS?" I ASKED.

Sarah shrugged. "Better than yours, I bet."

"I've had worse."

Sarah searched my face. I put on a brave smile. She tried to do the same but fell short.

"What happened to us, Frank? I don't even recognize my life anymore."

Sarah looked away. She was in casual clothing and light makeup. Jeans, a long leather coat, and a pale green sweater that picked up her eyes. I breathed deep to catch her scent. Jasmine and citrus. Held on to it for as long as I could before exhaling.

It was the Wednesday after Christmas. We were in a

DC Jail visiting stall, talking through scratched plexiglass. I was on the inside of the glass, Sarah on the outside. Gerry Gonzalez had called ADA Calderon with my surrender offer and he'd jumped at it. Things had moved rapidly after that. Sarah had protested my sacrifice, but I had made up my mind and things were already in motion. I was booked into DC Jail on Saturday morning; Sarah had been released seven hours later. All this had happened over Christmas weekend. We'd paid Gonzalez for the inconvenience. It amused me how fast the government had moved, how many rules they'd bent and broken to get me behind bars so quickly. Rules were made for rule followers, not the people who make the rules. The rule makers have always done as they pleased.

Sarah was my first jail visit. Gonzalez had negotiated this as part of my surrender. He said it was the best he could do, that we would have to meet behind glass instead of the standard open visit. Apparently, this was a new rule just for me; I would soon come to appreciate how much the rules didn't apply to me and my case. The invisible hand of power was behind it all. Prisha's hand. It infuriated Gonzalez. Another thing I found amusing: righteous indignation from a man who staged fake car accidents for a living.

But none of this mattered to me now, because I was staring through milky glass at the woman I loved. I was grateful for that. Grateful that she and Doyle were back in my life. Grateful for my son Teddy, the lone secret I still held back from Sarah and Doyle. For the first time in years, I had hope, real hope—while locked away in a place that breeds hopelessness.

The bruises on Sarah's face had almost healed, now just trace blotches of pale yellow and blue. The scratches on her neck were dried and scabbed over. Her crying had run her eyeliner. She hadn't slept well since she was released back into the mess that was now her life. She still looked beautiful to me. I ached to hold her.

"How are things at home?" I asked. "How's Victor taking all this?"

Sarah grunted. "Not good. He's catching a lot of shit at work." She ran her hands through her blonde hair, which she was wearing down around her shoulders for our visit. "At least he has a job."

"Sorry about that."

Sarah waved me off. "WRY boxed my office up the day the cops walked me out. Peter won't even talk to me. What do you call it when they expel you?"

"PNG. *Persona non grata.* 'Person not welcomed' in Latin."

"Well, I got PNG'd from WRY, that's for sure."

Sarah blew out a big sigh. She combed her fingers through her hair, then tucked it behind her ears. That gorgeous blonde hair was luminous, even in this dark place.

"I don't know, Frank. I haven't been happy for a long time. You've been a lightning bolt into my life. Burning out old growth, regenerating new. I think I needed that."

"So you and Victor... are you two...?"

"We're getting divorced. I filed on him yesterday."

My heart fluttered. I suppressed a smile.

"How are you feeling, Frank?"

"I'm okay." I tugged at the collar of my white cotton shirt under my prison orange V-neck.

"I mean with your cancer. Are you going to be able to get treatment in here?"

"Haven't told them yet. Thought I'd wait until after I get my life sentence to tell them. To see the look on their faces."

Sarah snorted, then teared up again. She paused to swipe at her eyes with the back of her hand. A hand that no longer wore her wedding ring.

"That's not funny, Frank." She sniffed.

I got another smile out of her.

"Seriously, Frank. You promised Quinn and me that you would seek treatment next year—which is next week. And now you're in here. You *need* treatment, Frank."

"I don't plan on being in here long enough for treatment. Me, Quinn and Gerry are working on something."

Sarah leaned into the glass. "What?"

"I don't want you involved in it," I whispered. "I've put you through enough already."

"But Frank—"

"No. It's for the best, Sarah. I want you to go to Quinn, up in Boston. He'll protect you."

"What about you?" Sarah asked. "Quinn said Prisha would have you killed in here, and that he couldn't protect you."

"I've got a plan. That's not how I'm going to go out."

Sarah put both elbows on the table, pressed her face up to the glass.

"Why don't we just run, Frank? Me and Quinn bust you out of here, maybe when they transport you for sentencing. Then we run to South America. I've got enough money stashed away. We could..."

I smiled and shook my head. "And you were pissed at me for robbing an armored car?" She reddened and grinned sheepishly.

"Seriously, Sarah," I said, "It's too dangerous. I don't

want us to be fugitives, looking over our shoulders for the rest of our lives."

"Maybe if we just give Prisha all her ODYSSEUS shit back, she'll leave us alone."

"And what about my money? My reputation? Making things right again?" I asked. "Running away from this won't solve that. This thing ain't gonna go away until we put her down." We locked eyes. "She's never going to stop. You know that."

Sarah sat back and dropped her head.

"Look, I know things didn't work out as we planned," I said. "I'm in here and Prisha's still out there. But I have you and Quinn back in my life. And now I have a life worth living. You've given me my faith and hope back, Sarah. I'm strong again. I know we can do this. But you have to trust me. Go to Quinn." I sat forward, trying to catch her eyes. "Leave now."

Sarah raised her head. She tried to smile, tears rolling down her cheeks.

An obese guard barged in, keys jangling, and announced that our visit was over. I stood and he cuffed me, brusquely, mouth-breathing down the back of my neck. My eyes never left Sarah's face. She mouthed *I love you.* I mouthed it back.

Sarah kissed her two fingertips, then reached out and pressed them against the glass. She held them there for a moment, then turned and left without looking back.

I stared at that smudge of lipstick on the glass until the guard jerked me away.

CHAPTER FORTY-FIVE

December 31, 2016
CDF/DC Jail
Washington, DC

I LAY ON MY BACK IN THE TOP BUNK OF MY FORTY-eight-square-foot cell. My cellie Jamal was finishing up his business on the steel toilet next to our bed. It was a few minutes shy of midnight. New Year's Eve. The inmates were whooping and hollering more than usual, their screams and catcalls echoing off the steel and concrete of our housing unit. All hard surfaces. All hard men.

Our cell was never dark, even at night, due to the hall light right outside our door. It too was encased in steel bars. Darkness was a privilege inmates here would never earn. I had been in DC Jail now for exactly one week and had yet to find my sleeping rhythm. Jamal could sleep through anything. Most nights I lay awake, listening to his breathing. And thinking.

I hoped Sarah and Doyle would be safe in Boston. She had arrived there yesterday. Doyle still had plenty of old friends in the city. They would build a moat around him and Sarah. They would be okay up there for the time being, I told myself.

Robinson had hidden all the ODYSSEUS data; Doyle had his copies of it. Robinson had dismissed Khabir Ahmad out of hand as a rank amateur, said he and his team would never crack his virus and uncorrupt the data. I wasn't so sure, but Robinson promised me it would take Prisha months to get ODYSSEUS fully back online. I intended to make good use of that time.

Prisha was counting on killing me in here, and on Robinson and Doyle not picking up the ODYSSEUS fight after my death. But even if ODYSSEUS was exposed, history proved it would be covered up well before it ever reached Prisha and the White House. Power always protects itself. Lies would be spun, scapegoats held up and skewered. I realized this now. Prisha had made this a zero-sum game. It was now me against her. One winner, one loser. She would never give me my money back, make me whole, then pat me on the head and watch me ride off into the sunset. I would have to destroy her to get what I wanted. I was ready to do so.

I'd had an attorney visit yesterday. No surprises. ADA Calderon had filed his sentencing motion and was seeking a life sentence for me. Gonzalez wanted to argue five years, citing my cancer. I'd told him not to fight Calderon's sentencing recommendation, but instead to push off the sentencing hearing for as long as he could. I told him I needed a couple more months to work things out. He didn't ask any questions.

This cancer thing sucked. I'd promised Sarah and Doyle I would seek treatment next year, but that was before everything went to shit. My bones still ached, and the night sweats had gotten worse. Since I'd been in jail, I'd broken out in tiny red spots all over my chest and thighs. I blamed it on the coarse jail scrubs, but I knew better. I didn't want to die, not anymore. I had Sarah and Doyle now. And Teddy. I would keep my promise and seek treatment for my leukemia. As soon as I could.

The doctors had given me a twenty-seven percent chance of beating it. In five years, and with treatment. But I had a bigger problem. There was a one hundred percent chance Prisha would have me killed in jail in the next few months.

Gonzalez had argued for me to be put in isolation, but of course they'd put me in general population instead. Right where Prisha wanted me. I felt the eyes on me, as if every inmate was taking my measure. Old Frank would have just put his head down and faced this alone. I knew better now. No man's an island. Doyle knew it. Sun Tzu, too. But it was Sarah who'd taught me this. Made me feel it. If I was going to survive in this place, I would need to put my faith in something. Trust someone.

I leaned down over the side of my bunk. Jamal was on his back, rereading a letter he had received last week from his six-year-old daughter. Jamal was a dark-skinned African American, tall and rail thin. He wore large oval-framed prescription glasses that magnified his chocolate eyes. He cussed incessantly, and his farts smelled like spoiled meat, but otherwise he was a good enough cellie.

"Hey, Jamal—who's the biggest badass in this place?"

"Whaddaya mean?"

"Who's the guy you want on your back when shit's about to get real in here?"

Jamal thought it over. He took a deep breath and sat up. "Shit... that'd be Duckie."

"His name's Duckie?" I asked with a chuckle.

"Yeah, you wouldn't be laughin' if you be seeing him."

"Why's he called Duckie?"

"'Cause motherfuckers be duckin' every time they around him, that's why." Jamal bobbed and weaved his head and shoulders in pantomime. "Trying not to get hit and shit. Dude's a scary motherfucker."

"You know him?"

"Shit, everybody know Duckie in here."

"Good," I said. "Go see Duckie tomorrow and tell him I gotta talk to him."

Jamal screwed up his face. His eyes narrowed behind his big plastic frames.

"Are you shitting me? I'll get me a fuckin' beat-down if I step to Duckie like that."

"Just tell him he's gonna wanna hear what I got to say. Get me in with him—quick—and I'll put fifty bucks on your books. Deal?"

"I ain't stepping to Duckie for no fifty bucks, tell you that right now."

"Hundred then?" I hung my hand down to shake on it.

"Fuck," Jamal groaned. He slapped my hand. "Okay, man. Money up front." He blew out a long breath, sounding out another *Fuck*. "Gonna get my ass beat, that's what's gonna happen. Be eatin' my damn commissary through a straw."

I smiled and thanked him. Jamal pursed his lips and nodded. I pulled back up into my bunk. Stared at the ceiling as my fellow inmates counted down the new year.

I knew it would be a good one, this coming year. Despite having two death sentences hanging over me and a pending sentence of life in prison. I don't know how I knew, but I did. Couldn't put it into words or explain it to anyone so that it made sense. But deep down, wherever one's soul resides, I knew everything was going to be all right.

Faith and hope. Hope and faith.

I let loose a howl as the clock struck twelve. Jamal joined me and the other inmates in revelry. No more ladder stepping. I would come at Prisha hard this year. A direct hit. Old Frontal Assault Frank was back. I howled again, the "lonesome howl" I'd first heard about sitting next to Teddy at the National Zoo. The deep, even howl of a wolf seeking its pack.

I was getting out of here. I would make things right again. I would rejoin my pack.

Because evil thrives when good men do nothing.

AFTERWORD

I hope you enjoyed my second novel, *Talion Justice*, the first book in my Frank Luce thriller series.

The sequel to *Talion Justice* will be published by end of year 2020.

Let's stay in touch. Click here (newsletter) to sign up for my free monthly newsletter and receive exclusive updates and insights on me and my author adventure.

Visit my Amazon Author Page (author page) to check out my other novels, including *First Citizen*, my stand-alone fast-paced thriller about an army general seeking absolute power, and the FBI agent who opposes him.

And lastly, if you enjoyed *Talion Justice*, please consider leaving me a review on my Amazon book page. It would help other readers find the book, and would also really make my day.

Enjoy.

ABOUT THE AUTHOR

Rick Bosworth is an attorney and retired FBI agent who worked and supervised street gang, drug, terrorism, and intelligence cases in six different offices during his 25-year bureau career. He survived the LA Riots, South Central, and the Northridge Earthquake as a street agent, and paper cuts, endless meetings, and ceaseless vexation as a squad supervisor and program manager. Rick has walked dark alleys and Beltway power corridors, arrested killer gang members and briefed Cabinet members, all the while asking himself the same two questions: Why? What if? His answers became the basis for his first novel, *First Citizen*.

Rick writes page-turning novels that make you think and feel. Juicy tenderloin thrillers, sautéed in literary prose and served with a buttery side of history and philosophy.

He lives with his wife on the shore of Lake Superior in Michigan's Upper Peninsula. When he is not writing, Rick enjoys hiking in the woods, sipping good bourbon, and slapping at his acoustic guitar. See what he's up to at his website, rickbosworth.com.

TALION JUSTICE

Copyright © 2020 by Rick Bosworth

All rights reserved.

ISBN Number: 978-1-7341412-8-3 (eBook)

ISBN Number: 978-1-7341412-9-0 (Paperback)

Published by UPrising Publishing, LLC 2020

Upper Peninsula, Michigan

This is a work of fiction. Names, characters, places, and incidents either are the product of the author's imagination or are used fictitiously, and any resemblance to actual persons, living or dead, business establishments, events, or locales is entirely coincidental.

www.ingramcontent.com/pod-product-compliance
Lightning Source LLC
Chambersburg PA
CBHW030553180626
46816CB00005B/1526